CROSSROADS

Just Creative Writing

Greensboro, Maryland

Also by Judith Reveal

FICTION

The Brownstone

The Writer's Bloc

Soon to be Rereleased:

The Music Room

A House To Kill For

NonFiction

The Four Elements of Fiction: Character, Setting, Situation, and Theme

Growing Up Middle Class in Post World War II America

Copyright © 2021

The scanning, uploading, and distribution of this book without permission is a theft of the author's intellectual property. For permissions contact jreveal@me.com.

Just Creative Writing
301 Wood Duck Drive
Greensboro, MD 21639

First edition January 2021

ISBN: 9798573415017

DEDICATION

This book is dedicated to Margaret
Gauthier, of Little Lake Michigan,
a woman of humor whose laughter
rings true even after many years.

CROSSROADS

By

Judith Reveal

Chapter One

I am not a risk-taker, and yet I stood at the registration desk of the Portsborough Inn wondering what drew me here.

"May I help you?" the clerk said.

"I have a reservation, Charlotte Sunday." I looked at the name tag. Carol. She smiled, her nose just a little crooked.

She typed my name into her computer. "Oh, yes, Ms. Sunday. How long will you be staying?"

"I'm not sure. A few days at most."

Carol checked me in, handed me the key, and asked, "Is there was anything else I can help you with?"

I reached into my purse and retrieved a wrinkled business envelope with an address scribbled on the front. A glance at my father's scratchy handwriting on the envelope brought sad memories. I showed her the envelope. "I'd like to know if you can give me some directions."

She looked at the address, glanced up at me, and the smile suddenly seemed glued to her face; not quite genuine, but more inquisitive. "Ah, yes. Varcoe Manor." She reached across the counter to a brochure holder, grabbed a map, and unfolded it. She took a yellow highlighter and marked the route for me.

Varcoe Manor? The place has a name? What the hell is a manor? I thanked Carol, placed the envelope back in my purse and as I left, I had the uncomfortable feeling of being watched.

* * *

As I stood on the balcony overlooking Penobscot River, several peculiar sensations washed over me. The difference between Portsborough Maine and Washington DC stood in stark contrast. The crashing traffic sounds of Washington; the smells of gasoline and garbage that I had taken for granted for my entire life receded into my memory.

I felt a calm in the air; the smells of pine and wisteria floated up to greet me. I thought about how I ended up here—in a town I didn't even know existed until two months ago. I returned to the room, sat on the bed, and took the crumpled envelope from my purse. The letter inside brought the events of the recent weeks to the front of my mind.

My Dear Charlotte

I asked George not to talk to you about the property until you had a chance to read about it for yourself. There is a large piece of property in Portsborough Maine that has been in your mother's family for more generations than I can even account for. It is where we lived when she died, and yet I doubt that you have much of a memory of it since you were only two years old. I have not been able to part with it, although I have not seen it since we left. I have renovated and maintained it with the able assistance of local help and now it is yours. George has the paperwork that you will need to sign to become its new owner.

I am sorry I did not tell you about this throughout your life, but your mother's death was, and still is, a difficult issue for me. I am sorry that this is being sprung on you as such a surprise, and I trust that you will do whatever is appropriate with it, as you are now the official owner.

Your Loving Father

The past weeks since father's law partner, George Breckenridge, read the will and provided me with this most confusing situation, had blown past me in a blur.

I stared at the letter and recalled my conversation with George.

"When Walter took me into the firm forty years ago, he was very open about what happened in his life. He was especially

concerned about you and the effect your mother's death may have had on you. He did tell me about the property but no details about your mother's death."

"But what is this?" I asked looking from George to the letter and back to George. "What exactly does this mean? Are there people living there? Is it even livable? Does it have any value?" I felt the questions tumble out of my mouth before I even finished forming them.

"The property is about 200 acres, mostly forested land. The house itself is a large building with some great historic value. It sits atop a high cliff, for lack of another word, overlooking the Penobscot River. There are several outbuildings—I'm not sure what they are or were used for. Storage probably. And there is a lighthouse just to the northside of the property itself. The lighthouse has not been used in years.

"Your father wrote this letter recently and gave it to me for safe keeping. There is a local man, Charles Beasley, who has been taking care of the property for many years. His father was an acquaintance of Walter's and took care of it initially. Over the years Walter rented the property and Beasley did his best to take care of it, but that was difficult considering the distance involved and that Walter never returned.

"I don't know what you may want to do," he reached into the middle desk drawer and retrieved an envelope, "but here are the keys. If you don't want to have anything to do with this, I can handle selling it for you. I'm sure I can find a realtor who would be willing to take it on." He shoved the envelope across the desk and changed the subject. "I have just a few things for you to sign. Your father had a life insurance policy of $500,000 with you as the beneficiary. Any thoughts?"

I signed the papers, picked up the envelope, and placed it in my purse. "George, I have nothing of my mother's. When she died, father packed us up almost immediately and moved down here to DC. I've never known any other home; I've traveled through my work, but never northeast. But now my curiosity is piqued, and I sense that I should at least go and see this mysterious property. Perhaps I can *reconnect with my mother, or at least put my mind to peace. I will pack up my father's belongings and I'll decide where to go from here."*

I put these thoughts aside. I had not even been here one day, and yet I experienced an excitement that had never entered my life in 50 years. The only thing that held me to Washington, DC, was my own business, and for several years I had been growing tired of it. *Perhaps it is time to move on.* And now there was something new pricking at me. Maybe it was a memory of my mother that existed only in vague recollections that darted through my mind and then evaporated.

Chapter Two

Sleep came to me in fits that night and I awoke at seven o'clock to see a heavy fog lying across the land. The river had all but disappeared, except for the sound. As I left the Inn and set out toward this mysterious property, I became more excited; I felt an odd draw to this unknown place.

Several miles north of the town limits I turned onto a small private road. Although overgrown with an abundance of weeds on both sides, the road remained in passable condition. I slowed the car to a crawl, looking from the map to the road and back again when I saw a gate about ten feet off to the right. I stopped my Jeep and walked toward the gate as a puff of cool air swirled around me. In the quiet of the morning, I was surrounded only by the distant roar of the river, a sound that was becoming more familiar with every minute. I spied a sign that hung by a thin wire thread from a wrought iron post next to the gate. "Varcoe Manor, 1875, The Crossroads" was printed in delicate calligraphy. The sign swung in the morning breeze. Curiosity tickled the back of my mind. *I wonder why people named their homes and properties.* I shook my head and the thoughts dissolved like crystals melting into the air.

I began a slow drive up toward the manor. The limbs at the top of the large trees reached across the drive forming a high arch, blotting out any sun except at brief moments when a breeze scuttled through the leaves. The spidery fingers of spring growth—spindly shrubs devoid of sunlight—clung to the trunks and the bark.

As I left the canopy of trees, I stared beyond the driveway. My eyes opened wide and I smiled. My gaze wandered across the façade of the Georgian style red brick building that arose before me. A freshly bricked circular drive wound past the front of the manor and six brick steps led up to the front door. The house brickwork was newly tuck-pointed and bright white shutters clung beside each tall widow. A brick walk stretched past French doors across the length of the house. The pristine white colonial front door, with its side window panels and overhead lintel, gleamed in the sunlight.

God, I hope this was not a mistake.

It was not! a voice seemed to answer. I looked around but saw no one.

I retrieved the set of keys George had given me and approached the large front door. The door swung open on silent hinges. My steps echoed as I walked through the empty parlor and library at the front of the building. A subdued morning light filtered through the tall windows, warming each room. I wandered slowly into the dining room and kitchen at the back of the manor. *Hmm, plenty of room for that large oak table that is squashed in my kitchen in Georgetown. And the view is fantastic! The forest, the lighthouse, and the river. I could live in this kitchen!*

Yes, it's really lovely, isn't it? Charlie did wonderful work.

I turned at the question but saw no one.

I felt drawn further into the house, as though someone gently put a hand on my arm and drew me in. My excitement built as I approached the staircase leading up to the second floor. I took slow steps as though I were intruding on a private place that belonged to someone else. The master bedroom in the southeast corner looked out on the river below and two tall French doors opened to a balcony that traveled the length of the house; the view swept across the back lawn and engulfed the cliff and the river beyond.

As I returned toward the stairs, I passed a door I had not noticed. One turn of the knob and I discovered the door was locked. I rummaged through my purse and retrieved the keys again. After several moments of fidgeting, I located the right key. "Might as well see it while I'm here," I said.

I swung open the door and a gust of musty air blew past me. I flipped the light switch and the single bulb above the steps emitted an eerie light. I felt as though I had walked into another era when I found several pieces of furniture in various states of disrepair that appealed to me. Eclectic items including boxes of papers, knick-knacks, pictures, and a clothes tree, cluttered the path. *Lovely pieces,* I thought. *Fixed up they could be perfect for the library or sitting room.* "So, I wonder if some of this furniture can be saved? I like this clothes tree," I said, touching the tall thin piece of furniture. I walked around a corner, into a spider web that curled on my shoulder. I brushed it off.

I touched a small cabinet and ran my hand over it. "It looks like everything needs a bit of overhauling, but I'm sure a good antique shop could probably give me some advice. I must investigate this further." I stopped and realized that I was talking out loud.

Decades of accumulation greeted me as I slowly turned around, absorbing, and wondering where to start; what I could do away with and what was worth keeping. I made a path through boxes of books and papers, pushing them to one side or another when a thought entered my mind: *under the eaves.* Not sure why that thought popped into my mind, I followed it and came upon a large wooden camelback trunk shoved far under the attic eaves. A vague memory of this trunk crawled through my mind.

The leather handle on one side of the trunk creaked as I nudged it into a spot clear of the attic's clutter. A heavy metal latch, rusty, with no lock, sat on the trunk's face and after some pushing and pulling, the latch yielded. Dust billowed out through the air, encircling me as dust mites blew around my head in the dim light.

As the dust began to settle, I lifted the lid and peered at its contents. Glued to the inside of the lid I found a piece of cardboard with faded cursive handwriting that spoke of a time past. I could not determine what was written, but something told me that the chest must be special—must contain things buried that had a particular meaning for its owner. I wondered about interfering with ghosts of the past.

I removed a shelf that nestled on a rail below the opening and found several small boxes and a few books neatly tucked away. The boxes contained jewelry, and I wondered if they had any value or if they were simply costume, reminiscent of the times. Three attractive bracelets and several pairs of clip-on earrings rested in boxes, but it was a ring that caught my attention. The initials *E.C.G.* wound around in a flourish inside the back. I turned it over several times. A lovely antique, I wondered if it belonged to a grandmother or an aunt. It would need attention, but I hoped desperately that it would clean up well.

At the bottom of the trunk, I found several pieces of women's clothing. I picked up a housedress that dated back several decades. Stylish for the times and well constructed, but its value to today's woman was questionable. I would donate the clothes and let someone else determine their value. The trunk itself would not be so easy to part with.

She wore that dress the last time we met.

Startled, I looked up to see an apparition hovering on the far side of the attic. I could not speak. The vision, without form, floated toward me but stopped several yards away. I took a deep breath and held it, unable to speak.

Her death was incomprehensible. I knew she would help me. She has now passed that on to you. Read the books. The vision appeared to speak, and yet it did not.

As I sat immobile, this vague shape dissipated. I stared across the room for several moments before I quickly turned my attention back to the trunk. I set the boxes aside and wondered about my imagination, when I saw several books and found a diary with the name Lyda Sunday written in that same neat cursive writing. I took another deep breath! My mother. My first instinct was to put it back and let the contents remain asleep. Of course, I did not do that. Instead, I opened a whole new world and was about to meet Emmaline.

* * *

May 31, 1967 – I had the most unusual dream last night. Walter and I had enjoyed a lovely dinner at a small diner in town – it was a lovely drive in the warm spring air. I think we may have a warmer than usual summer this year. That will be refreshing.

But my dream – I was not very tired when we returned home and I thought I would read a bit since Walter had already gone to bed, but I found my eyes drooping after the first page of the book. Before I knew it, I was asleep in the chair. I was awakened more by a 'feeling' than by a 'noise' and when I looked across the room, I thought I saw a figure of some sort sitting in the old rocker by the fireplace. It did not say anything, and I could not really tell what this figure was, but I sensed it might be a woman. I tried to speak, but its head slowly moved back and forth as if to tell me not to say anything. I stared at it for several moments then it just evaporated. Needless to say, I did not mention this to Walter. He would have laughed at me.

June 2, 1967 – I could not get that dream out of my mind. Even as I played with little Charlotte today, my mind kept revisiting that appearance. I wonder what it meant.

June 3, 1967 – This is becoming somewhat bothersome. Last night I went to bed early and fell right to sleep. I did not feel Walter get into bed; I must have been quite tired. At some point I rolled over and opened my eyes, and there was that vision again! She—I'm assuming it was she—stood wrapped in a fog-like shroud. She stretched out her hand and motioned for me to follow her. It was with the most uncontrollable urge that I rose from bed and walked into the living room behind this image. In the living room, I sat on the couch and she stood before me. I heard her speak—well, not exactly speak as much as think—and she said that I must help her. I asked, 'Help you what?' and her response was most unusual: help her find herself.

I did not share this dream with Walter. He would have me committed!

June 5, 1967 – I really do think I'm losing my mind. My vision reappeared last night and repeated her need for me to find her. I have no idea what this means, or where to even start – that is, if I were going to start! I asked who she was, and she said Emmaline Varcoe. I don't know anyone named Emmaline– never have—and Varcoe is not a familiar name to me either. When I attempted to get more information from her, she again disappeared in a most peculiar way. She just dissolved like crystals of breath on a cold day. Tomorrow I am going to the library and see if they have any information on anyone by that name, perhaps a relationship with the town. I know this is silly, but I am intrigued.

June 12, 1967 – this is most disconcerting! The library was of little help to me other than to direct me to the Genealogical Society where I found a nice young man—a volunteer—who helped me with some research. I fear we were both novices at this research, but Peter...that was his name, did help me find something very interesting. It seems that I had a distant great aunt (I really don't know how many greats she shared with me!) who lived in our home. Peter said he would search further and see if he could find some details. My Emmaline has not visited me for several days. I wonder if this is the same person! I'll see Peter tomorrow and we'll do some more research. How exciting. Walter still doesn't know!

The date shot through my head like a bolt of lighting. The day following the last entry, June 13, 1967, was the day my mother was struck by a car and killed.

I bolted out of my thoughts when I heard a noise from downstairs. I closed the trunk, looked around to see if I was still alone, and clutching the diary in my hand, I left the attic and slowly went back to the first floor. I found the front door open and when I looked out, I saw a large white van parked in front of the house with the words "Charles Beasley, LLC" printed on the side.

From behind me I heard a noise and turned abruptly to see a man with a paintbrush in his hand. A smudge of yellow paint dotted his nose and he smeared it with the back of his hand. He smiled—a warm smile that made the skin around his dark brown eyes crinkle. I took him to be in his fifties by the gray at his temples and that crinkle at his eyes. *Hmmm, attractive,* I thought.

He spoke first. You're Charlotte Sunday, aren't you?" he asked. "Hi, I'm Charlie. Charlie Beasley. Sorry we're meeting under such circumstances," he said, smiling. "Your father was a nice man and I enjoyed working with him. Truth is, I've been expecting you for several weeks. I had a few last-minute things to take care of and hoped I'd get them done before you arrived." He spoke quickly, obviously as surprised to find me as I was to find him. He placed the paintbrush on the tarp.

I stopped for a moment before responding. *Charlie?* I said to myself. "I am, and you've been expecting me for weeks? Have you indeed?" I took a deep breath. "And why have you been expecting me?" I asked and smiled.

"Walter called me several months ago and told me about his health. He asked me to do everything possible to restore the manor not only to its previous livability, but to its dignity."

I struggle to find the right words. "You'll have to excuse me, but until after my father died two months ago, I did not even know this place existed. I had no recollection of it from my childhood," I said. It seemed that everyone knew more about my father and Varcoe Manor than I did.

He waved his hand around a full turn. "It was not a difficult or time-consuming task. I've been familiar with Varcoe Manor all my life, and although there were a number of people living here at various times, I did the best I could to keep it up for Walter."

"My father's death, his secrecy, and my inheritance, well—it's all overwhelmed me. I've just been familiarizing myself with the house; it's quite lovely," I added as an afterthought.

Charlie allowed me a moment of privacy and we remained silent then I slowly turned around in the hallway and took one last view of the manor. With each step I had taken in the house that warm day, a feeling of comfort and familiarity grew within me, as if I was not alone. The more I considered my options to stay here or go back to DC, the more I knew I wanted to make this work. I was strangely comforted in my decision. "Charlie," I said, "I'm very happy with what you've done. I think this is exactly what I need."

"You're serious?" Charlie beamed. "That's good to know. This house needs someone to love it." Charlie folded the tarp and removed his equipment to the van.

As I approached my car, I smiled at him then turned back to look at the house and grounds one more time. "Yes, I believe I am serious. This will do just fine for me. I need to get back to the hotel. I have some calls to make and some planning to do. "

You are exactly the right person.

"Thank you," I answered.

"For what?" Charlie asked.

I turned and looked around, but Charlie stared at me in silence. My attention was drawn to a vague shape in the window of the sitting room. I ignored it.

Chapter Three

"George? Hi, this is Charlotte. I need your help."

"Charlotte, how wonderful to hear from you. Of course, I'll help with anything I can."

I was comforted by the sound of his voice. "I've gone through the manor...did you know it was a manor? I'm really quite taken with it," I said. "It's hard to describe why, but I've given a lot of thought over the past few days and I've made my decision and I am definitely moving into the manor."

He laughed. "I don't know why, but I thought you would make that decision. But what about your magazine? Walter was very proud of what you made of your life with that enterprise."

I stopped for a moment. *The Wave* – my artists' magazine had engulfed me for 25 years, but I now realized that I was growing weary of managing it to the cost of any personal life. "Yes, there is that. I've spoken to my friend Theodore Wolff, he's the Managing Editor and is going to continue to operate it for me. He's thrilled; I'm thrilled, and I know I can count on him. I need you to draw up some papers for me."

George remained silent for a moment. "If you're sure that's what you want to do, we can handle that for you. What else can we do?"

"I would now like you to sell both townhouses – mine and my father's. After my meeting with you I went through both places. I donated my father's clothes and packed and marked everything else. His furniture is in storage, I'll leave them there for the time being. His personal belongings are in my safety deposit box. Ted has a key to my house, and he will pack everything for me to be shipped up here. I've already packed the clothes and personal items." As I spoke to George, I realized that I had made the decision before I even saw the manor. "I don't think I'll be returning, and if I cut the cord now, that option will not linger. If you could contact Valliant and Associates and have them deposit the proceeds in my investment account in DC, I'll decide what to do with it later. Right now, I just want to move forward. I have enough in the account to cover any costs I might incur, but that cushion will be helpful."

"Charlotte, I doubt that you will incur very many costs. Walter took care of everything. Your personal expenses notwithstanding, you will be fine. The life insurance will clear in a few weeks and I'll make sure that money gets deposited also. What else do you need from us?"

"Nothing, George. You've been more help than you could imagine. I'm very grateful."

He exhaled a heavy sigh. "Don't be a stranger. Stay in touch and let me know if there is anything else I can do."

"I'll do that. Thanks again." As I ended the call, I felt a tear wander down my cheek. I wasn't sure if I would ever speak to George Breckenridge again, and that would be my loss.

Next, I called Ted Wolff. Our relationship had been close for many years and I could not think of anyone I trusted more with this task. We finalized the details of the townhouses, and I informed him of my decision about *The Wave*. I knew he and his husband, Greg, would be careful with my belongings and that *The Wave* would be in good hands. It would soon be his although I did not share that with him. It would be part of the agreement. It had served me well and now needed new management.

I asked Ted to make arrangements with National Storage to have my belongings moved to the manor once everything was concluded. When I ended the call, a strange sense of foreboding curled up my spine. Had I made these decisions too quickly? I shook the thought from my mind. It was time to move forward.

I made my last call of the day to Charlie Beasley. For some odd reason, I suddenly felt a rush of warm air swirl around me. "I've just finished making arrangements for my belongings to be packed and readied to be moved up here. As soon as my friend handles everything at that end, I'll set the date with the storage company. They will handle everything, and they told me I should expect delivery in four days from the date we agree on. I'm hoping to have that done within the next two weeks."

"I have a full team of very strong men. I'm sure I could convince them to help. We'll just need some direction from you."

I thought about his offer for a moment. I realized that I didn't know anyone here beside Charlie, and I hardly knew him. But if my father trusted him, I saw no reason why I should not.

"I'd be grateful for any help. I'll finalize the date and let you know when they will arrive."

"That will be great. I'll look forward to seeing you." The air in the room remained warm.

As I finished my calls, my phone rang. Carol at the front desk asked if I was available to meet with the director of the Genealogical Society.

How odd, I thought. I hesitated for just a moment before agreeing to see him in the lobby. I arrived at the front desk a few moments later and Carol was talking to a man several years older than me. She waved me over and the man turned and quickly walked toward me and smiled, showing a top row of ragged teeth on the yellowish side of white. Wisps of long gray hair lifted in the light air-conditioned breeze and he put his hand on his head to smooth them back in place.

"Miss Sunday, I'm Peter Tidewater, Director of the Portsborough Genealogical Society and I wanted to thank you so much for taking care of the lovely old manor. I realize this is probably an inconvenience, but I thought perhaps we could talk about the manor and the people..." His words drifted into the air.

I thought back to my mother's diary. *Peter? Could this be the same man my mother referred to?* Curiosity nudged me forward. I nodded and reached out toward him. "Of course, Mr. Tidewater." I had no idea what to expect next and turned toward a small alcove off the front hallway. "What can I do for you?"

We sat at a small table where he placed a briefcase.

"I had several discussions with your father over the years, and although he never led me to believe it, I have always hoped that the manor would return to its former beauty, and that certainly appears to be the case."

My eyes grew wide. "Excuse me, Mr. Tidewater, but when were you out there? When did you see the house?"

A tinge of red crept up over his collar. "I visited it while Charlie Beasley was working on it. He told me I should probably approach you with my proposal."

My eyes remained wide. *Proposal? How curious. Small town news does travel fast,* I thought. "Proposal? What would that be?" I asked.

"I am trying to encourage more people to become interested in the original settlers in this area, and your manor is certainly one of the oldest and one of the most well-preserved homes. I would like to know if the Genealogical Society might impose and have an open house to introduce the property and its original habitants back to the community." He stopped.

"Mr. Tidewater, I haven't even moved into the manor. My belongings will be on the way soon, but I'm in no position to plan an open house."

"Oh! No, no, I'm so sorry. I've approached this all wrong. I thought perhaps later, once you've become accustomed to the manor and the property..." He spoke quickly, obviously at a loss for words.

I thought for a minute, unsure of how to answer him. Cautiously I said, "Mr. Tidewater, that might not be such a bad idea, and I really do want to know more about the manor. It belonged to my mother and I really didn't even know it existed until recently."

"Oh, my, yes." He suddenly bubbled with enthusiasm. "I was sure you would want to familiarize yourself and I took the liberty to bring some background for you. Do you have a few minutes to spare? And please, it's Peter."

I smiled. "Yes, Peter. I do. What can you tell me about the manor?"

"Well, let me be upfront first. The Genealogical Society deals in people, not places. That's the Historical Society. So, my information is primarily about your family."

He now had my full attention. I waited anxiously while he withdrew a folder of papers from his briefcase.

"Well, let me start with John Varcoe. He was the original owner. John Varcoe arrived from England as a baby with his family. Must have been around 1840 or 41. He was the second son. He had two brothers, one was 10 years older, and a second one a year younger, then three sisters, and another brother." He flipped through several pieces of paper then continued. "The middle brother and two of the sisters did not survive to adulthood. His father, Waterman Varcoe, had a successful tailor business in London and when he arrived here, he turned that into a successful trapping and fur trading business. The oldest brother, Thomas, ran the business.

"As the second son, John would not inherit, but his father had enough money to send him to college in Boston where he learned the ins and outs of business. When he returned to Portsborough, he brought this knowledge back with him and started the family lumber business. Between him and his father and older brother, they built quite a little empire."

Peter was talking fast, as if he feared losing my attention if he paused. I listened carefully, wondering about my mother's connection to the manor.

"Apparently, he was quite the ladies' man. We don't have a picture of him; but as I was pulling together these notes...er...I found a story about him—well, really it was just a paragraph in the society section of an old Bangor newspaper that described him as tall, lithe, with a swarthy complexion. Curly brown hair, a smile that beguiled the ladies, and the longest eyelashes anyone had ever seen. Now, this society writer might have gilded the lily a bit, but he sounds like quite the looker."

He sat back and smiled.

I did not want to stop the flow of information and I held my breath waiting for more. Nothing more came.

"Is that all? There isn't any more information?" I asked, bewildered.

Peter raised his eyebrows and sat up straight. "Oh, yes, actually there is more information back at the society, but I was in such a hurry to meet you, and a lot of our information is fragile and, well, needs some organization." He looked anxious. "I can gather the information and organize it into a presentation that we could do at the open house—"

How very creative of him! I thought. I took a deep breath. He had piqued my interest. "Okay Peter. You go back and gather whatever you have on John and the manor. I'm anxious to know more about my mother's relationship to this property and I'll think about an open house. I'm going to be busy the next few weeks, so I won't make a decision immediately, but I will consider it once I'm more settled. Can I call you when I make that decision?"

Peter relaxed and bowed his head. "Most certainly. And I'll see what else I can get together for you. Um, one other thing—had you given any thought to selling the manor, it would be perfect for the Genealogical Society."

I smiled at him and said, "No. No thoughts about that at all."

Chapter Four

The next day, as I thought about my conversation with Peter Tidewater, my phone rang.

"Charlotte? Charlie Beasley."

"Hi Charlie. How are you?"

A brief silence preceded his words. "I think you should come out to the manor."

There was something in his voice that told me this was not going to be a good call. "Of course, has something happened?"

"Actually yes. But I'd rather not discuss it over the phone. Can you come out?"

"I'll be there in about fifteen minutes. Are you sure you can't tell me what's happened?"

"Just come here as fast as you can."

I disconnected the call, grabbed my sweater, and raced out of the Inn. I arrived within ten minutes and rushed up the steps. Charlie greeted me at the front door. "What in the world is going on?" I asked.

"Well, it seems—well, there was an incident overnight."

"An incident?" I asked. My mind raced over a cache of different definitions for that one word.

"Yes. Apparently, someone broke into the manor last night. There was some minor damage…nothing that couldn't be repaired quickly."

A wave of fear rolled across me. My eyes opened wide as I listened. "A break-in? What in the world happened?" I looked around the hallway.

Charlie said, "Your alarm system activated, alerting the police. They got out here and called me. When I came out to inspect the house,

I found a few things messed up. I've been out here since early this morning, but I felt it would be better not to upset you until I had some facts."

"So, do you know what happened?"

Charlie drew me toward the sitting room on the left side of the foyer. "We're not sure. I was hoping there was just a glitch in the alarm system, but when I got here, I saw that there had been some damage done to the sitting room. Nothing major; just some graffiti on the walls."

"Graffiti?" I asked, my voice rising. "What kind of graffiti?"

"I hate to bother you with this since we've already gotten this cleaned up…"

"You're not bothering me. What graffiti?" I repeated, my level of annoyance rising. A small wrench of panic settled in my gut. I realized I was staring at him and I felt the blood rise above my collar.

"Some not-so-nice words. I took a picture for the police, but there was nothing they could really do but a cursory investigation and write a report."

He reached into his pocket and retrieved his cell phone. He scrolled through several photographs then turned the phone toward me.

Across the bright yellow walls, in dark paint, were scrawled the words: *You don't belong here, bitch. You need to leave.*

"Who would do this?" I felt the words catch in my throat. "I don't know anyone well enough to make them angry. Hell, I don't know anyone at all except you." I mumbled the last sentence as I allowed my gaze to sweep across the room.

I turned my attention back to Charlie who said, "Mostly it appears that the walls were messed up. It doesn't look like there was any other damage. After I arrived and saw what had happened, I took it upon myself to just clean it up."

"That was very kind of you," I stammered. "I appreciate it."

"The same thing was done to the kitchen, but the other rooms seem to not have been touched. Might be because the alarm went off and the police came quickly."

"Why didn't they stay? Why didn't they call me?" I asked as I gazed around the room. I realized that my time in Washington DC had poisoned me to events like this, and I felt a pang of fear that the police did not remain.

"They knew I had been working here and had access. I don't think they even know you're here. When I arrived, we walked through the house and I told them I'd check to make sure nothing else was messed up or damaged and I'd remain to clean up. I'm sure they'll contact you shortly. Do you want to check out anything, just to see if something got missed?"

I realized I had been holding my breath. I felt myself begin to breathe again. "I'm sure you didn't miss anything. But perhaps I should just look at the rooms upstairs—just to be sure." I wasn't at all sure why I thought I needed to do this but moved toward the stairs.

Charlie followed. We looked in each room, in each closet, in each bathroom, but everything was in order. As we walked back toward the stairs, my mind cleared, and I thought about all the things that had happened since I arrived. Almost as an aside I asked, "Charlie, what do you know about Peter Tidewater?"

He stopped abruptly. "Peter? He's the Director of the Genealogical Society. A little odd, but he loves his work and tries to gather as much information about the families from this area as he can. Why do you ask?"

I told him about my encounter with Peter.

His eyes grew wide and he smiled. "I think an open house would be a great way for you to get to know the people," he said. He remained quiet for a moment, then asked, "Did Peter mention them?"

I turned and looked at him. I felt a bewildering frown cross my face. "Mention whom?" I asked.

"The stories," he responded.

"Stories? What stories?"

He stared at me for just a moment. "The stories about the manor."

I fell silent as I attempted to get my head around his comment. "Charlie, I've not heard any stories. Peter didn't say anything about any stories. What kind of stories are you talking about?" I felt my gut tighten.

Charlie swallowed hard. I sensed that he felt that he might have walked into a hornet's nest, but he was there now and could not go back.

"There have been some odd things that have happened at the manor. I don't really know any details, but if you want to know more about the history of the manor, you might go to the library or the Historical Society. Between them and Peter, you could probably get more information..." He let his sentence slide off into oblivion.

"Well, nothing odd other than this has happened in my first days and no one I've encountered has mentioned anything out of the ordinary." I did not mention the apparition in the attic. I was certain that my imagination had worked overtime because of the entries in my mother's diary. It really was not something I needed to mention to Charlie...not really.

Chapter Five

The next day I thought about Charlie's suggestion and put the library and the Historical Society on my list of visits. I found the library on the town square. It was typical of what I expected to find in a small town with a long history; probably a bank or government building at one time. The red brick building façade rose three stories above me. Tall stone pillars stood guard on either side of the heavy wooden door. Two tall first-floor windows rose on either side of the entryway and directly above, two equally tall second-floor windows. The small square windows on the third floor I assumed hid an attic or storage. Old shutters, painted red, nestled tight against the walls, embracing the windows.

I recalled going to the library in Washington with my father when I was a child. It was so much bigger, and impersonal, but he encouraged me to read and my love for words began early. I held that memory close throughout my life and now I realized that the slight sense of foreboding about Charlie's mysterious stories that I carried with me, had diminished. The door swung open soundlessly on well-oiled hinges and a 'Silence!' sign immediately greeted me. I grinned at the exclamation point's implied demand. The library was neatly planned with overloaded bookshelves that covered every inch of wall space. The open room was clustered with tables and chairs for computers and printers; small tables and chairs for children; easy chairs and sofas for reading, and two tables for writing. Tucked on the right, next to the entryway, was the Information Desk.

As I entered, a rush of cool spring air blew past me and I noticed several people lift their attention to stare at me, a new, unfamiliar face in town, then slowly returned their attention to their primary tasks.

Two women sat behind the long Information Desk. A young woman, perhaps in her early thirties, sat stamping books while an older woman with dull, gray-streaked brown hair, matted into an unruly bun at the nape of her neck, sat upright, doing nothing. *My librarian*, I assumed. The nameplate on the desk introduced her as Claudia Cooper.

I walked up to the older woman and smiled. "Hi," I said. "I'm new in town and would like to get a library card, please."

She looked at me without smiling, reached over to a drawer on her left, retrieved a form, and slid it across the desk at me. When I'd filled out the form and returned to the desk, I slid the form back toward the woman.

"May I ask you a question?"

The older woman leaned forward and whispered, "Certainly, what can I help you with?"

I found myself leaning forward in an equally conspiratorial manner. I whispered, "I just moved into a house here in Portsborough, and Charlie Beasley suggested I come here. He said that you might be able to answer some questions about my property."

She nodded her head in a knowing way. She eyed me up and down. "Charles, yes of course. What is your question?" She sat up straight in her chair and waited.

I edged closer, as if the question required more confidentiality. "My name is Charlotte Sunday. I own Varcoe Manor, and I'll be moving in shortly. Charlie asked me if the rumors about the house bothered me."

"I heard that someone had occupied that old place," Claudia said. She moved in close, whispering again. "My goodness, it's not been lived in for some time, not since the Sheraton affair."

"The Sheraton affair?"

"Come with me," she directed, as she left her place behind the desk. She looked at the younger woman hovering at the far end of the desk. "Madelyn, come here and watch the desk. I'll be in the office with this lady."

Madelyn slowly moved toward the librarian's chair, never taking her eyes off me. "Yes, Mother. Can I help you with anything?" she whispered.

"No dear, just keep an eye on the desk." She motioned me to follow her to the far end of the room.

We entered a cramped office and sat at a miniscule round table.

"My name is Claudia Cooper, Mrs. Sunday. Now, what did Charles say?"

"It's Ms. Sunday," I corrected her. "Actually, I prefer Charlotte. Charlie knows I want to get some history on the manor, and he mentioned that there were some stories that might fill in some of the blank spots—well, all I seem to have are blank spots. I got the impression he really did not want to talk about it, and perhaps even regretted bringing the subject up."

She sat back and smiled. "I see."

I waited and I said nothing more. I just waited—a habit I was forming.

After a moment of silence, Claudia coughed. "Ahem, well let me see now."

She spun her chair around to face a row of old, rusty file cabinets. A label on each drawer indicated a span between years. She ran her finger over each until she stopped at one labeled just '1975.' She opened the drawer and the smell of old, stale paper billowed out through the room. We both coughed.

She thumbed through folders, pulled one out, spun back around to the table, and placed it in front of her. When she opened the folder, I felt my eyebrows rise. Even upside down the headline blasted at me – CHILDREN DIE AT VARCOE MANOR.

"Yes, here is one of them," she said, more to herself than to me. "It was 1975 when the Sheraton family rented the manor. They never really fit in with the town. We had no idea why they chose to live here."

"Had you been to the manor?" I asked.

Claudia turned red and cleared her throat. "Oh, my, no, not really. That is, children used to go there and do who-knows-what, and when they were caught by the police—well, of course the children would tell about the manor's state of, well, being." A nervous twitch crept into her hand as she pointed at the paper.

I took it, turned it around, and reread the headline tracing my finger down through the details of the story. The air became oppressive as if the small room were closing around me. When I finished, I looked up at Claudia.

"This story says that two little girls fell from the cliff and tumbled down to the beach below. But it doesn't say what they were doing there. I noticed a steep wooden staircase leading down from the grounds on one side and up to the lighthouse on the other. Were they trying to go up or down the steps?"

Claudia's eyes wandered. "No one really knows. The parents had left the property to go to town to do some shopping, and when they came back, they couldn't find the girls. They searched and finally called the police to come out and help. That's when the bodies were found at the base of the steps." She thought for a moment then added, "It was directly below the lighthouse if I recall correctly."

"This story says they were seven and nine years old! Who leaves children of that age alone? What were they thinking?" I sensed anger in my own words, and quickly stopped.

"Again, no one knows the answer to that question either. When asked, Rachel Sheraton said the girls had always been very responsible, and that she and Timothy were only making a quick run into town for groceries. They gave the girls specific directions to remain indoors."

"Well now, how'd that work out?" I said half to Claudia and half to myself as I continued to read the story. Then thinking back to Charlie's comments, I said, "But why would Charlie think such a story would bother me as an occupant of the house? Tragic, yes, but it has nothing to do with me."

"Well…." Claudia looked around the room avoiding my eyes.

"Well, what?" I asked.

"There were more accidents."

I raised my eyebrows; my interest piqued. "Like what?"

She spun around again and went deeper into the historical newspaper files. She retrieved a musty copy of a previous, but now defunct, town newspaper, the *Portsborough Gazette*. The date was

1929 – the year of the big crash. She carefully laid it flat on the table and turned several brittle, yellow pages until she arrived at the local news section, where another headline screamed about one Mr. Elliot Spindler who resided at the manor at that time. He had apparently committed suicide in much the same way the Sheraton girls had died. Claudia gently turned the fragile paper around and poked at the story with a shaking finger.

I focused my attention on the few details. I looked up at Claudia. "This doesn't really say very much."

"The police said that everyone they spoke to talked about how despondent he was about the stock market crash, and the local sheriff closed the case as a suicide for that reason." She sat back and pursed her lips.

"But you don't think that was the real story? In either case?" *This is becoming quite fascinating. I wonder if my father knew these stories.*

"Most us, the the people of Portsborough, have lived here all our lives; we understand a little bit more about what's going on. The police have to be very careful how they relate stories, especially stories about Varcoe Manor." She fumbled with her fingers. "There was Miss Sarah Close who got caught in a rainstorm and a tree crashed down on her as she was hurrying up the driveway; and then that odd little man— what was his name?" She paused for a moment as if searching a file in her mind. "Oh, yes, Virgil Bulley. He fell down the attic steps. Stories tend to take on a life of their own, you know." She sat back, folded her arms across her chest and waited.

"No, actually, I don't know. These stories seem to be very straightforward, regardless of how tragic their outcomes. I don't see any patterns connecting the deaths."

Claudia reached over to the desk and grabbed the telephone. She pushed a button and a second line lit up on the base. "Madelyn, would you please get the copy of that Varcoe Manor book and bring it into the office for me? Thank you, dear." Thirty seconds later the door opened, and Madelyn Cooper poked her head in. She said nothing but stared at me with wide, questioning eyes as she reached around the door and handed a book to her mother. She closed the door and left.

Claudia wiped her hand over the book to remove a thick layer of dust then set the book down in front of me. "We generally don't let this out of our control—it's a reference book not to be taken out—but under the circumstances, I think you might want to take it and read it." She tapped the cover just above the name of the book: *VARCOE MANOR: THE SAD LIFE OF EMMALINE CATHERINE VARCOE.*

Emmaline...I thought.

I turned to the copyright page and saw the publication date was 1910. The author was one Simeon Barkley, a name that meant nothing to me.

I looked from the cover of the book to Claudia's face. It was clear she did not want to speak about this, but equally clear that she wanted me to know something that only this book could tell. I could not resist the temptation. "Who *was* Emmaline Varcoe?"

Claudia shifted in her chair. "She was the first death at the manor. After you read this, I suggest you go to the Historical Society if you have any more questions. Belinda Stapleford is the director, and she is may be more knowledgeable about the manor."

Emmaline Catherine Varcoe. The initials on the ring. Emmaline. Mother's apparition. I felt a piece of a puzzle beginning to fall into place, but it was a big puzzle, and this was only one piece.

Chapter Six

I placed the book on the passenger seat next to my purse and stared at it. The cracked spine and faded cover appeared to show more age than wear. I ran my hand gently over the cover, *I wonder if anyone had ever really read this.*

When I arrived at the Inn, I sat at the small table in my suite and began reading the book. Its yellow, brittle pages required careful handling and I started with the very first title page then cautiously turned to the next: *Dedicated to my aunt, Emmaline Catherine Varcoe. May she rest in piece.*

I reread the dedication, and when I got to the last word, I realized it was wrong. It should have been "peace." *How odd that no one would have caught that,* I thought.

Not odd when you know the story.

Startled, I looked around the room but saw nothing. *I must pay less attention to these stories*, I thought.

I spent the next hour reading about Emmaline Catherine Varcoe. It was a poorly written story based mostly on family lore. The basics simply stated that Emmaline Varcoe was the wife of one John Varcoe, a timber baron whose wealth grew with each year. In 1870 he, a Catholic, married Emmaline Grimes, a Methodist, and built Varcoe Manor for her. I knew that much from my conversation with Peter and was disappointed at the start of the story.

The story unfolded that Emmaline had miscarried and was so unhappy living at the manor and being away from her family and friends, 180 miles away in Portsmouth that she fell into a state of 'the vapors' and she took her own life.

As I read on, the question of religion and suicide and consecrated ground became somewhat jumbled in the telling, but it was clear that Emmaline's body had been placed in an unknown location. *How awful, to be in a state of depression to the point of taking your own life, and then not even be laid to rest properly.* There was no discussion about where John was buried. I assumed there was a town cemetery where his grave would be found. My curiosity piqued; I called Peter Tidewater at the Genealogy Society.

"Hello, Peter? It's Charlotte Sunday. I know I said I would call you in a few weeks, but some things have come up and I'm wondering if you got any other information about John Varcoe and Varcoe Manor? I just returned from the library and have gathered some information on my own. I also found a diary in the attic at the manor; a diary that belonged to my mother. She talks about an encounter with an Emmaline Varcoe. I thought we could share?"

The excitement in his voice pealed through the phone and he invited me to the Genealogical Society. We agreed to meet the following morning.

* * *

I spent a fitful night dreaming about break-ins one moment, and specters the next. I arose at 8:00 a.m. grateful to know I would not have many more nights in the Inn sleeping on a hotel mattress. As I gathered my few belongings I glanced at the diary on the nightstand. The previous night I had scanned through it but learned nothing more. I had so few things that belonged to my mother, and I cherished this one small item.

By 9:30 I was ready to meet Peter and learn more about my family.

The Portsborough Genealogical Society was located in an old storefront a block off Main Street. It was clear that the members worked hard to put up a good front, but the smell of old papers and the dust mites that flew around the room left me with an impression of age. *Of course, that's what a Genealogical Society deals in,* I thought.

Peter greeted me with a smile. I sensed it was the first time in a long time that he felt a positive push to his work.

"Charlotte, I am so pleased that you called. And very excited to hear about your visit to the library and what you've discovered." He led me to a small table at the back of the room. "If I might, let me tell you what additional information I've dug up." He laughed at his joke. "Then I want to hear all about the library and more importantly about this diary you discovered!"

"That's fine. You start, then I'll show you the book I got from the library and my mother's diary."

"Okay, let me start with Emmaline." He rubbed his hands together and opened a folder on the desk. "Emmaline enters the scene under peculiar circumstances. It appears that her father was quite wealthy in his own right, and Emmaline was his oldest daughter. Apparently, she was not a beauty, but her appearance was not totally unflattering. And she came with a huge dowry, so her popularity soared as she neared the marrying age. John Varcoe did not need a wealthy wife, but he did need the social standing she brought, so he put on his best face and wooed her. Must have wooed her father as well, because John and Emmaline were married in 1870 when she was 23 and John was 29. There's not enough information, or I haven't found it yet, to indicate how he really felt about Emmaline, but it's a good bet that he wanted at least one son to carry on the name. And she brought good genes with her."

Peter shuffled through more papers. "Didn't learn very much. She had trouble conceiving, and then when she finally did, she lost that child to a miscarriage and became very despondent…ended up killing herself. Apparently threw herself off the cliff according to a newspaper report. Something about a lighthouse? Her husband found her, but she was pretty badly torn apart from the fall. The brief newspaper obit indicated that she was physically broken up, especially around her head and shoulders."

I waited for a moment then asked, "You mean, she was in pieces?" I thought back to the dedication page of the book. *Another piece of the puzzle,* I thought.

"That's what I got from the report. Not exactly sure how to interpret that." Peter scratched his head. "According to the paper's report, apparently the local doctor wasn't summoned for several hours, which I thought was strange. When he finally got there, there was nothing he could do, so he just wrote it up as a suicide due to despair and filed it with the state. Her husband remarried. I'm just guessing here, but I think he was a bit of a cad. Just sayin'..." Peter let the sentence drop off, unfinished.

"Well, this really is a puzzle, isn't it? Lots of information and not sure how it all fits together!

"Yep, it is," Peter answered. "Now, your turn."

I took the diary and the library book out of my briefcase and put them on the table. Peter stared at both and whistled. He first picked up Simeon's book; his eyes closely scanned each page. I was pleased that he handled the book with such care although I was curious about why he did not seem to be familiar with it. *He had to have known about it...perhaps he just never focused on it.* I recalled how Claudia had wiped off a layer of dust and wondered just how close she kept her reference books. It was about an hour later when Peter finished Simeon's book. He took a deep breath and exhaled slowly. I just smiled and nodded my head. I suggested he try to convince Claudia Cooper to let the society have the library book. It was apparent to me that no line was forming to take it out. He agreed that he would try that.

But now I was more interested in his reaction to the diary. I watched him closely, wondering how he would react to the very last entry. I let him scan the part of the diary that related to mother's unusual dream and when he read the last entry, he gently placed the book on the table. He stared at it for several moments, then looked up at me.

"I had completely forgotten about that meeting, but now as I read this, the memory of that day comes back to me as if it were yesterday. I remember hearing about the accident. It was a terrible event. I don't believe anyone ever paid for that. My day with your mother was very short, and I was new at the society, just a teenager at my first job, trying to make an impression. She was probably more helpful to me than I was to her. She did not tell me about the apparition; I'm sure she thought I'd have directed her to the door. Actually, I find this very interesting." He left his words floating in the air, not expecting any response from me.

I felt a tear welling in my eye, and quickly changed the subject. "Oh, and Peter," I added. "I like your idea about an open house, and I'd like to do that. I'll figure out a date and make it happen. I need to get to know my new neighbors."

He clasped his hands together and looked toward the ceiling. I said nothing more.

* * *

I placed the Emmaline book and my mother's diary into my bag and left the Genealogical Society. My next stop would be Belinda Stapleford at the Historical Society.

The Historical Society was located in an old barn-like structure; it appeared structurally sound, but I suspected that money was an issue and maintenance was something provided by volunteers. *How similar the two societies are*, I thought, *and yet how distant*. I opened the door to the sound of scraping hinges, metal on metal. *No sneaking in here*. I entered a cool room with a high ceiling. Several people sat at tables culling through piles of paper stacked in front of them.

A woman in her early thirties looked up from her desk, rose, and approached me, with her hand out. "I'm Belinda Stapleford, director of the society. How can I help you?" She spoke with a mild whine and just a small nasal nudge to her voice. She released my hand and immediately moved her right hand to an errant strand of blond hair, which she tucked behind her ear.

"I would like to know if you have any details on Varcoe Manor." I reached into my purse and retrieved the Emmaline book. "I was at the library yesterday and Claudia Cooper loaned me this book."

Belinda's right eyebrow rose high as she took the book out of my hands and turned it over several times. "I must say I'm surprised. I've tried borrowing this book several times and Claudia wouldn't let it out of her sight. I wonder why she gave it to *you*." Her comment snarked across the quiet air almost as an afterthought.

Her attitude told me that there may be issues there, but I really did not want to get involved with the local drama. "Probably because I'm the owner of the Varcoe Manor, and it would only seem normal for me to be curious about its history." My response was sharper than I wanted it to be.

"So," she drew out the word for emphasis, "you're the new owner. We heard someone had inherited it. The society offered to buy the manor a few years ago, but the owner wouldn't sell. Would you be interested?" Her comment was short and curt.

Small town communications, indeed! This was the second unsolicited offer to buy the manor in two days. Surprised, I blinked several times. "No, I'm not interested in selling."

She shrugged her shoulders and proceeded to offer nothing more about the manor than Peter had shared that morning.

"Well, do you know anything about these accidents that have happened at the manor?" I asked. "I've been told of four that all resulted in deaths. That's a little disturbing."

"Only four? I thought there were more than that." She stared at the ceiling as if mentally counting accidents. "Let me introduce you to someone who might have more information." She took my arm and walked me to the far side of the room where a tall, handsome man, in his mid-thirties, sat alone at a table and a computer. "Ms. Sunday, this is Tom Greene. Tom, this is Ms. Sunday, the new owner of Varcoe Manor."

He sat up straight and stared at me, almost an angry stare.

"Tom's doing some research—interestingly enough, he's researching Varcoe Manor. I've been trying to collect information on the house and its dark history, but I've not been able to get anything concrete. Tom had expressed an interest in the house several months ago and I convinced him to help me. Everyone who's been here any length of time thinks there is something definitely wrong with the house. I mean, it's just not natural for so many deaths to have occurred in one place."

"It seems that this house just has unfortunate things that happen in it," Tom said. "It's an old house, buildings settle, things happen." He returned his stare to the computer screen. "But it could be as if the original occupants don't want others living there."

I stared at Tom. "Original occupants? Are you trying to tell me that this house is haunted?" I asked.

"Well, I'm not sure that's the right word, but I guess it would work. A lot of town people think just that," Tom mumbled.

I realized the conversation had taken a serious turn. "Well, I don't believe in ghosts." I failed to mention the ethereal vision that visited me in the attic. I felt there was a logical explanation for that—dust mites, spider webs, shadows through dirty glass—but ghosts and goblins were not the answer. "I've not been here long, but long enough to know that I'm not ready to commit suicide or throw myself off a cliff. I'm very happy with this place. I do have a question, however. This book that Claudia loaned me about Emmaline Varcoe indicated that the manor was built in 1870. But the sign by the gate has the date as 1875."

Tom answered. "Oh, the house *was* built in 1870. That was the year they were married. But 1875 was the year that Emmaline died, the year she committed suicide." He issued a slight snort.

I raised my eyebrows and slowly nodded my head. *That makes sense to me,* I thought. *No unexplained movements in the night.*

Then Tom added, "The interesting folklore that seems to stick to the manor is that no one knows where Emmaline is buried."

I felt a cold chill blow through the room. I shivered. "Yes, I read that in this book, but isn't there a community or church cemetery around somewhere? Where is John buried?" I asked. *Puzzles.*

Tom shrugged. "So, you know about John? No one really knows that either. There is a town cemetery, and the Methodist and Catholic churches both have cemeteries, but neither John nor his second wife, Ellen, are buried there either."

Tom looked directly at me and continued, "Ellen and John were married less than a year when she died. Then John remained here until he died around the turn of the century. His older brother inherited the manor but had no use for it. He buried John…somewhere…and boarded up the house and left. The property somehow traveled through several different hands till it presumably ended up with you." He turned back to the computer and mumbled, "No knowing what would have happened to the property if you hadn't come along. I guess money can buy a lot, even a house that belongs to someone else." His tone took a dark turn. Tom stiffened and I thought I saw a small frown pass quickly across his face.

Presumably? I thought. *An odd word to use.* A small sensation of fear scuttled up my spine and I took a step backward. Tom had made no outward signs of hostility, but there was something in his look that startled me. I took a deep breath and turned to Belinda. "I don't know what to say to the town lore, Belinda. But as I said, I don't believe in ghosts. If you happen to come across any additional factual information about the history of the house, its grounds, or its owners, I'd appreciate it if you would let me know." I was particularly interested in Tom's puzzling comment about ownership but thought better of pursuing it.

"I don't know that there is really anything more to know about the manor. It's all just dark history." She thrust the book into my hands and turned away. *Well, that's a curious thing to come from the Director of the Historical Society!*

I arrived back at the Inn and dialed a familiar number and waited.

"Hello?"

"George? This is Charlotte. I need another favor from you."

"Of course, what can I do?"

"If I remember correctly, you told me that Dad said that this manor had been in Mother's family for decades. You said you checked every detail, and the house is definitely mine. Do you recall that conversation?"

"Clearly. We did do that and there is no doubt that the manor is yours. Why do you ask?"

"Well, I met a man today who is researching Varcoe Manor, and he told me that when the original owner died, his brother inherited the property. If that is true, then how did it come into my mother's family's possession? This man also seemed to question ownership."

"I don't know about any of that, Charlotte, but I can promise you that while Walter was alive, we spent quite a bit of time pursuing the ownership. But since this question has arisen, I'll get someone on it, and we will go through all the the papers again. Did this person say anything more about the ownership of the other person?"

"Not much. The brother's name was Thomas Varcoe. That's about all I know. I really appreciate anything you can learn about this. My father went to a lot of trouble to keep this place up, and I don't want to be surprised by anyone appearing making a claim."

"Charlotte, I'm going to tell you not to worry, but I will look into this. I'll get back to you with anything that I find."

Chapter Seven

The call from Ted Wolff was a welcome diversion from banking, electric power, and a myriad of other activities.

"Ted! How great to hear your voice!"

"And yours, Charlotte. We miss you a lot and hope everything is settling in nicely."

I laughed. "Well, for someone living out of a suitcase in a hotel, it's about as well as can be expected! What news have you for me? Please – nothing bad; I've had enough of that!"

"Greg and I have spent the past few days working at your house and have just about everything packed. I appreciate you trusting me with the key to your safety deposit box. I'll pack that up and insure it for a million bucks before we send it up."

I smiled at his comment. Ted and Greg have been best friends with me for 20 years and we've been through a lot together. I couldn't think of anyone I trusted more.

"I talked to National Storage and Moving, and I just need to know when you want to move, and I'll finalize it."

"As soon as possible!!" I answered with more enthusiasm than I'd had in several days.

Ted called me back that afternoon and my weekend was now planned, with my furniture arriving on Saturday. I called Charlie and asked if his offer was still good, and to my relief he assured me it was.

* * *

By eight o'clock on Saturday morning I was at the manor. My entire life in an eighteen-wheeler would come rumbling up the drive by 10:30.

Relief washed over me, knowing that this would be my first night in my new house, and yet there was an anticipation that ran through me, both hot and cold. My strange conversation with Tom and Belinda seemed to linger. I tried to disregard my strange visitor in the attic, but it continued to hover in the back of my mind. I wondered if there could be something more to the ownership of Varcoe Manor.

I opened windows and a gentle June breeze wafted across the air, bringing with it the sting of brackish air. I stood on the kitchen deck looking out across the yard toward the river when a movement caught my eyes and I looked toward the lighthouse, where I thought I saw a shadow in the distance. But before I could move toward it, a muffled sound drew my attention away and I hurried out the front door to see a van with "Charles Beasley, LLC" written across the doors. Charlie jumped out of the van and hurried up the stairs.

"Hope you don't mind me showing up early. Thought maybe you could use some help prepping for the arrival of your entire life!" A grin crossed his face.

"Of course, not! I'm grateful that you agreed to come."

Within moments of his arrival, another loud sound greeted us as a large moving van rolled up the drive. Charlie shouted directions to the driver, helping turn the monstrous vehicle around to back up close to the porch and through a beehive of activity the manor began to take on a life of its own. Four hours rushed by, and by 2:30 the moving van was empty and on its way back to Washington. Charlie remained, helping where needed.

We stood in the kitchen where boxes sat stacked along the wall, in the pantry, and on the counters. I took a deep breath, realizing the work that lay ahead of me.

I looked out across the river. "Thanks for helping. Lots of things still to do, but your thinking of me…well, I'm very grateful. Oh, and thanks for sending me to the library. I picked up some interesting information about those events you mentioned, and Claudia Cooper loaned me a book about Emmaline Varcoe, the wife of the first owner."

"Interesting. I'd like to see it. I find myself becoming more curious about the history of the manor than I ever was growing up here!" he said.

I looked for the book but could not find it among the disarray of the house. I searched around the rooms but did not find it. "Well, that's odd. It was right here in my purse." *What in the world did I do with that book?*

A small frown crossed his face. "It'll turn up once you've become more settled. I'll see it then."

I put the thought out of my mind and continued. "Then I went to see Belinda Stapleford, who offered to buy the manor for the Historical Society. She seemed most anxious to do that."

Charlie's frown disappeared replaced by a small, crooked smile as if he were teasing me. "Between Peter Tidewater and Belinda, you seem to have quite a few people interested in purchasing the manor. I'm glad you turned down both offers." He coughed and I noticed a slight discoloration rise to his ears. "That is, this house needs someone to live in it." He stood with his hands in his pockets and slowly rocked back and forth on his heels and toes. He looked around and said, "It's been my pleasure to work on this house. We've kept it up as best we could over the years, but each new tenant seemed worse than the last. I think it's finally coming back to life. I rather enjoyed this work. Is there anything left you need taken care of?" he asked.

"Not right now, Charlie, but can I rely on you if I need something in the future?"

He smiled again. "Of course."

I waited a moment, then asked, "Do you know Tom Greene? I met him yesterday at the Historical Society and apparently he has been doing some research on the manor."

"Really?" Charlie said. "I don't know him very well. He came to Portsborough several months ago, maybe six or eight. He's a sort of 'handy-man'—I don't think he has a regular job. I've used him once in a while when I've been short-staffed but not regularly. Not sure where he's from. He seems to see a lot of Belinda. At least that's what the rumor mill says." The small frown returned. "So, he's been researching your home, eh? I wonder why."

"He told me some things about the original owner, John Varcoe, and his wives. Then he made the most curious comment about the ownership of the manor."

"Curious? How?" he asked.

"I don't recall his exact words, but he seemed to question whether I really held ownership."

"I doubt there is any validity to that. I wouldn't worry about it if I were you. I've been doing maintenance for your father for years, and my dad before me. There was never any question during that whole time about ownership. But that is a curious comment from someone who is so new to the area."

I sensed a moment of worry in his comment. We both remained quiet as a warm breeze fluttered through the manor and seemed to wrap itself around us.

I turned and walked out on the deck and Charlie followed me at a distance.

"What can you tell me about the lighthouse?" I pointed to the tall building on a hill about two hundred feet north of the manor.

He chuckled. "Yes, Walter and I had several conversations about that. It's not been in use for decades. I asked him if he wanted to tear it down or refinish it for some other use. He told me not to do anything with it, that someone else would make that decision. I didn't understand that sort of cryptic comment, but now I guess I do. That will be your decision."

I looked back at the building, with the mismatched, deteriorating wooden steps leading up to the building, and its state of disrepair. "That will be something I will decide later on—much later on." I continued to stare at the decrepit building. "The view from that lighthouse must be spectacular," I said.

It depends! Not all views are spectacular. The comment seemed to whisper in my ear. I looked up quickly but found no one else on the deck except Charlie staring up at the lighthouse.

"It's a dangerous place, that lighthouse." he said. "I haven't gone into it recently, but as I mentioned before, it's been inactive for decades and needs some major repair work. Of course, you might not be interested in that—it will require quite a bit of attention."

For a long moment my attention was drawn back to the lighthouse.

You must see that building, Charlotte. If nothing else, you must see that building.

I turned around and saw a vague vision in the kitchen doorway, behind Charlie. It was the same vision I saw in the attic.

Charlie looked at me with a questioning look on his face. "Of course, I'll be happy to help with whatever you decide." The sentence faded off into dry air.

"It's locked, right?" I asked, thinking about the shadow I saw earlier.

"No, not really necessary. But you don't want anyone marching around up there. Too dangerous."

* * *

My first night at the manor was not uncomfortable, and yet an uneasiness crept into my thoughts. Recent conversations and the history of the manor and its residents weighed heavily. I turned toward the French doors and stared out into the night made bright by a full moon. My eyes grew heavy, and I thought I saw a familiar shadow standing at the foot of the bed.

Welcome, and thank you.

I smiled as I drifted off into a deep sleep.

* * *

I awoke to almost-warm air drifting through the bedroom window, lifting the sheer curtains then releasing them to float back down and be sucked against the window screen. I rolled over, pulled the quilt up to my neck and watched the hypnotizing motion repeat itself. The movement lulled me back into a quiet daze; my eyelids became heavy and I wandered back toward a deep sleep when the breeze returned, cooler this time. I rose up onto my elbows. *I don't recall opening that window.*

I rubbed the sleep from my eyes and rose, placing my feet on the floor, searching for my slippers. I grabbed for the thick chenille robe at the foot of the bed, only to find that the robe was neatly hung on the old clothes tree that I rescued from the attic, and my slippers were carefully placed on the floor at the foot of the tree. I wrinkled my brow and walked toward the tall, thin piece of furniture. *I could have sworn I put the slippers at the side of the bed and the robe on the foot of the bed. I must have been more tired than I thought.*

I grabbed the robe and threw it across my shoulders, slid into the slippers, and wandered over to the window. The transparent sheers fluttered as I opened the screen door to the balcony. I closed my eyes and inhaled deeply the sweet fragrance of fresh lilacs. As I opened my eyes and walked to the edge of the balcony, I watched two hummingbirds hover on nearly invisible wings enjoying the fruit of the columbine flowers; a sign that mid-spring temperatures were warming as they made their way up the coast.

The clock on the nightstand read 7:16, and I knew my day would be a busy one. I showered and dressed and wandered down to the kitchen to try and find the French press and kettle.

* * *

I stood on the kitchen deck looking out across the lawn toward the Penobscot River, my hands wrapped around a warm mug of coffee. I gazed across the grounds until my eyes settled again on that lighthouse at the peak of the cliff. A light fog crawled up the cliff off the river and curled around the lighthouse, and a glow seemed to shine from the windows at its peak.

I thought about Mother's diary with its cryptic messages. I pushed away thoughts of my visitor in the attic—and again yesterday in the house—sure that was a carryover from the surprise of finding mother's belongings and the message of Simeon Barkley's book.

The temperature was not warm, not cold, but a welcoming morning cool, and in my jeans and sweatshirt, I felt more at home. I sat in a white Adirondack chair a short distance from the steps that led down to the river below. I had reread the diary after Charlie left and I found mother's reference to Emmaline Varcoe a little more off-putting than I had the first time I read the entry. The words Mother had put to paper grew more curious.

A light sound in the distance drew my attention and I looked up from the book, expecting to see some activity on the water, but the water was still. I returned to the book, and the sound occurred again. As I looked up, I glanced up toward the lighthouse and thought I saw a faint glow from the room just below the lantern room. I knew little about lighthouses but was aware that this room was used for storage. Of course, the house had not been in service for decades, and there would be no reason for maintaining supplies.

I placed the diary on the chair and walked toward the lighthouse steps, searching for that noise, but I heard only the waves slapping the rocks at the bottom of the cliff and the caws of the birds above. I approached the steps, my curiosity rising. I remembered the strange comment that I *must see this building*. I found the first step a bit wobbly, but it was the crack from the second step that brought me back to the conversation I had with Charlie about not going into the lighthouse until the steps could be checked and fixed. Despite his warning, I felt drawn to this building.

The stairs proved to be a challenge as I cautiously moved forward. Each stair was worn in different places and on some I found myself stepping to the side, others to the middle. As I approached the walk around the base of the lighthouse, I saw the railing broken in two when a gust of warm air blasted against me and I stumbled backward, grabbing the railing as my balance teetered. A splinter of wood jammed into the skin just below my thumb. *Enough investigating for now. Perhaps more when you're a little less careless!*

When I returned to the yard, I discovered my mother's diary had disappeared. I searched the ground around and beneath the furniture but found no trace of the book. I ventured toward the side of the cliff and sensed a slight vertigo as I looked down 30 feet to the river below but saw nothing of the diary. *First the Emmaline book, now Mother's diary.* A chill raced up my spine. I searched further but to my disappointment, found no diary.

Chapter Eight

As the days moved forward, I searched further for the diary. My sense of loss was greater than I could ever have expected. I spent the days sitting on the lawn and listening to the rolling waves below crash against the rocks. As I inhaled deeply, I had a growing sense that things were not quite right. The long, dark nights when shadows stretched across the grounds in odd configurations proved most troubling, but after several days of collecting myself and my belongings and sprinkling my own touch throughout the house, my comfort zone began to improve, with one exception: the books were still missing.

One morning at the beginning of my second week, as I followed my daily ritual and watched the breeze ruffle the grass below, I sensed a warming of the air. The air became still, the shrubs and trees stood motionless; the grass remained quiet as well. I focused on the scragginess of the lawn, in particular the heavy forest to the north when a thought entered my mind.

Ellen never cared for this land. She did not take care of it. She was not entitled to it.

I stood up straight at the sound of a voice slipping across the deck. *Ellen? Where have I heard that name before?* I turned and saw the vague form hovering at the far end of the deck. There was nothing distinct about it. It appeared like a cloud. I froze. *Ellen?* It was an unspoken word, and yet the start of a conversation.

Ellen was not a good woman, but then again, she did not marry a good man. The cloud began to take a vague form.

Cautiously my thoughts engaged in the conversation. *What do you mean she was not a good woman? Who was Ellen?*

The vision moved closer and I saw the unclear feature of a female face.

She was Thomas's second wife. She wanted this house because she thought it gave her standing in the community. But she never did anything to bring out its true beauty.

You said she did not marry a good man. That's a rather unfeeling thing to say. Why wasn't he a good man?

She remained quiet for a moment. Then, *I don't recall. That's something you'll have to learn.*

Then it turned and disappeared; where it went, I did not know, but it left. *Did I really just have a conversation with a vision? What more do I have to learn?* I asked myself, refusing to believe that my new home was haunted, as Tom Greene had suggested.

* * *

As the day progressed into evening, my eyes became weary and my head began to droop. I walked to the bedroom balcony and peeked out toward the cliff but saw nothing out of the ordinary. *Getting a little too taken up by stories of the house,* I thought and yet something stuck in the back of my mind and I thought about the accidents that occurred on the grounds. As I turned, a faint light drew my attention to the lighthouse above the cliff's edge. I squinted and stared, as the light seemed to waver through the upper floor of the building when suddenly it disappeared. *Did I really see that or is my imagination playing games?* Tired, I closed and locked the door and returned to the warmth of the room, where I neatly folded my robe and placed it at the foot of the bed. I removed my slippers and placed them on the floor directly next to the nightstand. *I will remember exactly where I put them tomorrow, and they had better be where they are right now!* I smiled at my thoughts.

My eyes grew heavy and the last thing I remembered was a cool breeze wafting through the room, circling gently through every corner, as if searching for a place to settle. My eyes closed and I did not dream.

Something happened. My mind became active and I sensed movement around me. I turned my head toward the nightstand and saw the time was 2:35 a.m. I lifted my hand to my face and rubbed my eyes.

It's all wrong, you know.

I stopped. Was I dreaming?

You might as well turn this way.

Unable to resist, I turned toward the other side of the bed and saw a vague, translucent, and yet familiar figure settled in the chair on the other side of the bed. I sensed a smile drape across the figure's face. My heartbeat increased, and I remained immobile.

Good morning, Charlotte.

I did not respond. I did not know how to respond. I just stared.

Are you afraid of me?

I crawled up on my elbows, edging backwards toward the far side of the bed. I continued to stare at this elusive image, the same image that told me about Ellen earlier; the same image that met me in the attic now sat in my bedroom chair, and yet 'sat' was not quite the right word.

You don't have to be afraid of me. I'll not hurt you. Actually, I need you.

My heartbeat slowed and I further skittered up into a sitting position. *What do you mean, you need me?* I thought the words rather than spoke them.

There have been so many before you, and with each I thought I would find the one who would help. I felt so strongly that Lyda could help me, and then— But not until you appeared did I ever really feel I had found the right one.

I'm afraid I don't understand. Who? How were the others not able to help you?

I sensed a sad grin wander across her face.

I need to find out where I am.

I stared for a moment, confused.

Well, first Simeon. As I said, he got it all wrong.

My gaze wandered through the figure; I shook my head as if to disturb this vision but when I looked back at the chair, it was still there, gauzelike in its appearance. *What's all wrong?*

Simeon's story. Of course, poor Simeon had none of the facts. He based his story on family lore, and we all know how wrong that can be, don't we?

The vision lifted two books from her lap, and gently placed them on the bed next to me. While the books sat in her lap, they had the same transparent appearance that my vision had, but once they left her hands and sat on the bed, they became three-dimensional.

I stared at the books—my mother's diary and Simeon's book. *I wondered what happened to these.* I gently touched my mother's diary; afraid it would disappear as quickly as it arrived.

I had to see what Simeon wrote. I know he was trying to do the best he could, but he just never got the facts right. The figure smiled that same sad smile. *I remember your mother. As much as she thought she was losing her mind, she believed in me. After so many attempts, I felt I had finally found someone to help me.*

Tears puddled in my eyes at the mention of my mother. I tried to speak but words failed me. I wiped the tear from my eye and picked up Simeon's book and thumbed through it. *What did he get wrong?* I found myself asking again, as if this conversation was normal.

I can't tell you – I'm afraid I can only guide you. You'll have to discover the truth for both of us.

The figure rose and retrieved my robe and slippers, which she placed at the clothes tree then began to glide toward the open French door.

Wait! Who—what—are you? I felt myself choke on the words.

The figure turned just as she arrived at the doors. The warm breeze floated through her, but not against her. When the sheers billowed, her dress did not. Again, I felt that transparent smile. *I thought you knew.* She pointed to Mother's diary and commented, *I'm Emmaline; Emmaline Varcoe. I enjoyed revisiting your mother.* And with that declaration, she disappeared through the screen.

I struggled to remain awake, but my eyes grew heavy. Against all rationality, I lowered myself back onto my feather pillow and fell into a deep sleep.

Chapter Nine

I awoke to the boom of thunder and rain beating against the windows. Through foggy eyes I read 7:38 a.m. on the clock just as a strong wind blew open the French doors. Rain poured into the room, soaking and lifting the sheers. I threw back the covers and rushed to the doors, closing and locking them. The water-soaked sheers fell back and clung to the windows and doors. The sky darkened and lightning shards brought only brief moments of light before plunging the morning back into a gloomy darkness. Heavy clouds traveled quickly across the ground and out over the river below. Thunder pounded the air with a heavy rhythm that shook the house.

My head ached as if a small drum beat just behind my eyes. Turning back toward the bed, I stopped in the middle of the room, and noticed my robe and slippers. They were not where I had left them last night but were once again at the clothes tree. My eyes widened as I recalled the scene from earlier. *Did I really see her move my robe and slippers?* I also recalled my mother's prophetic question about her own sanity.

The sounds of the storm drifted away as the thoughts of an unusual dream passed through my mind. I turned and looked at the chair next to the bed but saw nothing that would indicate it had been recently occupied. However, my gaze drifted to the side of the bed, where I saw Mother's diary. Next to it, Simeon Barkley's book sat face down, open to a particular page. I picked it up and turned it over.

The book was open to a chapter titled 'Emmaline's Death.' I flopped down in the chair and began to read. The chapter proved light in detail, but the emotion of Simeon's writing blew off the pages. The earlier chapters I read had not engaged me, but it was clear that Simeon had lost a favorite relative and it caused him great distress. I picked up mother's diary and reread the last entries before placing it on my nightstand. I considered how Mother thought she might be losing her mind and wondered if that could be hereditary. Unable to concentrate, I put the book down, rose, and prepared for a new day.

* * *

As I stood at the kitchen counter, I looked out the door toward the river. The sturdy shrubs at the edge of the cliff withstood the storm, but they waved back and forth with the stiff wind. I wasn't sure what I expected to see, and yet as I looked at the lighthouse, buried in fog, I sensed that the cliff and the lighthouse were pivotal to events that had occurred in this house.

The fuzz of sleep began to dissipate, and my mind went back to the visit that so rudely awakened me. Even in the vague light of a day beginning with an onslaught of wind and rain and thunder, that visit remained vivid in my mind. I wondered if this had been anything more than a dream brought on by a combination of old newspaper stories, two books, and some historical research that peppered my imagination. And yet, the reality of the encounter settled in my head and would not let go. I was drawn out of my reverie when the phone rang.

"Hi Charlotte, Charlie here. Hope you're making it through the storm okay."

"Other than the wind blowing open my bedroom doors and the rain soaking the carpet, I'm fine. What can I do for you?"

"I was thinking about that area below the lighthouse—I think it needs to be cleared. Walter and I had talked about it, but I never pursued it. I'd like to get all of the heavy undergrowth removed; quite a few roots are under a thick layer of soil. We could probably restructure it without too much trouble."

"Do you have any idea how long it will take to do that job?" I asked.

He thought for a minute, then said, "Cleaning the shrubbery out will probably take about two weeks. I had planned to come out today, but I think the weather has other ideas. I'll get back to you as soon as I can. Just wanted to share that with you."

A thought skittered across my mind as I remembered my conversation with Peter Tidewater. "Do you recall that I mentioned Peter Tidewater's suggestion for an open house one day in the not-too-distant future? I've been giving that some thought. Do you think anyone from the town would come? It would be a good way for me to get to know people and maybe show them that there is nothing mysterious about the house."

A smile rose in his voice when he said, "Yes, I remember and I think that's a great idea, and believe me, you would not be able to keep the townspeople away. Maybe you should limit that to the Historical Society, the Library, the Town Council—people like that. If you don't, you'll have the entire town wandering around your grounds."

"Perhaps you could help me identify who to invite?" I asked. I looked at the calendar on my counter and flipped a few pages forward. "How about Thursday? You could help me with a guest list, and I could pick your brain about the town and this house in particular."

He rustled through some papers, then said, "Thursday it is. I have it on my calendar. How about 10 a.m.? If you want me to, I could look at the bedroom door and make sure the latch is okay."

"I'm sure there is nothing wrong with it and ten sounds good. And thanks for calling about the lawn work."

We finished the call and I thought perhaps Charlie could answer questions about the house that I should be asking the Historical Society or the library. For some reason I was comfortable with Charlie, even though I'd known him for such a short time. I was certain that if Charlie could not help me get to know this house better, he could send me to the right person.

* * *

Time dragged slowly, and I felt trapped by a wet, noisy day. The wind pounded and the rain pitched sideways, striking the windows and sending water cascading from side to side, when I heard a loud noise from the second floor. I rushed upstairs and found the attic door open. I flipped the light switch and took careful steps into the dark attic. The musty smell of old papers and older wood accosted me. Rain pelted the roof, but I saw no damage. The small windows were secure, and no water leaked into the room. I wandered around, fingered several items, when a small figurine caught my attention. I picked it up and was surprised to find two little pink piglets looking at me from the palm of my hand. *Hm, supposed to be good luck.* I smiled to myself as I put it in my sweater pocket.

As I turned to leave, a large hutch on the far side of the attic caught my attention. I walked over to it and discovered a treasure. "This will need some attention, but it would fit perfectly against the far wall in the kitchen. I'll have to talk to Charlie about this," I mumbled out loud. I realized that Charlie was beginning to take a larger role in Varcoe Manor than I had anticipated, and I wondered about bringing a man into my life at this time. The thought intrigued me, but that door seemed to be securely closed.

I ran my hand over the lower back of the hutch and felt wood that moved at my touch. I struggled to move the hutch forward a few inches and discovered what appeared to be a picture frame hidden behind it. It took several minutes of wiggling and pushing and prodding before I was able to free the oval frame from its resting place.

Filthy with dust and grime, and in the dim light of the attic, I could not distinguish its contents, but I believed that the frame, once cleaned up, would be lovely. I left the attic and returned to the library with the picture frame tucked under my arm. I placed the frame on several large pieces of newspaper on the library floor and went to the kitchen for an early dinner.

As evening drifted into night, the storm did not pass completely, but rather changed to a steady rain. The wind and thunder and lightning had moved on further north leaving rain-cooled temperatures. I yawned. My gaze wandered toward the kitchen door and I found myself looking across the lawn toward the lighthouse and the cliff. That curious light reappeared, stopped for a moment, then extinguished. I wondered if someone could be up there. *I'll find out soon enough once the repairs had been completed.* I felt a cold chill wander up my spine. *Somebody must be walking on my grave,* I thought. And that uncomfortable dream from the previous night returned and haunted my thoughts.

I quickly turned out the light and scurried up to my room. I washed and changed clothes and found myself drawn to the French doors. The weather continued to move north, and night settled in without a moon. I wondered briefly about my dreams, and if I was letting my imagination run amok. I put the thoughts of boogeymen out of my mind, walked over to the clothes tree, hung up my robe, and placed my shoes at the foot of the tree.

I stopped and looked back at what I had done. Never in my entire life had I used a clothes tree, and suddenly this small, upright piece of furniture had taken on a new meaning in my life. I just wasn't sure what that meaning was. I climbed into the bed and pulled the warm flannel sheets tight up to my neck. The steady rain cooled the air, and I lowered my already drowsy mind into a deep sleep.

Chapter Ten

The next two days remained damp, with brief rains skittering on and off as though through a plugged spigot. The days passed in gloom, although the distant skies to the south carried only thin, wispy clouds and the faint promise of a warm sun.

Thoughts about Emmaline remained tucked just at the edge of my mind and on Wednesday night I punched up my pillow and closed my eyes. Sleep did not come easily, but eventually it did come, when a light sound raised me from a deep sleep to a level closer to the edge of reality. I rolled over and looked at the clock. Two thirty in the morning.

Good morning, Charlotte. I hope I did not startle you.

I spun around to the other side and sat bolt upright. I felt an unspoken response rise. *Well, yes, actually you did.* I had no idea why I was engaging in a mental conversation with this aura that sat in my bedroom chair, and yet I was not uncomfortable or frightened, just curious and annoyed.

I apologize for that. I do realize that you must think this odd.

I'm not sure I know what I think. My common sense tells me I'm having a dream, and that it's probably the result of hearing stories.

But you don't believe that entirely, do you?"

I thought for a moment, afraid to answer for fear I would commit myself to something that just didn't make any sense. And yet, I felt an urge to move forward. *No, I don't believe that entirely. But I don't know why. You told me the other night that you are Emmaline. Is that correct?* I pulled myself up to a full sitting position and allowed my mind to take control of the conversation.

Yes, that's correct. I am Emmaline.

I took a deep breath. *And so, you're telling me you're a ghost, haunting my new home?*

A cold breeze blew through the room. *My old home—and no, I am not a ghost. At least I don't choose to consider myself that. I'm not even sure what a ghost is, but I prefer to consider myself the essence of this house.* Her answer was not angry, but rather determined.

I stopped to consider this. *Does this mean that you will remain here forever, and visit me every night?*

No, and no. But I can't leave until some things are set right and you are the first person to set foot on these grounds in many decades who I believe can help me. Simeon lived here for a short time—I suspect to get a feeling for where I died. I thought he would be a good candidate to help me, but I'm afraid he did not take kindly to my essence. And as far as visiting you every night? No, although you should not be surprised to see me during the day.

I felt a sad smile rise through her aura.

Can I ask what you expect me to do? My curiosity piqued, I began to feel that perhaps I'd been drawn to Varcoe Manor to accomplish a task, and now I was on the verge of finding out about that task. Perhaps I would put my mother's memory to rest as well.

Charlotte, you have to get to the truth, but I fear you will find many stumbling blocks in your path. Be careful of those around you but call upon your friends for help.

Are you going to tell me what these stumbling blocks may be?

I suspect I will be one of them.

Her response reminded me of the quizzical comments inside a fortune cookie. *Do you plan on giving me any hints as to what truth I'm looking for?* I sensed Emmaline smile at me.

I can direct you, but you must find the answers. I do desperately need your help. Charlotte, I am unable to leave this world because I don't know where to leave from. I don't know where I am buried—or for that matter, even if I was ever buried. Regardless, in order to move on, I have to know what happened.

Emmaline—I am baffled by this whole situation. I'm not even sure that this is anything more than a dream.

Her sad smile once again appeared, and she nodded her head. *When you find the answer, you will know this is not a dream.*

My eyes became heavy again, and although my mind was awake and racing through this odd conversation, my body curled down onto the bed and the last thing I remembered was tugging the warm flannel sheet up around my neck and falling back into a deep slumber.

* * *

I awoke early Thursday morning confused. My dream had begun to dissolve but had not completely evaporated. Emmaline remained in the back of my mind and I wondered about the reality of her visit. Twice this visitation appeared at my bedside, and yet I was unable to determine if something unearthly had happened, or if I was, indeed, simply plagued by dreams based on town rumors and bad events that occurred on this property. I found myself intrigued that there was a history here that needed to be opened.

A stiff breeze off the river blew the humidity out of the air. Several small, high clouds dotted the sky; I sensed a good day on the rise. At 10:00 a.m. sharp I heard the sound of a vehicle approaching and opened the door just as Charlie arrived.

The rain of the previous several days had skittered off to the north and left a mild day in its wake. We spent the next hour walking the grounds. We approached the large swath of lawn surrounding the manor and Charlie nodded his head several times. We finished at the north side of the manor where the trees and shrubs formed a deep forest.

"This is going to take some work," Charlie said. He pointed to the long tree roots that crept toward the house. "You don't want to have this much growth creeping toward the house, it could damage the foundation." I nodded in silent agreement, relying on his knowledge. As we turned and walked along the cliff, the lighthouse rose before us.

Charlie leaned in close and looked at the first few steps. "These should be easy enough to fix," Charlie said. "It will take a few weeks, but I have the men and material I need back at my shop."

Embarrassed, I did not mention my mishap when I ventured up the stairs.

* * *

We finished the tour and returned to the house. I stood back and opened the door wide then said, "I think I have another task for you if you have any extra time."

"I've got time. What is it?"

"The other day during the height of the storm, I heard a loud noise on the second floor. When I went to investigate, I found the door to the attic at the far end of the hall was open. So, I went snooping and found several items of furniture up there that I'd like you to take a look at. I think they might have some potential. Among these pieces was an old hutch that I am particularly interested in seeing if it can be restored. I have the perfect place for it in the kitchen."

He scratched his chin and thought for a moment. "I seem to remember seeing a hutch. Didn't take a really close look, but I do recall it being there. Let's take a look at it"

"Well, there's more…behind the hutch I found a large, oval shaped antique picture frame. I brought it downstairs. It's in terrible shape; well by that I mean it's filthy dirty, covered in years of grease and grime, and I can see there is a picture there, but I can't make out any details. I need to clean it up but maybe you can tell me if it needs any additional refurbishing or special care. I don't know what kind of wood it's made of and I don't want to damage it by using some vile cleaning agent that will eat away at it, and I wondered if you would be able to give me some help cleaning it up. It looks really quite lovely and I think I can probably find some nice art to place in it."

I listened to Charlie chuckle, a soft, knowing sound. I rather liked it. "Sure, be glad to take a look. I don't recall seeing anything like that while we were there, but we were pretty well distracted with other things. Let's head toward the attic. Now I'm curious and anxious to see that hutch and that frame you found."

I flipped the light switch, and we climbed the stairs. The hutch sat against a far wall and Charlie pulled out his measuring tape and a flashlight for a closer look.

"Seems to be some damage here on the top of the carving board shelf but this is good, solid ash and should be easy to fix. Someone must have used this a lot; I see lots of stains and slices from sharp carving knives. Those things always add a certain amount of character to a piece of furniture, I think."

I watched as he pointed out the gashes in the board. My mind wandered to what could have done this damage. "This is a rather large piece. Do you think you'll have any trouble moving it downstairs?"

"Might take some pushing and prodding. We might have to take it apart, but someone got it up here, so I guess we can get it down."

I led Charlie downstairs to the library where the frame was laid out in the middle of the floor. Charlie walked around it, looking at it from all angles but not touching it. He bent over and looked closely, then got down on his hands and knees and slowly edged his way around it. He gingerly lifted the frame off the newspaper and moved it around; then slunk closer, lowering his face almost to touching it. He removed a handkerchief from his back pocket and slowly drew it across a small area of the frame, moving it back and forth with gentle strokes. Slowly a dark shine emerged as he wiped away years of grime.

I watched this one-man dance with curiosity. Although the area he cleaned was no longer than two inches, the gentle swirls he used to clean it brought that small piece of wood to life. He waved me down to the floor next to him and pointed to the spot. He shined his flashlight at it. I squinted at the small piece of burled wood.

"This is an amazing piece of work," he said, "and I suspect that whoever created this frame spent a great deal of time locating just the right wood, applying just the right finish, and carving the wood to create such a beautiful, individual piece. The craftsman must have spent hours, if not days, on it."

"How old do you think it is?" I asked.

Charlie sat back and his glance washed over the whole frame. "Assuming that there's no damage that would have required mending— and if my suspicions are correct regarding how it was created and what wood was used—the style dates back to well over a century ago. There were a lot of craftsmen in this area and wood was certainly accessible. I'd like to take it with me, if I may, and see what I can do with it."

We were both still low to the ground and when I turned and looked at Charlie; his face was comfortably close to mine. I smiled. "Of course. I'll be excited to see what you can do with it." We both remained silent for a moment until a slow smile crept across his face. His smile warmed me. He rose onto his knees and gave me a hand.

"If this is what I think it is, there may be some real value to it as well. There was a furniture craftsman in Bangor who specialized in pieces like this besides his regular furniture work. I believe he was sought after for pieces just like this. I'll have to check into that."

I stared at him, my eyes wide, and my mouth slightly agape. "Charles Beasley, you amaze me. I suspect there is more to you than meets the eye."

He smiled, and I saw a slight flush rise from under his color. At the same moment a cool breeze wrapped around me.

He likes you.

I turned around quickly at the sound of the voice; Emmaline stood in the hallway just outside the library. I felt annoyed at her interruption of a special moment.

"Are you okay, Charlotte?" Charlie asked.

I turned to him and the moment passed. "Oh, yes, yes, I'm just fine. Got a little dizzy getting up so quickly."

There was a moment of stillness that came between us then he bent forward and picked up the frame. "Let's take this into the kitchen and see if we can clean up the glass."

I followed him and placed the newspaper on the island countertop, and he laid the frame on it.

"I'd like to see what is under the glass. I can tell it is some kind of photo or perhaps a portrait. Whatever it is, it's very dark. I need to be very careful because this glass is gently convex and if it is as old as I think, it might be quite fragile."

I looked at the frame as it lay on its back. "I didn't realize it when I brought it down from the attic. My God, I could have destroyed this with just one bump." I had already taken a personal ownership of the item and did not wish to see it ruined.

"Well, if you had broken the glass, that would not be as bad as breaking the frame or destroying whatever is under it. I could get the glass replaced."

I laughed, a short, almost snorting laugh. "It's probably a picture of Elvis on velvet!"

Charlie rolled back and bellowed out a hearty laugh. "I would never have thought of that! Well, shall we get started? This could take some time. And while we're at it, let's talk about your open house."

"What do you need to start cleaning?" I asked as I retrieved a pencil and notebook from a drawer.

"Let's start with the glass itself. I'd like to see what's under the glass. I have some gentle cleaning agents at the office to clean the wood. I'll need a small bucket of warm water—and do you have any Murphy's Oil Soap?"

"I do."

"While you're getting that ready, I'll write some ideas about invitations."

As I rummaged around in the back of the pantry, Charlie began throwing out names and ideas.

"Any idea when you want to do this soiree?" he asked.

I smiled to myself. I wouldn't have pictured 'soiree' in his vocabulary.

"I was thinking perhaps in the next month. Do you think that's too soon?"

"The people in this town will begin getting ready for it the instant it becomes known, and it will take them all of thirty minutes to shower, shave, and dress!" He laughed at his own comment. "Mind if I make a few notes for you?" he asked.

"No please do." I moved several items around in the pantry until I found a small green plastic bucket, some rubber gloves, and a sponge while I continued to search for the Murphy's Oil.

"Okay," he called to me. "You'll want to be sure to invite the full town council and their administrative staff. They control permits and we'll be needing those over the next few months."

I stood up straight when he used the word 'we.' That cool breeze engulfed me again.

He likes you. The mantra repeated in my ear.

I turned quickly but was alone in the pantry.

"Oh, and the sheriff's office – don't want to forget Lorelei Tuttle, our first female State Sheriff; and the Historical Society. Belinda gets her nose out of joint if she is snubbed or ignored."

I returned from the pantry with all the cleaning paraphernalia in hand, including several clean white cotton cloths. I put the sponge, cloths, and Murphy's Oil on the counter next to the frame and took the pail to the sink.

Charlie stopped writing and turned toward me. "She kept a real tight grasp on what we were doing here. Especially after word got out that the owner passed—er—your father. Made quite a pest of herself."

I stopped and turned toward Charlie. "That's odd. I didn't know she had been out here at all. She didn't mention it when I met her the other day."

Charlie continued, "She was here almost every day. I caught her a few times snooping around through the house and had to ask her kindly to leave. The maintenance on this property is a major task, and the last thing I needed was for some nosy citizen to fall and injure herself. I finally got rid of her during the last week while we put everything in order for you."

I brought the bucket over to the counter. "Well, whatever her reason was, she seemed quite disappointed that she couldn't sway me to sell."

Charlie just raised his eyebrows. "Your property seems to be high on the buyer's list these days! Well, I'm glad you did not succumb to her prodding!"

I cleared my voice and changed the subject. "So, who else should I invite?" I took the paper and pencil from him as he poured the soap into the warm water.

As he swirled the mixture, he looked off into the distance, quickly running names through his mind. "Okay, Claudia and Martin Cooper from the library and of course, Madelyn, their daughter. You might consider the school principal and maybe some of the teachers— history and English and all that! Those invitations would put you in good stead. Chamber of Commerce staff and members – don't worry, there aren't that many members and most of them are business leaders, so that could be a double invite."

I quickly scribbled Charlie's thoughts as his distant gaze remained glued to the cabinet in front of him. He turned and smiled at me as if he realized he had wandered, mentally. "I'll get a list of names drawn up. Did you have a number in mind? This is such a small community that to leave someone important out would be the kiss of death. We circle our wagons a lot!"

I laughed out loud. "I don't have a number in mind. As a matter of fact, this was just a last-minute thought from Peter Tidewater—" I let the remainder of the sentence drift off unfinished.

He really does like you!

I shook my head again, this time to remove the pesky little voice.

Charlie ignored the rubber gloves, just picked up the sponge and dipped it into the water. He approached the glass as if he were a surgeon getting ready to operate. He tackled the top middle of the convex glass and began a slow swirling movement, moving only centimeters at a time. He took a cotton rag and wiped the area, repeating this process several times. I noticed the strength in his hands, yet his gentle touch moved in one small circle, over and over and over.

It took only minutes before the glass began to shine. We hovered over the frame, each staring into the oval as it gained more and more clarity. Charlie increased the area he cleaned from one small circle until after fifteen minutes of continued gentle rubbing he had most of the glass cleaned. I ran my index finger over one small area on the side where the glass that touched the frame remained grimy.

"When I get this back to the shop, I'll take the glass off the frame and get those small places cleaned up. Don't want to do it here in case I drop it!"

"No, that's fine. I agree. So, what do we think is under this glass?" I asked, my voice betraying my excitement.

Charlie picked up the frame and carried it over to where the sun streamed in from the French doors. We moved our heads close together to see who or what was under the glass.

"Oh!" I said. I did not want to tell Charlie that I recognized exactly whose picture we were looking at. Emmaline. The vague vision of the woman who visited me so often these days became clear.

I took a quick step back and Charlie raised his head. "Are you okay?" he asked.

"Yes, yes, I'm fine."

We both looked back at the frame. The sepia photo stared back at us, void of color except for the varying degrees of browns and grays, typical of the pictures taken during and after the Civil War. A young woman stared back at us through the cleared glass. Her dark hair above her brow was drawn back away from her square face and tied into a full bun at the top of her head. Unruly curls and waves fell to the sides, just above her ears. Her heavy, dark eyebrows sat above narrow, dark eyes, and a small, delicate nose pointed barely upward. Her lips, devoid of artificial color, protruded into a slight pout as if she wanted to smile but knew that pictures were serious, and smiling was discouraged. It was clear she wore no makeup.

Wrapped around her high collar was a small necklace that looked like a locket. It hung directly in the center of her chest, close to her throat. On the left side of the dress a small watch sat pinned just a few inches below the shoulder. It hung upside down to the observer, but as she would look down at it and lift it toward her face, it would be right side up for her to read the time. The dark dress did not appear to be formal; rather it looked like a blend of cottons or linen. The straight lines flowed down over her small body and disappeared under the frame of the photo.

"It's rather a plain dress, but I guess there were times and places for more formal wear," I said. I wondered if a plain dress was a sign of her character.

"I'll take this back with me and work on it. Maybe we'll find out something more once it's cleaned. And I'll work on this party list. Should have it done by early next week."

I smiled. "That would be great. How about dinner Tuesday? You could be my first guest."

Charlie smiled back. "I'd like that. Tuesday it is."

"Dinner at seven but come earlier if you find out anything about our picture frame." I flushed as I realized I referred to the picture frame as 'ours.'

"Oh, right. I'll let you know if I find out anything else, but otherwise I'll see you at seven."

I found an old quilt and we wrapped it around the frame and took it out to the truck. As Charlie drove off, I turned away from the door and saw Emmaline standing in the kitchen doorway, her face as clear as day.

I don't remember when that picture was taken. Another thing for you to discover. And she disappeared.

Chapter Eleven

I slept well that night with no visits from Emmaline, nor did she appear in my dreams. I thought about Mother and began to feel that her visions were just that, dreams. The fact that I awoke the next day having had a full night's sleep, somehow confirmed that belief.

I rose at 8:30 and my mind went directly to the picture frame. I wondered what else Charlie would find, if anything. Since the first frame contained Emmaline's picture, I wondered if there was also a picture of John…or so I supposed it would be normal.

The day started clear with a bright sun rising high overhead. I filled myself with a strong breakfast and a hearty cup of coffee and wandered into the library. I sat down at the computer and discovered an email from Madelyn Cooper.

Ms. Sunday. At your convenience could you come to the library? I think I have something of interest for you.

I read the message a second time, wondering what in the world Madelyn Cooper could have that would interest me, but since I needed to return the Simeon Barkley book I might as well see what she had in mind.

The temperature had begun a steady rise and it felt good to be outside with something to occupy my time besides some unaccountable dreams wandering through the recesses of my mind.

When I entered the library, I noticed that Claudia was not at her perch, but Madelyn was at hers at the end of the desk. Madelyn looked up and her eyes grew wide. She shifted her glance from left to right, then toward the office, picked up an envelope, and hurried over toward me. I found her state of anxiety curious.

"Good morning, Madelyn," I said. Apparently, my voice carried, as three nearby patrons raised their heads in unison and stared at me.

As Madelyn came around to the front of the desk, I saw she held the large envelope close to her body. She grabbed my elbow and nudged me back out the door and into the hallway and closed the door behind us. Again, she looked from one direction to the other. *How odd,* I thought. *This hallway is only five feet wide!* But I waited.

"Miss Sunday, I thought you might be interested in this." She waved the envelope but did not give it to me. "The other day when you were here—well, after you left—Mother told me about your conversation, and—well, I did a little investigating on my own."

"Investigating?" I asked.

She leaned in close. "About Emmaline. There isn't really very much, but I thought these might help answer any questions you might have about the house and property." She handed me the envelope.

I opened it and several pieces of paper slid out into my hand. All were Xerox copies of other documents, but the first one I looked at was a copy of a photograph. It was the same woman whose picture was in the frame Charlie and I cleaned yesterday – Emmaline.

"That's Emmaline Varcoe," Madelyn said. She suddenly looked like the proverbial cat with canary feathers in its mouth.

"Where did you find this?" I asked. I did not tell her I already knew.

"It was in the Historical Society archives." Again, she leaned in toward me in a conspiratorial manner. "I snuck it out and brought it back here to copy. I didn't want Belinda to know."

"Know what?" I asked.

"That I took it. I've since returned it and she never knew!" She chuckled.

"Why would Belinda care?" I asked. "Surely this is public information."

"No, not if Belinda has anything to say about it. As soon as she learned about you inheriting the manor, she went into a panic. Of course, there wasn't much she could do about it. But she got Tom to researching it right away."

My mind flew into overtime with questions. "Why would it matter to her if I own it or not?" My curiosity inched up as she spoke.

A deep red hue flushed up from under her collar and she just stared at me. "Oh, well, I don't know, exactly, she just—" Madelyn rushed to change the subject. "The other things in the envelope might help you with anything else you need to know about the property. I made some copies of the property plats. They are quite old; dating back to when the manor was originally built, but I don't think there has been any change to the property lines. I don't think anyone else has ever bought any of the surrounding property. So, nothing has been changed unless the grounds changed over the years by nature."

I was at a loss to know why she thought the property lines would interest me, but something in the back of my mind told me to keep and study them. "Well, thank you for doing this, Madelyn. May I ask why you thought I'd be interested?"

She unfolded her arms and straightened her blouse, pulling it down over her hips. She looked at the floor and said, "I just thought, as a new neighbor, you'd be interested."

It was obvious she knew, or thought she knew more than she was willing to share. I remained silent for a minute and nodded my head. I reached into my tote, retrieved the book and handed it to her.

"Well, thank you for that. And, before I forget, I want to return this. Please thank your mother for sharing it with me." I did not mention that an ethereal figure from the netherworld also read it. I was certain that that information would get around town in a heartbeat! She took the book and held it close to her chest.

"Thank you, I'll let mother know you returned it." With that short response, she spun around and hurried back into the library.

I walked back to my car and sat in it for several minutes, looking at the photograph. I started the car and drove to Charlie's business. There was one person talking to Charlie and one of his employees in the small conference room. At the sound of the door closing behind me, Charlie looked up, said something to the others, and left the room to greet me.

"Charlotte, what a pleasant surprise. What can I do for you?"

"Madelyn Cooper gave me this envelope. Take a look at this picture." I handed the copy of the picture to him.

He looked at it, then at me. He blinked several times then walked over to a workbench at the far end of the room. I moved close to him and we both stared at the picture under the glass. Charlie put the smaller copy next to it.

"This is the same woman," he said, moving his eyes from one to the other and back again.

"This is Emmaline Varcoe, the wife of John Varcoe who built Varcoe Manor."

"How do you know that?" he asked, looking up at me.

"Well, that's what she told me." I realized I could not tell him that I knew because Emmaline told me!

"What makes you think she knows what she's talking about?" he asked as a half-smirk darted across his face.

I repeated my conversation with Madelyn, adding, "She made some cryptic remarks about Belinda being all upset about me inheriting the manor and coming here to live but could not do anything about it. When I asked her why Belinda would be upset, she didn't answer me. It was like she felt she had said too much."

Charlie laughed. "There's always been a competition of sorts between Madelyn and Belinda. Fighting over boyfriends, buying the best dress, whatever. Right now, they're in a huge wrangle over Tom Greene. When he moved here Belinda snatched him right up! Made Maddie crazy!" Charlie lifted his head and laughed, his deep, throaty laugh. "You know, this is a small town, and whenever something like this occurs, it travels through the rumor mill at warp speed."

Small town, indeed, I thought. "What would these two women, arguing over a man, have to do with Varcoe Manor?"

"Probably nothing, but if Belinda was upset about something to do with the manor, that would be something Madelyn would pounce on. Maybe she thought that by giving you this picture she could make sure that you wouldn't sell the house and that would really upset Belinda. I honestly don't know what goes through their minds, but it's a benefit that she did this because now we know, or are pretty sure, who the woman is." He looked at the envelope in my hand. "What else did she give you?" he asked.

I opened the envelope and slid out several other pieces of paper. "Apparently these are old property lines. I can't imagine what good they will do, but she thought I should have them."

He pulled a pair of glasses out of his shirt pocket, took the papers from my hand and turned his attention to the property papers. "I had these when we were working on the house, but I returned them to the town archives. These copies might come in handy when we're cleaning out that driveway. Oh, and speaking of that, I've thought about that heavy shrubbery and forest encroaching the property close to the north side of the house. We only gave it a cursory glance the other day, but I should take a closer look at that at some time if you want me to. I doubt that anyone has done anything with that forested land and it's really crawling toward the house."

"Let's talk about that. I'll take this stuff home unless you think you need them."

"No, you find a safe place for them. Maybe we can look at them more closely when I come out on Tuesday. Also, I want to make arrangements to get that hutch moved. I can get a few of my heftier men to come out and help me."

"That would be great. Do you think it will take very long to get the hutch refinished?"

Charlie thought for a moment. I watched his brown eyes dart around as if he were checking some mental calendar. "Depends on the amount of damage and how heavy the piece is. But if I put some additional time into working on it, a few weeks."

"Well, don't make any special arrangements for me. I just think it will be a lovely piece in the kitchen."

"I'm anxious to see how it turns out also." He turned and looked at the two people in the conference room then turned back to me. "I'd better get back to Frank. He's new at negotiating with clients. He has a lot of potential but needs some guidance."

I slipped the papers back into the envelope. "I'll see you Tuesday."

Chapter Twelve

The house was warm when I entered, and I set my purse and the envelope on the counter while I prepared a cup of coffee. I took a moment to stare out toward the lighthouse. I saw no activity other than a slight breeze moving the limbs of the trees and shrubbery in the yard and yet I felt as though I was not alone.

I placed the cup of coffee on the counter, went into the pantry, and grabbed the large flashlight from a top shelf. I walked slowly toward the cliff and the lighthouse beyond. Upon close inspection, it was obvious that the steps were in need of not just repair, but total replacement. Using the lighthouse for anything would be out of the question, and the repairs would be costly, and yet something tugged at that curiosity trait and I indulged myself to move forward.

The climb required extreme caution as I placed each foot first on one side then on the other side then in the middle of each step. When I reached the top step, I followed the deck that led a full circle around the base of the lighthouse until I reached a door on the river side.

When I opened the door, the smell of must and dirt greeted me, and yet something else. Food. I peered inside to find a room with just three small windows around the three sides of the room, allowing only a small amount of light to enter. It was obvious that the room had been used for storage many decades in the past, and yet I saw bundles of clothes and boxes of food stuffed in one corner. A sensation of panic grabbed me, and I quickly looked around, but saw no one else. *Take a deep breath, Charlotte! For heaven's sake. This is probably stuff left from years ago.* I wasn't sure I had convinced myself of that, and the idea of strange lights appearing in or near the lighthouse at night suddenly took on a whole new meaning.

On the north side of the room a staircase rose to the light room on the next floor. I climbed the stairs slowly and as I stepped into the light room, I found myself facing the river at the highest point on the property. Until now, the view from the cliff, or from my own bedroom, had taken my breath away. But the sight before me now was incomparable. The wide distance of water stretched out before me as I saw the land across the Penobscot River blend with the water and the sky. The idea of someone being here, uninvited, disappeared as I stared at the beauty before me.

A moment of vertigo took away my sense of balance and I almost felt at though I was falling. It was then that I felt a stiff breeze from my right and discovered that every window that overlooked the river was shattered and as the draft swirled in, dust and dirt whirled throughout the room. Only one window on the south side that overlooked the manor remained intact.

Let's just not talk about this for the time being, I thought. *When you're ready to tackle this building, you can ask Charlie to remove these remnants of squatters, or kids making mischief from years past.* Oddly enough, I did not fully convince myself that the clothes and food were that old, but I chose to believe it as much as I could. I would deal with it later!

As I returned to the staircase, I noticed a small swatch of cloth caught in a corner under the wooden floorboard. I picked it up and placed it in my pocket. Despite the massive amount of dirt and grime, I felt a sense of tidiness as I retrieved that cloth.

In the kitchen, I took the cloth from my pocket and held it for just a moment. Heavy cotton, a rough texture, of a dull brown color, it looked like it could have come from a shirt or jacket. My mind went back to what I had seen in the lighthouse. *What in the world are you going to do with this?* I asked myself and placed it in a drawer. I opened the kitchen windows and the French door, took the cup of coffee and the envelope, and wandered back into the library where I opened the windows. Immediately the air began to move through the house. A rush of warm but not uncomfortable air crisscrossed the first floor. I sat on the small loveseat and put my feet up on the coffee table then grabbed the envelope and opened it once again. The contents slid out onto my lap and I again picked up the picture and looked at it. *Why is this so important to me?* I asked myself.

Because it's important to me, and I've asked you for help.

I sat up immediately and looked around to see Emmaline's vague, translucent figure standing in the French doorway. The sheers blew gently around her, drifting back to the screens as she moved into the room. My eyes grew quite large as she moved closer.

Please don't be afraid. I thought we had gotten beyond that. I told you, you might see me during the day. This isn't the first time, although we have not talked except in the dark of night.

I remained silent for a moment and wondered if I had fallen asleep.

No, you're not asleep. Go ahead, take a drink from your coffee cup; you'll see.

I looked at the mug sitting on the table next to me and slowly raised my hand to pick it up. I took a sip of the lukewarm liquid.

There, you see. You would not be able to do that if you were asleep, now, would you?

I waited for a moment then responded. *No, I guess I would not. And you have a question?*

I took a deep breath. *I have many questions. I supposed those were your cryptic comments about Charlie?*

A smile teased her face and she nodded. Emmaline moved closer and seemed to sit in the chair across from me. *Yes, I'm sure you do know that he likes you.*

I sensed a movement as Emmaline moved her head and looked at the picture in my hand.

That's my picture. Where did you get it?

I looked from Emmaline to the picture, and when I looked back at her she clarified before my eyes. She transformed into the mirror image of the picture I held in my hand, right down to the locket and the timepiece on the bodice of the dress. I told myself I should be terrified but did not experience that sensation.

No, you should not be afraid of me. I'll not hurt you. It's my fear that you really sense.

I wrinkled my brow. *Your fear? But what are you afraid of?*

The image was complete, and I sat across from Emmaline Varcoe.

I've waited over 145 years to find someone who could help me come to peace, and no one ever has. The fear of death is more than most people can stand, but the fear of not knowing…well, that's even worse. When you first appeared to look at the house, I watched you; walked with you; listened to your enthusiasm about Varcoe Manor, and I knew then that you were the person I waited for all those years. I knew my fear would disappear as you brought me peace.

My gaze flitted around the room, settling on objects only to jump from one to another. I failed to grasp this conversation. Then Emmaline smiled.

I know how confusing this must be. I've started this conversation so many times, always with failed results.

Without realizing it, I asked, *you also asked my mother for help?* I pointed to the diary on the table. *She referenced your visit in her diary and she said she was going to help you.*

She looked down at her hands, folded neatly in her lap and I sensed an overwhelming sadness. *That was the last time I felt I had found someone to help me. Her loss was tragic on so many levels. I had such hope for her.* She gazed up at me and I watched as a tear seemed to wander down her cheek.

What is it that you think I can do to help you? I tried to make light of the conversation. *I've never helped a ghost before.* My attempt at levity failed before the words were out of my mind.

I told you before…I am not a ghost! she insisted, and the house momentarily grew cold. She paused for a moment then continued. *I am the essence of this house, its spirit.*

Her words remained unclear to me and apparently the confusion appeared across my face. The cold air blew out of the room and once again a warm, humid breeze wrapped gently around my shoulders.

She continued. *It's difficult to explain what I mean by that, but I think it is easier for you to grasp if you think of me in those terms.*

If I understand you from our other discussions, you don't know how you died or where you were buried? And you want me to find out?

Her glance returned to her hands as if considering her answer. *Yes, I need you to tell me what happened to me.*

My eyes blinked rapidly. *What happened to you? I don't understand. Surely you know what happened to you. I'm told you committed suicide.*

There was a long moment of silence, then, *I don't believe that. But the important thing is that I don't know where I'm buried, and that is the key to my departure.*

I wouldn't know where to even begin.

She smiled. *But you've already begun that journey, haven't you? Don't you think there was a reason why selling the manor did not appeal to you?*

I allowed my head to rest back onto the chair. *I am not interested in selling the manor, at least not now that I'm learning about it. And from what Charlie tells me, this house needs someone to live in it.*

Yes, Charles. She repeated his name not as a question as much as a formal, yet warm, familiar statement.

Charlie Beasley. He's the man who did all the renovations to the manor. He's the one who kept the manor for you.

She looked around the library then brought her attention back to me. *I like what he did. He brought life back into the manor—life much better than what I experienced.* Her comment was blunt. *He likes you; you know.* She repeated the often-said words.

I watched her countenance change as she smiled. *I seem to recall hearing that several times before!*

She nodded her head. *Yes, I was in the room when he was cleaning the picture frame. I like him. You should too.*

I felt that warmth rise through my body again. *I think I am getting there. But this is not about me—*

She interrupted me. *Not yet perhaps, but soon.*

Another cryptic remark. I wondered if I would ever understand her fully. I took a deep breath. *But that's not what we're here to discuss.*

By all means, ask your questions. I look forward to this conversation.

I took a deep breath. *You said you need my help, but I'm still not clear what exactly that means. Help with what? How do you want me to find out what happened? And why do you not know?*

A heavy sigh rose from the other side of the coffee table. *Something happened here and although you may think that we 'ghosts' know all about death, the truth of the matter is that once I passed, my thoughts and knowledge splintered, and much went on without me. And I am still here, unable to move forward. I've been here so long, and I am so weary. I just want to be able to leave. I only know that I can't until I learn the truth about what happened.*

My heart became heavy as she spoke. I wrinkled my brow and leaned forward in the loveseat as I listened to her. I realized I would take on my mother's challenge. *All right, I will do what I can, but I have to tell you, I make no promises. I will take any guidance I can. We're talking about over 145 years ago. I have no idea what kind of success I'll see.*

She nodded. *I will guide you as best I can, but you will be the real leader in this search.*

Any ideas? I asked her.

I believe you already have a good start. You found the picture and the books. There are documents around that need to be uncovered; stories that need to be told and people that you must meet. She stopped at these vague directions.

I'm having an open house in a few weeks. I'll be meeting more people; maybe something will turn up. Charlie is coming to dinner next Tuesday. He may have some information on the pictures. It's the best I can do to start.

She repeated the now familiar mantra, *He does like you, you know.* And I watched as she faded away and the air remained warm and still in the room.

Crossroads

What have you gotten yourself involved in? I asked, but there was no one to answer the question.

Chapter Thirteen

The following day I received a large envelope from the Genealogical Society in the mail. A flurry of papers slid out across my desk and appeared to have no particular order. I looked around, wondering if my friend, Emmaline, would return to help me decipher the many papers, but I found myself alone. The next two hours flew by as I methodically organized the material and attempted to put some chronological sense to Peter's research. The bulk of the information was what he had read to me during our last meeting, and I found a list of names he included for the open house.

I could do nothing more until I heard from Charlie about the picture, or from Emmaline, should she decide that she could give me some direction. I recalled my conversation with her and her reference to Charlie. I had not realized it, but I did feel a fondness growing for him. I shook my head to clear my thoughts. If my past experiences were any indication, I was now much too old for romance to come wandering into my life, and perhaps it was time to close that door.

The phone rang, yanking me out of my thoughts of younger years and lost chances.

"Hi Charlotte," Charlie said. His voice rang with warmth.

I felt that closed door nudge open just a sliver. I smiled at my foolish reaction. "Good evening, Charlie. What's up?"

"I finished cleaning up the frame with Emmaline's picture in it. The frame is beautiful and cleaned up without a scratch. I took the back off and wanted to see if there is any damage to the photo."

"And?" I inquired.

He remained quiet for a moment then said, "Well, although I couldn't see it through the glass when the picture was in the frame, it does look like someone attempted to do some damage."

"Oh, no! How badly?" I asked.

"Not a lot of damage, just some lines scratched across the photo. I actually think it could be fixed if a professional photographer got his hands on it. But there is something odd about this."

My curiosity rose at his comment. "Oh? What's that?"

"When I first cleaned the glass—I don't mean at your house, but rather when I got it back to the shop and gave it a good cleaning—it didn't look like there was any damage at all. When I took the back off, I didn't take a close look at it, but left it lying on the counter. I had several customers come in, so the photo took a back seat. When I went back to it several hours later, that's when I noticed the lines."

"That doesn't sound good. Is it possible someone could have done that when you were elsewhere?"

"Could be. I was in and out of the shop all afternoon and I have no idea who might have come in, but the frame was at the far end of the room on the worktable."

"Was there any damage to the frame?" I asked.

"No, it wasn't really out in the open near the front of the office. Anyone who wanted to do damage would have to have actually walked back to the far counter where I was working on it."

"What happens now?" I asked. I was curious about this turn of events and angry that someone would damage such a lovely piece.

"I plan to bring it out to dinner and thought we could take a better look at it then. I'll have everything put back in place and if you want me to see about getting the photo fixed, I can always bring it back here."

"No, let's see what it's like. I'd like to get it hung up for the open house. If we have to take it down again, we can do that later."

"Okay. I'll bring it with me. I'm looking forward to dinner."

"I'm looking forward to my first official dinner party."

"Me too. Best way to christen a house, with just two attending."

And that door nudged open just a few more inches.

* * *

That afternoon, a noise caught my attention. I walked out onto the deck and turned toward the lighthouse where I saw Tom Greene standing at the base of the step.

"Tom?" I called. "What are you doing here?"

He turned, startled to see me. I left the deck and hurried toward him. He did not move, made no attempt to leave, and did not answer my question.

"Tom!" I repeated. "Do you want something? Can I help you with something?"

He took a deep breath. "No, I'm just doing some of my research."

His excuse sounded vague. "What do you mean? What are you researching?" I asked.

"The manor. I'm helping Belinda research the manor."

"I know that," I said. "She told me that when I was the Historical Society, but I don't understand why you're here doing your research. This is private property. What is it you're looking for?" I felt my anger growing.

He turned and looked up at the lighthouse. It was apparent to me that he knew he was caught where he should not be. He spun around and stood up straight and I felt his demeanor change. "I'm looking for information on the ownership of the manor."

I raised my eyebrows. "Well, since I'm the owner, I think you should come to me about ownership. I have the papers showing that this is my property."

He stepped toward me in a menacing way. "From my research, I think you are not the rightful owner. I'm trying to establish the correct provenance of the property."

I found his use of the word 'provenance' an odd one. "I can assure you that there is no question about my ownership. I'm a little confused. Why do you think there is, or should be, any question about that?"

He curled his hand into a fist, then took a deep breath and his glance flitted around the property. "I've been doing this for several months, and it just seems to me that there are unanswered questions about who should be living here."

"Such as?"

He stumbled and did not have a good answer. "My research has shown me that there might be some additional information in the lighthouse, and I was going to look there."

"No, actually, you are not going to look there. I've been in the lighthouse and there is nothing there of any interest. Certainly, there are no papers or other information."

"You've been in the lighthouse?" he asked. "What did you find?" He took another step toward me.

Panic raced through me and my adrenaline level rose; I backed up one short step. "Yes, I have. And I found nothing other than garbage. The place is a mess. There is nothing to find."

"I think you're wrong and I'd like to go up there and see for myself." His voice moved down an octave to almost a growl.

"No, Tom. That place is dangerous, and I won't have strangers waltzing around there. You could fall, you could be hurt. No, you need to leave." I tried to reason with him, to convince him that my argument was for his safety. I wasn't sure I succeeded.

The anger returned to his eyes. "You're mistaken. The ownership of Varcoe Manor is still not settled."

Before I could respond, he pushed past me and rushed toward the driveway and I watched him hurry away from the manor.

Chapter Fourteen

I spent the remainder of the day busying myself with thoughts about my planned open house. I had no idea why I was so excited, but my stomach churned every time I thought about it. I experienced an unusual anxiety because I had not seen or heard from Emmaline. We had no more conversations, and I began to think that perhaps these events were nothing but a wild imagination in the mind of a woman who just embarked on a new life, moved over six hundred miles away from the only home she had known for over 50 years, and missed her friends.

I put my encounter with Tom out of my mind, but not so far that the thoughts didn't linger and rise when least expected. I found myself looking out the kitchen door toward the cliff with some frequency. And yet, I did not spot Emmaline anywhere and Tom did not return.

The days passed quickly and on Tuesday I slipped the chicken Kiev into the oven and stood looking at my meager wine caddy when I heard a knock at the front door. I looked at my watch, and it was 6:00 p.m. I hurried through the kitchen into the hallway and glanced at myself in the mirror. I smoothed a wayward wrinkle from my linen pants and raised the collar of my matching blouse, then reached for the door. I jerked it open, just a bit too fast, and looked into Charlie's smiling face.

I stood back and admired him, in his blue suit, light blue shirt, and dark blue tie. "Well, aren't you a picture to behold!" I said, opening the door wider. "Come in, please."

"Something for the lady of the house," he said as he handed me two bottles of wine—a Vidal blanc, and a zinfandel. "Wasn't sure which would be right, so I brought both." He handed them to me then continued, "I have the picture frame in the truck. Let me go get it and after dinner we can take a better look at it."

I took the wine and waited at the door while he returned to the truck.

He dresses up quite nice.

I spun around to see Emmaline standing in the doorway to the kitchen.

"I also brought the party list; in case you want to go over it."

I spun back around just as Charlie arrived at the door.

"Is there something wrong, Charlotte? You look like you've seen a ghost."

You have no idea! "No, no, nothing wrong." I pointed him toward the library and said, "Why not put that frame in the library and we'll look at it later."

I turned and hurried toward the kitchen. Emmaline was gone.

"Something smells very good. Hope the wine is okay."

Still looking around for Emmaline and not seeing her, I turned to him. "I'm sure the Vidal blanc will complete the meal nicely. We're having chicken Kiev, asparagus with hollandaise sauce, and baguettes. Your timing was just right, dinner will be on the table in about five minutes." I took a bottle opener out of the drawer and handed it to him along with the bottle. "Do you mind?" I asked?

"Not at all." He opened the wine, passed the bottle under his nose and took a deep breath. "Perfect. Where are your glasses?"

I motioned him toward the table at the far end of the kitchen where the place settings were ready. I removed the chicken and placed it on the stove.

"Can I help?" Charlie asked, approaching my side. He peered over my shoulder and inhaled deeply. "Ummm, smells good.

I took a deep breath and handed him the two hot pads. "Yes, you can take this over and put it on the table. The baguettes are in a basket in the breadbox. I'll have the asparagus ready in a moment."

Charlie followed my directions and by the time he had the bread on the table, I arrived with the asparagus. We sat at the table across from one another, and he lifted his glass toward me.

"Thank you for inviting me. I've been looking forward to this."

I smiled, picked up my glass and nodded. We tapped the glasses together. I chalked up the warm sensation that rose through my body as nothing more than a warm kitchen. Dinner was comfortable and we chatted about mundane things as if we were old friends. *I could get to enjoy this,* I thought.

We finished our meal and Charlie refilled our wine glasses. "So, do you want to see what you salvaged from the attic?" he asked.

"Absolutely. I'm really excited about seeing this picture."

We took our wine into the library and Charlie unwrapped the package and removed the frame. I was stunned at the beauty of the wood. "Did you stain this?" I asked.

"Nope, I didn't do anything to it except use some very fine cleaner. I was actually concerned that if I used anything strong, it could damage the wood."

He lifted the frame and held it in front of himself so I could get the full effect. I leaned in close to take a better look at the photograph and I saw the lines marked through the photo that Charlie had mentioned. He put the frame back down on the desk.

"Here, let me take the photo out of the frame. You can see the markings better."

He turned the frame over and gently removed the photo. As soon as he did, the lines in the photo took on a darker tone. We leaned over the photo and at the same time, we both gently stroked a line that ran across Emmaline's brow.

He does like you... the gentle voice whispered in my ear. I sensed a trend taking hold.

I stood up straight and looked around the room. I saw Emmaline standing five feet behind us. I felt my eyes grow large, wondering how in the world I could get past this moment. Had Charlie heard her whispered comment? Surely, he could not have heard it.

"Charlotte? Are you okay?"

I took a sip of my wine and answered, "Yes, I'm fine. I'm just stunned at the damage to the picture, I guess." I looked toward the other side of the room, but Emmaline had gone. I focused my attention back to the picture. "Do you know what happened?" I asked.

"No, I can't imagine how this could have happened in the shop. No one really knew I had the frame. I wonder if it was damaged years ago. I think I can get it repaired—probably not to perfection, but I can inquire around and see."

I looked at the photo again. "No, let's just leave it like it is. When it's in the frame, the marks are not quite as apparent. I'd like to wait."

"So be it. Where would you like to place this picture?"

"Come with me," I said, and I led the way into the sitting room. I pointed to the mantle over the fireplace. "I thought it would look nice centered over the fireplace."

Charlie walked across the room and moved from one side of the hearth to the other. The wall was bare; he turned and nodded.

"I think that would be a perfect place." He smiled at me. "You've become quite besotted about this woman, haven't you?"

I coughed out an uncomfortable laugh. "Well, I'm not sure 'besotted' is quite the right word, but I do think there are some issues left unanswered about her. This was, after all, her home and since the picture is of her—" I found it hard to finish the sentence. My eyes darted around the room as I expected an appearance. There were so many things I was not telling Charlie, and I wasn't even sure I knew how to tell him.

Charlie seemed to recognize my confusion. "The fireplace it is, then. I'll leave the picture here, but if you would allow me, I'll return and hang it for you."

"I'd be grateful. Thanks Charlie."

"Now, if you have a few more minutes, maybe we can go over this tentative guest list." Charlie reached into his pocket and removed an envelope. He opened it and withdrew several sheets of paper.

"I received a note from Peter Tidewater with a list of names also. Perhaps we can compare them?"

We sat side-by-side at the kitchen table and Charlie laid out the pieces of paper in front of us. He placed Peter's list on the right, next to his. I leaned in close and studied the lists as Charlie pointed to each name.

"I see quite a few duplicates, so I guess Peter and I are thinking along the same lines. Now, these are just the folks I think you really need to invite—they're mostly the old families, or newer arrivals within the past one hundred years." He smiled at his joke.

"Okay," I smiled back. "So, who are these people?"

"You've already met some of them and we've already talked about many of them. Belinda Stapleford, and I'm sure she will bring Tom Greene." He chuckled. "Should make for an interesting evening because Madelyn will come with her parents and I'm sure Maddie will be furious. Always entertaining."

At the mention of Tom Greene, I thought about telling Charlie about my encounter, but decided it would do no good to bring him into it, and it would not happen again. At least I convinced myself it would not happen again.

He moved his finger down the two lists making his own comparisons. "Sheriff Lorelei Tuttle, I think I mentioned her before...works out of Bangor but has an office in Portsborough and lives here. A good woman to know. You'll like her."

I glanced quickly down the list but did not see any other names I recognized other than Peter Tidewater.

"Father Peabody, he's the Catholic priest, and Reverend Smithers—he's the Methodist preacher. The Catholic community is sizable, but mostly local churchgoers, not many from out of town. The Methodist congregation is about the same size as the Catholic. Both churches keep us all on our toes." He laughed again.

I smiled. "Do you attend one or the other?"

"No. My mother tried her darndest to ingrain religion into my soul, but I'm afraid it didn't take. You?"

"No, no religious sensibilities in my life."

The room remained quiet for just a moment, and then Charlie turned his attention back to the list.

"Okay, here's the list of the Mayor and Town Council. They will all bring their spouses. I saw the mayor the other day and she was beside herself with curiosity about 'the new lady of the manor'. God, this is going to be fun!" The skin around his eyes crinkled as he laughed.

"This looks like a telephone directory of the entire town!" I said.

"Well, not quite, but these are the people you'll want to get to know first. Where that takes you from there is your own path. But these people control the gossip as well as the ordinances, and we'll need them in our pocket."

Our pocket?

I turned at the words whispered in my ear but saw no reaction from Charlie.

"Ah, yes, Peter Tidewater and the board of the Genealogical Society." Charlie laughed. "His name is at the top of his list. They work with the Historical Society but seem to retain a distance. I sometimes think that Peter and Belinda are at odds, but that may just be an impression I have."

"Don't they like each other?" I asked.

"It's not that, I just suspect that Belinda would like to have her hands in more of the ancestry of the area, and Peter is not always willing to share. I mean, hell, he's been doing this for over 50 years, he's not about to give up now!"

We had reached the end of the list. "Is that all? It's really not as big as I thought it might be."

Charlie turned and smiled at me. "Trust me, once the word gets out, people will be coming out of the woodwork to wrangle an invitation."

"In that case, I'd better find a good caterer. Any ideas?"

"Well, I don't have any reason to hire a caterer, but Lucius Bartels has a good reputation. I've been to some of the parties he's catered and he's never disappointed. I'm sure you can also find some good ones in Bangor. I'll ask around but don't want to start that fire before we have to."

We.

The word slipped into my ear and again I looked around but saw no one.

"Before I go, let me ask you something else. That hutch in the attic—where were you thinking of putting it?"

I turned around and pointed to the blank wall behind us. "I thought it might look nice here. This kitchen is long and large, and the wall at this end of the room feels bare. What do you think?"

Charlie rose from the table and paced off the length of the wall similar to what he had done in the sitting room. "I'll have to re-measure the hutch. I seem to recall that it was pretty sizable, but we may be able to do it. Are you going to be around tomorrow? I can get some of my guys to come out and we'll see what it takes to get the thing down from the attic. I'd also like to take another look at those lighthouse stairs. I think it will take some anchoring to fix them and there are a few different ways to go about this task."

I hesitated for only a moment. "I'll be here trying to figure out what I've gotten myself into with this party! I have some things I want to do around here, so I expect to be here all day."

"Okay, I'll be out maybe around 10:00 a.m.?"

"That'll work out just fine." Again, I found myself reluctant to mention my encounter with Tom and I wasn't sure why.

I walked Charlie to the door. "I want to thank you for joining me tonight. Moving into a new place where you don't know anyone can be daunting. My shopping trips have been mostly just for groceries, or I've gone up to Bangor for a few things. I've not really gotten to know anyone. You've been very helpful, and I hope I'm not taking advantage of your kindness."

Charlie leaned in and kissed my cheek. "Not at all. I'm pleased to help. Besides, how else would I get an invitation to the party of the year if I didn't help out?" He smiled, turned, and bounced down the steps to his truck.

I felt a rush of warm air surround me. I brushed my cheek and when I turned around, I saw Emmaline standing in the kitchen doorway. She smiled and disappeared.

Chapter Fifteen

By 9:00 p.m. the last vestiges of the sun settled into the horizon leaving a light purple haze in the distance. I stared at the lighthouse but saw nothing but a lighthouse. No wavering lights, no creaking stairs, no Emmaline. I wondered why I had avoided telling Charlie about my encounter with Tom, and yet I realized that that is exactly what I did – I intentionally avoided telling him.

I stretched and walked back into the sitting room. The desk lamp glowed a light yellow, warming the room. I stood and looked at the blank space above the mantel imagining Emmaline's picture gracing the wall.

Thank you.

I spun around, almost losing my balance, to see Emmaline standing at the far end of the room by the pocket doors. She nodded her approval.

I appreciate you deciding to hang my picture there. She moved toward the loveseat in the middle of the room across from the fireplace and sat, not taking her eyes off the wall.

I sat in the Queen Anne chair next to the loveseat. *I felt it only appropriate to put it there. Besides, I've been unable to find anything else suitable. This is, after all, your house.*

She looked at me and I sensed rather than saw a grateful smile. *Perhaps, but it's your home. There is a difference. I don't know that this was ever a home to me.*

I considered her words. After several very long moments, I asked, *Why do you feel that way? I thought this house was built for you.*

She took a deep breath, and I felt the air in the room chill.

Have you ever been in love, Charlotte?

Startled at the change of subject, I opened my eyes wide. *I'm not sure I understand what that has to do with you living in this house.*

She smiled. *Perhaps it has everything to do with moving forward. Have you?*

I thought for a moment about the men who had wandered through my life. *I thought so...* I said, letting the sentence go unfinished; not looking at her but rather staring at the floor, still lost in my memories.

You're not married, she said.

I was becoming both uncomfortable and more than a bit annoyed with the turn this conversation was taking, but there seemed to be no escaping her knowledge of what was going on in my head.

I'm not trying to make you uncomfortable, just trying to understand you, she added.

Why is that important to you? I asked.

She tilted her head to the left as if considering her conversation and the direction it was taking.

We come from two different worlds—two different times. As I've followed the people who have lived here, I've become more curious about the changes in culture that I've seen. Marriage doesn't seem to have the same value that it once had.

I thought about her observation. *I suppose you're right. But women have more freedom to choose today that they did 145 years ago. It might not be a matter of value as much as a matter of fact...a fact that women are more independent.*

She looked up at me and furrowed her brow. *But why would women look differently on marriage today than they did then?"*

I found myself being drawn into this debate. I leaned forward. *Let me turn the question around and rephrase it somewhat. Why did you marry John Varcoe?*

Her eyes darted around the room as she considered my retort. *I was not an attractive woman. The men who courted me did so not because of my beauty, but because of who I was and the money I would bring to the marriage. I married John because it was expected,* she said. *Father and John made the decision.*

Well, you see, I replied, *today it is not expected. It's a choice we make and there may be many factors moving us to make that decision.*

And what factors affected your decisions? She asked. *Was love one of those factors?*

Your questions make me uncomfortable. I stopped and sat back in the chair. Memories I thought I had buried began to rise to the surface. *Several years ago, there was a man named David,* I said. *When I first met him, he was all charm. I suppose at the beginning I thought David was the big love of my life. We were together for five years.*

And you never married? she asked. *I'm sorry if I'm making you uncomfortable, but I'm trying to understand the difference between us, and yet I sense a kinship.*

I considered her last comment and realized that I also sensed several growing relationships that confused me and and yet drew me in. I thought about her question. *Well, no. I have always been independent and never believed marriage would be part of my life. I tried to explain that to David from the onset of the relationship, but it did not take long for me to realize that he either didn't understand me or chose to ignore me. I'm a wealthy woman and I learned too late that David pursued me for that reason.* I felt myself making excuses and moving deeper into my own life than I chose to.

Well, then it probably was not meant to be. I understand your position. I did not have the opportunity to make such a decision.

I realized that her comment raised my understanding of something that sat dormant for many years in my life. An odd sense of relief washed over me. *Did John love you?* I asked.

She took a deep breath. *No,* she responded, short and tart. *Social standing and wealth were important to John, and I came with both.* Her tone was matter of fact, not one of discovery or sudden awareness. It carried no sadness, no anger, no glee. It was what it was. John did not love her.

I thought you did not have memories of your life before death, I said.

Oh, that is not a memory as much as a fact that seems to sit in my mind; a fact that I can't get rid of.

I felt I had intruded. *I'm sorry, Emmaline. I did not mean to pry.*

Do not apologize. It's this conversation and others like it that will help direct you to the answers I seek.

She rose from the chair and moved toward the kitchen. I followed her in silence and watched her walk out of the house and across the lawn toward the cliff. She turned; a sad smile graced her face. I had more questions, and as she disappeared, I sensed the conversation was not finished.

The light glow drifted across the lawn until it disappeared at the cliff. The clock on the stove read 10:00 p.m.; I locked the house and wandered up to the bedroom. My mind was alive with our conversation. I thought about the men in my life and I realized that not marrying was a good thing. My feelings toward Emmaline were beginning to coalesce into a genuine need to help her. I realized that I no longer thought of her as a dream—she had become a reality and she needed my help. I knew Emmaline would not return tonight and as I laid my head on the pillow and wondered where my journey would take me. And I thought of Charlie as a quiet sense of peace enveloped me.

Chapter Sixteen

I had not opened the windows before lying down the previous evening and the room felt stuffy. I opened the French doors, and a light breeze blew through, billowing the sheers in a graceful move. The room began to cool just a few degrees.

I stretched and took a deep breath. The aroma of sweet white violets floated through the air from the wooded area below. I could have returned to bed for the rest of the day, but one glance at the clock on the nightstand and I knew that Charlie and his men would be arriving in just under two hours to collect the hutch.

By 9:30 a large mug of coffee warmed my hands, and I wandered into the library and glanced at Emmaline's picture. Still in its frame, it seemed that the marks across the photograph had diminished. I wondered if that was my imagination, or another sense of reality about Emmaline.

Charlie's list lay before me on the kitchen table and again I noticed his nearly perfect writing. The letters slanted gently to the right—not calligraphy, but more than cursive. I retrieved the telephone book and began to look up caterers. Four in Bangor and one in Portsborough stood out. I called the local caterer, Lucius Bartels. *Might as well test the local businesses first.*

I explained about the open house, and he agreed to come out and visit the manor and help me determine what I needed, how much I needed, and what this event would cost. We spoke for twenty minutes and agreed to meet the following Tuesday at 2:00 p.m. The conversation ended just as I heard a knock on the door.

I opened the door to see Charlie in his jeans and a sky-blue Welcome to Portsborough Maine sweatshirt. I smiled. He smiled back.

"Good morning, Charlotte. As you can see, I've brought my sturdy workers with me. We'll see what it takes to get that hutch down from the attic."

His crew paid regular courtesies to me as they unloaded straps and blankets. I backed away from the door and Charlie led them through the house.

I remained on the first floor and in the distance, I heard Charlie throwing directions around as well as several grunts and shouts from his crew. It was obvious that the hutch was being difficult.

I returned to the kitchen and opened the door. A soft breeze stirred the leaves and, as much as I hoped to see her, I saw no movement across the grounds, no image of Emmaline. The temperature had risen since the early morning and with it, the humidity and the scent of fresh Rosemary moved through the kitchen.

My attention returned to the guest list and I began to write my invitations. My handwriting skills lacked the graceful slope so clear in Charlie's, but a handwritten invitation presented a warmth that would be lost in a printed one, regardless of how professionally it was done.

I became lost in my writing as I struggled for the right adverbs and adjectives—trying to make each invitation personal, avoiding repetition. The sounds of a scuffle with the hutch remained in the distance as I buried myself in my task.

"Charlotte?"

Startled, I jumped and turned to see Charlie at the hallway door.

"Oh!" I said, embarrassed. "Sorry. I got involved with these invitations. I heard your men wrestling with that hutch. Everything ok?"

Charlie laughed. "Yeah. That staircase is a little narrow. It must have been a real challenge to move that thing up. It doesn't come apart except for the cutting board top, so its size and weight made it difficult to move. But we prevailed!"

I nodded and smiled. "Any thoughts on refinishing it?" I asked.

Charlie looked around the kitchen. "Well, we painted the walls a stark, matte white, so I would suggest something with color. Either a colonial forest green, or blueberry blue."

I turned and looked at the wall. "I think I would like the blue."

"Blue it is," he said.

"Any idea how long it will take? I'm not rushing you, just curious."

"I understand. I think at least two weeks. It looks like the back needs some reconstructing, and that carving board is a mess. Some shaving and planing; nail replacement, glue—"

I laughed and held up my hand to stop him. "Enough! Take as much time as you need."

"I'd like to finish it before your open house, but no promises."

"Like I said, take as much time as you need."

"By the way, while we were nudging this beast, I found a second picture frame. It was under the hutch. It's identical to the one of Emmaline. I'd like to clean it up also but left it up there—a job for another time. I think the Emmaline frame is the more important one. "

"Oh my gosh! I wonder if that could be John's picture. If it's an identical frame, I can't imagine it would be anyone other than John."

"We'll get to it later if that's okay with you. I'm kind of swamped right now."

I nodded my head. "Of course. I'm just pleased with Emmaline's photo."

A voice from behind him called out, "Charlie, we got 'er loaded and tied town in the van. You left this bag on the front seat. You need it?" One of Charlie's crew handed a brown paper bag to him.

"Oh—this is for you." He handed me the bag and I withdrew a cotton tee shirt with the words Welcome to Portsborough Maine. The shirt was sky-blue.

I raised my eyebrows and looked at his shirt without saying a word.

A deep crimson crept up from below his collar. "It was the only color I could find."

I held it up to my body and looked down at it then looked up at Charlie and smiled. "It's perfect. My favorite color."

He returned the smile. The pink hue remained on his neck. "Well, I'll let you get back to your invitations. When do you want to hang Emmaline's picture? I can't do it today but could return at your convenience."

"Anytime is fine. I'd like to have it up for the party."

"Today is Wednesday. How about next Tuesday."

I didn't even look at a calendar. "Tuesday would be fine. The caterer is coming in the afternoon to look at everything and I'm sure we can work around him."

"Good—killing three birds with one stone."

"Three birds?" I asked.

"Hang the picture, get the caterer settled, and I get to see you again."

I smiled at the last comment. "That would be nice, in all cases." I felt a warmth rise above my collar.

As he turned to leave, I asked, "Should I invite your crew to the party? After all, they did all the work."

He turned toward me again and as he walked backward toward the door said, "That would be very nice. They've talked a lot about the manor and all four were anxious to come back and get the hutch. If you'll send the invite to me, I'll include them and their 'others' in my RSVP."

Charlie descended the steps and I watched as he and his crew drove down the long drive to the highway. I still had the tee in my hand and held it up to my body one more time.

He likes you.

I smiled and swatted at the air. It was good to know that Emmaline was in the neighborhood.

Chapter Seventeen

The weekend slipped by quickly with no calls from Charlie or visits from Emmaline. I almost felt that my life was moving toward normal. Tuesday morning arrived with a stiff breeze across the river; I stood by the cliff, mesmerized by the action as the water rushed in, roiled against the rocks below, and rapidly retreated to be followed within moments by a second wave.

The breeze carried a light mist that settled on my face. In the distance I heard the rumbling of a vehicle arriving and knew it would be Charlie. I left the cliff side and returned to the house just as I heard the knock at the front door.

"Good morning," I said, opening the door a little too quickly.

Charlie stood on the front steps holding his tool kit, a small tarp, and a short stepladder, while Tom Greene stood just below him with his tools and a large canvas bag.

"Good morning, Charlotte," Charlie said. "Tom came with me to look at the growth near the house, and I have the equipment to hang that picture."

I took a step backward and ushered them both in. I felt an uncomfortable anxiety wash over me, recalling my last encounter with Tom.

"'Morning," Tom mumbled. He looked around the hallway and into the two front rooms then walked through the house to the kitchen. I heard the back door open, I turned to Charlie, the silent question on my lips.

Charlie shrugged. "I was talking to Belinda the other day and she asked about the manor. She mentioned that Tom is looking for some work—he needs some extra money. I asked him if he wanted to do some landscaping work here and he agreed. He'll check out the grounds."

I wasn't sure if I was annoyed or curious, but I nodded my head. "I'm sure he'll work out just fine." I wasn't really sure at all, but I trusted Charlie and that trust calmed me.

Charlie did not react, and I let it go. "Shall we hang Emmaline?" he said.

I immediately looked around but did not see her—grateful for small favors. We walked into the sitting room, where Charlie placed the tarp on the floor in front of the fireplace and set the stepladder in the middle of it. He went into the library and retrieved the picture.

"Did you do something to this picture?" he asked, holding it away and staring at it.

"No, I've not touched it since we looked at it last week. Why?"

He took a handkerchief from his pocket and wiped it over the convex glass. "I don't know. It looks like these marks have lightened." He pointed to the marks across Emmaline's photo.

"That's odd. I did look at the picture the other day and thought the same thing, but I wrote it off to the convex glass playing tricks on my vision. But you're right, it does look like the marks have all but disappeared."

We said nothing more while Charlie climbed the ladder, pulled his ruler out of his pocket and measured precisely to the center of the mantle. "How far up do you want this?" he asked.

"Charlie, I have no idea. I assumed it should be centered."

He took a pencil from behind his ear, made an almost indistinguishable mark on the base of the wall at the mantle, then measured the height and determined the placement of the picture hanger. I watched in amazement as he moved quickly to determine the exact place. It would have taken me hours to do the same thing and even then, I could not be sure I wouldn't have erred by three inches to the left or right!

"That should be right. Can you hand me the picture?" he asked.

He fidgeted with it for several seconds and made sure the picture was not tilted one way or the other. When he stepped down from the ladder, he walked to the far end of the room and looked. I walked over and stood next to him. We both tilted our heads one way then the other.

"Looks good to me. What do you think, Charlotte?"

"I think it's lovely. And from this distance the photograph is quite clear. Yes, I think that is the perfect place for it. Thank you, Charlie. I'd have never been able to do this on my own. That'll work out just fine." Knowing that I had obligated myself, at least mentally, to research more about Emmaline, I asked him, "Do you know much about the Varcoe family? Emmaline, in particular? I understand she committed suicide." I stared at the picture instead of Charlie.

"That's the town lore," he said, adding nothing more.

"You don't seem entirely convinced." I said.

Silence. He hesitated then shook his head. "No, I only know the story about her committing suicide."

I did not totally believe him, but I had no reason to pursue it. The moment passed and I had no idea why I did it, but I leaned over and kissed him on his cheek.

He turned and smiled at me. "See…that's payment enough."

I threw my hand to my mouth. "I am so sorry! Charlie, I don't know what came over me!"

He laughed. "Don't apologize. I enjoyed that." He packed up his belongings and wandered over to look back at the picture. "I think the partygoers are going to love that. Gives them more to talk about!"

I wondered if he meant the picture or the kiss, but then, how would they know…An uncomfortable silence wrapped around me until I heard, *you like him too.* I quickly responded to Charlie's comment. "Good grief. I should be quelling these stories, not fueling them!"

"Oh, by the way. I told the guys about the invitation and they all said they would come. I guess their wives and girlfriends are beside themselves about the invitation. You're quite the talk of the town."

"You're the first person I've heard from. I hope I get the same enthusiastic response from the other guests."

"You will! Meeting with the caterer today?"

I looked at my watch. "Yes, Lucius Bartels, the local caterer you suggested. He's supposed to be here about two o'clock."

Charlie nodded his approval. "I understand he hardly has any openings on his calendar. What incentives did you have to give him to find space and say yes?"

I wrinkled my brow. "All I did was introduce myself over the phone and tell him what I was planning. He didn't even ask anything else before he said he'd be delighted to help."

Charlie nodded his head. "Everyone says Lucius is a good guy and you won't be disappointed. He has jobs up and down the coast—very popular for weddings and graduation parties—now open houses. I suspect he wants to see the house as much as anyone else in town. If you keep entertaining like this, we'll have to pave that driveway and clean up all of the growth down by the county road just to make room for all the traffic." He rolled his head back and laughed.

"How about some coffee?" I asked.

"Sounds good!" he answered.

As we entered the kitchen, Charlie stopped, then hurried to the window. "What's he doing?" he demanded, more to himself than to me.

I rushed over to Charlie and he pointed toward the cliff. Tom stood at the base of the lighthouse steps, staring up toward the building. He stepped on the first stair and through the open window we heard the snap. Charlie turned and rushed out the kitchen door with me on his tail.

"Tom! What are you doing?" he shouted.

I watched Tom teeter and trip backwards at Charlie's shout.

Tom caught his balance and spun around. A dark shadow crossed his face as though he did not expect to be interrupted. "I—er—thought I could get a better visual from the lighthouse." He attempted a failed excuse and quickly changed the subject. "But I can tell from here that you were right, Charlie. That forest needs tending to," he said, distracting the conversation.

I heard anger in Charlie's voice that I had not heard before. Charlie grabbed Tom's arm and drew him away from the steps. "These steps are dangerous in their present condition. Don't go up there until we can repair the steps and take a good look at the lighthouse and what state it's in! What were you thinking?"

Tom stood up straight and snapped, "I'm not doing anything wrong." I noticed his face flush. "I have a right to be here—that is, you asked for my help. I was just trying to get a better visual on the work needed." He spoke quickly and we all knew that his excuse was not true.

He glanced at me, and a silent message passed between us about his last visit. Had I told Charlie about that; we would not have encountered this situation. I averted his stare.

Charlie slowly took a deep breath and released the air. "Regardless, we don't need anyone falling down these steps—" His sentence did not end, but we all understood the intent.

I quickly added, "I'm sure Charlie is only concerned for everyone's safety. I appreciate your thought, but like Charlie said, we should get the repairs done first." I shared a further unspoken comment as I stared at Tom.

Tom grimaced then he just nodded his head. "Sorry I caused any problems." His attitude took a decided turn as if he had done nothing wrong.

The air calmed around us, and Charlie said, "Let's just agree to wait until the steps are fixed before we even think about the lighthouse."

My curiosity increased about Tom's last visit. With this second attempt I wondered if there was more to Tom's desire to see the lighthouse then he initially said.

He looked at me and added, "Belinda got your invitation and she asked me to respond for both of us. We'll definitely be here."

We left the yard and returned to the driveway. I thanked Charlie and waved them on their way. I walked down the driveway to the wrought iron gate and the mailbox. As I began my walk back, I took notice of the overgrown shrubbery. *Yes, I need to clear this all out before autumn sets in. So many things to do.*

* * *

Lucius Bartels arrived precisely at two o'clock, a large leather bag slung over his shoulder.

"Now, let me be clear right up front," he said. "I've been hearing about the resurrection of this house for months and as you might expect, everyone, absolutely every human being in this town, would kill to see what you've done. I've not been in town but ten years and that makes me an outsider, but even outsiders hear the stories. The manor and the grounds have been more or less forgotten—well, except, of course, for those ghastly stories, but then I'm sure you're familiar with them." He did not look at me but let his gaze pass slowly from one end of the manor to the other.

His sentences seemed to run on and on with no punctuation in between. I smiled and jumped into the middle of his conversation when he took a breath.

"Yes, I've heard them—at least I've heard a few of them. They're quite interesting and I suspect they add to the mystery of the place. But really, there is no mystery. Just unfortunate events."

Lucius raised an eyebrow and smiled. "Of course, my dear. Of course." He patted my arm as if to reassure me.

He must have been ten years younger than me and I found it amusing that he referred to me as 'my dear.' But I took no offense. I quite liked the man.

"Would you like a tour of the house or do you want to just get down to business?"

"I would never turn down a tour, but if you had not offered, I'd have been forward enough to ask." He grinned from ear to ear.

Once we returned to the first floor, I showed him the formal dining room and then we migrated to the library. In each room he nodded, mumbled 'ummmhmmm,' and made notes in his iPad. When we walked into the sitting room, he stopped in the doorway and his eyes grew wide.

"Is there something wrong?" I asked.

"Oh, my goodness, no. That photograph over the fireplace is gorgeous."

"I discovered it in the attic. Charlie Beasley cleaned it up. He was just here earlier and hung it for me. It's a photo of Emmaline Varcoe, the wife of the original owner."

He swung his head around and stared at me. "Is that right? How do you know?"

I found myself stammering. "Oh, I was given a similar photo only smaller by Madelyn Cooper at the library. She said she got it from the Historical Society."

"I'll bet Belinda doesn't know that Madelyn confiscated it! Belinda is very, very careful about what leaves the Historical Society." He laughed.

Small town gossip, indeed, I thought.

"Are they both coming to the open house?" he asked.

I nodded. "Yes, they've both been invited. Belinda has RSVP'd, haven't heard from the Coopers.

He laid a hand on my arm. "Oh, don't you worry, the only reason any of your invitees would not show up is death—their own. They wouldn't miss this for anything. Those RSVPs will begin flooding in. My dear, I can't tell you how delighted I am that you contacted me. I repeat—I wouldn't miss this for anything!"

He spent the next hour looking at the layout of the kitchen, the preparation areas, the best places for food to be laid out, and what the menu would consist of. By the time Lucius finished, I felt like I was serving dinner to the entire state, and yet an excitement rose through my body and I began looking forward to the event with more enthusiasm than I thought I could muster.

We ended our visit with a clear plan. The open house was a little over two weeks away, and I prayed to the weather persons for a lovely, warm, dry day.

Chapter Eighteen

Good morning, Charlotte.

The quiet notes of her voice carried across the room just as I turned over. My eyes opened and I looked at the clock: 5:30 in the morning. I stared through the early morning haze toward the sound. Her figure seemed to lean against the French doors without really touching them. I sat up in bed and rubbed my eyes.

Good morning, Emmaline. I sensed a closeness had developed over the days since she first appeared. Not quite a friendship, but some close feeling that allayed any fears. *I have missed our visits. You've not been to see me for several days.*

She flowed into the room and nestled in the chair on the far side of the bed. *Perhaps. Although I have been here, observing.*

I found that an odd comment. *Observing? Observing what?* I asked.

She let out a heavy sigh and waited for a moment. *I've been observing the picture. Someone did some damage to it. I tried to mend it.*

I pulled the light sheet up to my waist as I sat up further. *We saw that. I thought it was just a trick of the glass on my eyes. How did you do that?* I asked.

I don't know how. I just lightly brushed my hand over the photograph. The marks seemed to lighten.

I thought about the damage. *That seems unusual.*

Many things seem unusual. They happen, nonetheless. How's Charles?

The question left me uncomfortable as I ruffled and unruffled the bed linens around my legs. *He's fine.*

Emmaline smiled.

I changed the subject. *You know I'm having an open house here shortly?*

Yes. I saw your caterer come in. I'm pleased that he liked the renovations to the house, and he liked my picture. Who are you inviting?

I scratched my head thinking of the names. *Most of the city and businesspeople. The standard 'in' crowd.* I laughed at my description. *Oh, and the Methodist minister and the Catholic priest...they were both invited.*

She rustled in her seat. *The Catholic priest?* she asked. *What's his name?*

Father Peabody, I answered.

I don't know him. I'm glad it's not Father O'Brien. I sensed anger in her answer.

Father O'Brien?

Yes, he was our priest. He married us. A dark shadow passed over the room, yet the sun rose outside.

Emmaline, that would have been nearly 150 years ago. The church would have changed leadership numerous times since then.

She stared beyond me, as if wandering through the memories she claimed not to have. Slowly she returned her attention to me. *Oh, of course. I can't leave, you know, so those changes would be unknown to me. I remain here until you get me out.* I was startled by the anger in her voice and surprised at her use of the word 'out'.

Emmaline, I don't know that I'm making any progress on that at all. I'm still not sure where to look for answers or what to even look for. And as far as you not leaving the grounds, what about your conversations with Simeon? Did you meet him elsewhere?

I was shocked by the annoyance in my own voice. I had not meant to be cruel, and my confusion at this entire situation seemed to heighten.

No, he lived here for a short time. She released a heavy sigh. *Until your mother appeared, he was my last real chance. My only other options appeared when others moved in, and they had no idea how to help me. I frightened them. With your mother's death, I found myself encased at Varcoe Manor and its grounds with no options.*

I sucked in a lungful of air. *I'm sorry. I do not mean to ask so many questions, but this is a frustrating situation. I'll continue to search for an answer.* I had no idea why I made that promise, and no idea how in the world I would keep it. But there it was, said and done, and I was now locked into it.

You will, you will. Will Charles be at the party? She changed the subject to the relief of both of us.

Yes, of course he will, as well as the crew that helped him renovate the entire manor and the grounds.

He's not finished with the grounds, though, has he?

I stared at her image, wondering how she knew additional work needed to be done. *No, not entirely. He'll clear out overgrowth along the driveway and the forested area that runs north of the house along the cliff line by the lighthouse. He's concerned about roots encroaching on the base of the house.* I waved my hand in the general direction of the lighthouse. I seemed to be babbling.

She turned her head and stared at me. *Yes, those areas were both much less dense than they are today. But he mustn't damage the lighthouse.*

Why?

I think it holds some answers for me.

I wondered if her memory was clearing, or if those words were just images that lingered as foggy moments in her mind.

She rose and moved toward the French doors and the balcony. Although I perceived our conversation to be short, I glanced at the clock and saw it was 8:30. We had visited for longer than I thought, and I noticed that the sun had risen high. Emmaline turned back toward me. *I'll look forward to your open house. It will be nice to see Charles again.*

I wrinkled my brow, and a jolt of jealousy burst through me. Emmaline saw my reaction and smiled. She walked through the door and onto the balcony and disappeared.

* * *

As I finished washing my breakfast dishes, the phone rang.

"Good morning, Charlie," I said.

"'Morning, Charlotte. Do you have any plans for today?"

I took a quick glance at the calendar on the wall. "Nope. I'm free. What did you have in mind?"

"We're slow here, and I thought I'd bring a few of the guys out to take a closer look at that wooded area we've been talking about and figure out what the next step is. We could probably do a quick cutback, just to stem the flow of any roots. Then we can do a fuller clearing when we start the driveway work."

I remained silent for a moment. "How odd that you should comment about that. I was just talking about that this morning."

He stopped. "Really? Who were you talking to about it?"

I tried to laugh the comment off. "Well, I was actually thinking out loud about it. I happened to be in the yard and that area caught my attention and I remembered that you had mentioned taking a look at it—" I felt that my words were running together too rapidly, and I stopped. I did not like lying to Charlie but had no choice.

"Oh. That is a coincidence. Would you mind if we came out and looked at it?"

"No, not at all. I'm anxious to get these other things taken care of." I felt my face turn red. How embarrassing!

"Great. How about eleven o'clock? I'm not sure how long it will take so we could plan on the afternoon."

I nodded my head as if I thought he could see it. "That would be perfect. I'll look forward to seeing you."

"Me too."

* * *

The mail arrived shortly after 10:30 a.m. and I retrieved several RSVPs for the open house. The size of the party was growing and taking shape. I called Lucius to give him an early headcount.

At the sound of a vehicle approaching, I turned and saw Charlie's truck winding its way up the drive. He had his regular crew of workers who all jumped out of the truck and greeted me as old friends. Tom Greene slowly descended the truck last.

Charlie leaned out the window of the truck. "Mind if I drive over the lawn to that area? I have a heavy generator and some power tools that I think we're going to need to get through this brush. "And I promise he won't go near the lighthouse steps!" He smiled as he said that.

I returned the smile. "Not at all, by all means do what you have to, park where it is convenient."

"Tom will help us do as little damage as possible." His reference to Tom put a chill in the air. He parked the truck close to the forest and his workers started unloading the equipment. Charlie got out and walked toward the forest, scanning the growth from side to side.

"There is a lot more here than I thought there was. I guess I wasn't paying a lot of attention to the outside when we were working on the inside." He lifted the baseball cap off his head and ran his hand across his salt and pepper hair.

"I'll leave you to it. I'm making lunch for everyone, so just let me know when you're hungry."

Charlie smiled. "Thanks. That's nice of you."

He turned to the others and they began discussing the best way to move forward. Tom stood away from the group and contributed nothing. We shared a brief glance then I returned to the kitchen. The rest of the morning passed quickly, and I checked the RSVPs against the list of invitees. Among the people who had not responded were Father Peabody and Reverend Smithers. I did not expect the priest to bring a guest, but one never knew; I did expect Reverend Smithers might bring a guest.

I spent the next few hours on the plans for the open house, as saws buzzed outside, when suddenly my attention was snatched from the guest list as a commotion rose outside. I opened the kitchen door and stepped out on the deck just as Frank rushed up the steps.

"Charlie asked me to come and get you."

A moment of panic set in. "Is everything all right?" I asked, expecting to hear that someone had had an accident.

Frank just stared at me and waved me forward. I rushed down the steps just in time to see Charlie exiting from the forest. His clothes were filthy; dirt embedded in his hands and nails and streaked across his clothes. In one hand he carried a small garden trowel encrusted with mud; in the other he had a wire brush, with a long wooden handle and short bristles.

I raced toward him. "Charlie? What in the world is wrong? Is someone hurt?"

He shook his head. "No, but we've found something that I think you need to see."

He turned around and walked back into the forest and I followed close on his heels. The musty smell of wet earth and decomposing leaves rose to greet me. We hurried about thirty feet through dense brush until we came to a small glen that appeared to have been cleared at one time—the ground cover, although thick, was short. The growth had crept forward, and although under a canopy of trees, that particular area still remained less dense than the rest of the forest.

As we approached, I saw Tom Greene crouched down. His attention was focused on something on the ground. He was intent on his mission to uncover it, so absorbed with his task he failed to react to the sounds of rustling leaves as we approached.

"Tom," Charles called, but got no response. "Tom!" he called again, his voice a decibel higher.

Slowly Tom raised his head, his look distracted as if he heard Charlie call, yet did not understand what he was supposed to do. He stood tall and straight and wiped the back of his left hand across his brow, leaving a long line of wet dirt across his face. He remained silent as Charlie walked toward him.

Although the thick growth kept the entire area in dark shades of gray, small shafts of light flickered through the leaves above as a breeze caught them and swirled them back and forth. I felt a chill in the air and wrapped my arms around my body. Charlie removed a flashlight from his work belt and shined it on the ground. He motioned me to his side. Cautiously I moved forward around Tom who had not moved from where he stood.

"Take a look," Charlie said. He shined the light toward a patch of ground about six feet square.

I stepped in close and bent over. An earthy scent rose and lifted into my nose, my eyes, my throat, and I choked. Charlie bent down close to me and using the brush, removed some dirt from a stone. That's when I saw them…the letters, JOH….V..R…. I shot up from the ground and stumbled. Charlie caught me.

"Is this what I think it is?" I asked.

Charlie gave his head a tentative nod. "I think so, but we need to do more clearing. I don't think we want to move any more of this growth until we know exactly what we're about to uncover. But I think we've found John Varcoe's grave."

I immediately began looking at the ground around the marker, searching for another grave—one with the name Emmaline engraved on it. I stared at Charlie, and he read my mind.

"This is the only one we've found so far," he whispered. "I think you should go back in the house and let us see what else we can find."

I realized I would just be in the way and slowly returned to the house. As I approached the deck, I turned and stared at the entrance to the forest, as if I could actually see the work continuing. I turned and entered the kitchen and as I washed my hands, I felt a cold breeze waft through the room. I spun around and saw Emmaline standing by the kitchen window, looking at the beehive of activity outside.

She turned to me. *I told you, you would find the answers.*

I did not have the nerve to tell her that I still wasn't sure of the questions.

Chapter Nineteen

Emmaline retreated, leaving me with my confused thoughts. I felt an obligation to her but remained unclear as to what that obligation was and how I was to move forward. To clear my thoughts, I spent the next hour busying myself with lunch, and just finished the salads when I heard a knock on the door. I turned to see Charlie standing on the deck.

I opened the door, but he remained on the deck. "I'm pretty dirty; think I shouldn't come inside. Just thought you might want to see what we've uncovered."

His crew had cleared a wide pathway through the dense woods and into the small clearing. I noticed two headstones lying several feet apart from one another. All shrubbery and ground cover had been removed and the stones had been cleaned as much as possible, considering the conditions.

Charlie led me to the first one as the men around moved further back into the distance. Charlie switched the flashlight on and shined it on the first stone.

JOHN VARCOE
b. 1840 – d. 1902
He swung the light to the next one that read:
ELLEN VARCOE
b. 1856 – d. 1876

I looked from one to the other then I scanned the cleared area but found no other indications of graves. I looked at Charlie, a question settling on my face.

"We did not find any other graves. She's not here, or at least not in any marked plot." He read my mind. "But at least this is one mystery solved."

"Or deepened," I added.

"I don't think we should disturb any more of this land. At least not right here. We'll clear out more of the outside area and make sure the woods don't further encroach on the house."

"That's good. I'd like to empty this area when we can, but it's not my priority. They've been here all these years buried in all this undergrowth; I guess they can last a while longer."

"Any thoughts about what you would eventually want to do with them?" he asked.

I blanched at the term 'do with them,' then shook my head. "Have no idea," I answered. "I'm not ready to deal with it right now."

Charlie nodded his head slowly then redirected his attention to the crew. "Okay guys let's move the equipment back outside. We need to make sure all this shrubbery is cleaned out and any new growth removed."

The men began to move as one group, except Tom Greene. He remained behind, staring at the two graves. I watched him then turned my attention to Charlie.

Tom lifted his head and looked through a fog of thoughts. "Oh, sorry Charlie. This is just so sad. I wonder why these people weren't buried in the Catholic Cemetery in town."

"Don't know," Charlie answered. "In those days many people had their own family graveyards on their property."

I looked from Tom to the graves then to Charlie. "Did they have no children?" I asked.

"No idea," Charlie responded.

I turned to Tom and asked, "You've been researching this manor. Did you learn anything about these graves?

A slight tinge of red crept up his throat from his collar. He did not respond, just looked down at the ground and turned away. I let the question remain unanswered but wondered how much he really uncovered in his research.

The chill of the dark forest wrapped itself around me and I shivered. "Perhaps you should break for lunch? I have sandwiches and salad." I was at a loss how to break the mood.

Charlie smiled and wiped his hands on his pant legs. He lightly touched my arm, and we left the glen. A somber mood prevailed over the group. The bright sun and warm temperatures did not infiltrate the pall that settled. It soon became apparent that additional work would not continue on that day.

I thought it curious that there was no joy at discovering such long lost remembrances of someone passed. As the crew began reloading the truck, I turned to Charlie and said, "I feel as though this should not be such an unhappy event. Someone went to great lengths to bury these people properly, and the fact that over the decades their resting place has not been cared for shouldn't hide that fact."

Charlie nodded in agreement. "I'm just surprised there's no record of this anywhere in the town archives or the Historical Society records. I'm sure someone would have found records if they existed."

"And more often lost to memory," I added. "You said you didn't find any other graves. I guess Ellen and John didn't have any children either. Kind of sad," I said. "It would have been typical for a man of that day to want children to carry on his name, and both of his wives died without giving him that."

Charlie turned and looked at me with a curious glint in his eyes. "Why are you so caught up in this family?"

His question was almost humorous, but I sensed a serious side to it as well. I was not yet prepared to tell him about the entry in my mother's diary or about Emmaline...I still wasn't sure what I even *knew* about Emmaline.

"Oh, I think I'm just caught up in the history of this house and the more I find out about the various tragedies that have occurred here, the more I want to know. There is an attachment to my family, as you know." I wasn't sure that excuse would take hold, but it was the best I could come up with at the moment, and it was not entirely untrue. *Lying by omission.*

Charlie watched as his crew continued loading the truck then turned back to me. "So how are the party arrangements coming along?" he said, redirecting my thoughts.

I was grateful for the deflection. "Quite well. The invitation RSVPs are flying in and so far, no one has sent their regrets! I've been updating Lucius and he's very excited."

Charlie laughed. "I would have been surprised if anyone had said no. I hope we have good weather for it."

We.

I looked up as the word whispered through my ear, expecting to see Emmaline, but only Charlie and I stood in the yard.

"As do I," I answered, still watching for an appearance that did not occur. "Do you think Father Peabody would want to do some kind of blessing on the graves? Not at the open house, mind you, but perhaps just as a courtesy to the departed?" A cold breeze wrapped itself around me as I made the comment.

Charlie wrinkled his brow. "Charlotte, you surprise me. You said you weren't a religious person. I suppose it would be a nice thing to do, but it sounds like it is more important to you than to those in the graves."

I noticed that as I rubbed my hands across my arms for warmth, Charlie was sweating in the warm afternoon air. I stopped rubbing my arms, and the warm air quickly returned.

"I have to take the boys back to the office. I've been working on the hutch and I think it's going to be a beauty once it's been cleaned up, sanded, painted—you know, the works. The toughest part will be the cutting board. It was pretty well damaged, although not irreparable."

I was caught by the word damaged. "That's surprising. I only got a quick look at it in the attic, but it didn't look like there was a lot of damage. What kind?"

"Well, mostly from it being used as a chopping block." Then he laughed. "Funny thing though, as I was removing it from the hutch, Sheriff Tuttle came in and saw what I was doing. She asked if she could borrow it for some tests. It seems the forensics department in Bangor is working with some new equipment and she wants to see if it is possible to determine what kinds of animals were carved up on it by a blood match. Ducks, rabbits, deer, you know – the various hunter trophies."

I cringed. "Not sure I care to know. Can it be fixed? That is, can you remove all remnants of what animals were carved up on it? I'm not sure I care to have anything that obvious in the kitchen. I can promise you; I will not be using the carving board for much more than lettuce and tomatoes!"

Charlie laughed. "Not a problem. If I can't remove any duck fragments, I'll just replace it with something similar!"

I liked Charlie's laugh. It was genuine. I smiled and nodded. "That's what I like to hear." I turned my attention back to the opening to the cemetery, as I had begun thinking of it. "What about this? We can't disturb the graves; but we still need to do something with this whole hedgerow here." I pointed to the edge of the woods where undergrowth remained thick.

"Yeah, I agree. We won't do anything more around the graves in case the Genealogical Society wants to dip their fingers into this pie—and that would be up to you. But this edging still needs work. We can look at that later, maybe after the party. You've got a lot to deal with right now." He turned and saw that the crew had just finished loading the truck. "I'll look at what we need to do about this, and let you know, but let's not worry about it for now. These roots aren't going to take over in the next few weeks. In the meantime, are you going to be okay?" He nodded his head toward the opening to the cemetery.

"Yes, I'm just fine. I am glad we discovered these graves. I actually find it rather satisfying. Although, I'm more disturbed we didn't find Emmaline's grave. If this was intended to be a family cemetery, surely, she would have been buried there. She was, after all, the first wife."

The cold air blew in again and I looked toward the cliff. I thought I saw a light glow but realized it could just be a reflection off the water below.

"Well, I guess we'll never know. Let me know if you need anything more before the big soiree!" He laughed again. It was a movement and a sound I was becoming very fond of.

Chapter Twenty

As I watched Charlie leave the driveway, my phone rang. It was George Breckenridge.

"Charlotte, good day. I hope I'm not interrupting anything."

I enjoyed the familiarity of his deep voice. "Not at all. What can I do for you?"

"It's probably more 'what I can do for you,'" he said. "We went back and did some more research on the property and discovered some interesting facts."

"Oh, no. Don't tell me I don't own the house!" I felt a catch in my throat.

"No, not at all. In fact, I'm convinced even more that it is definitely yours."

"So, what's the news?" I asked.

"Well, as you know, after John Varcoe died, Thomas inherited the property, but he never returned to Maine. Or at least there is no record of him returning to Portsborough. I went back through the papers we found when Walter was verifying the ownership. My researcher had discovered some papers in Boston archives relating to a sale. A letter from Thomas to Harold Barkley very specifically laid out the details of the sale. That being, Barkley would take all responsibility for maintenance of the manor and at no time could he renege on the sale. It seems that Thomas was having some financial issues and the property was weighing heavily on his resources. Once the sale was complete, Thomas washed his hands of the entire property."

"I'm confused. Who was Harold Barkley?"

"He was Emmaline's brother-in-law. He married Lyda Grimes, Emmaline's sister."

"Of course! Simeon Barkley was their son!" The pieces of the puzzle were beginning to come together. "And there were never any other property sales?"

"No. The property remained in the Barkley hands and came down through several generations to your mother. You might want to trace that family genealogy for a better understanding."

"I know just who to call. George, thank you so much for this information. You have put my mind at rest."

* * *

"Peter? It's Charlotte Sunday. I need some genealogy help."

The intake of breath was palpable! "Of course. What do you need?" I heard the shuffling of papers in the background. "Tell me, who and what information do you have?"

"Well, this is going to be a chore. It's my genealogy that I need help with. In particular, through my mother. Her maiden name was Lyda Converse. She and my father married in 1964. This property came to her through several generations – I don't know how many. But I need you to track my genealogy and tell me what you find, if anything."

"This should be no problem at all. Does this have anything to do with Emmaline and John Varcoe?"

"Perhaps, and that would be a bonus, but right now I'm just curious about how my mother came to own the manor." I did not feel it was necessary to provide any additional information until I had a better understanding of my own history.

* * *

The remainder of the day flew by as I wrapped myself up in the final touches for the open house. Lucius Bartels called late in the afternoon to go over the menu, and he made a few suggestions regarding where to locate the wines and where to put the foods. We both decided the food should be served in the house, while the wine and liquor bars could be placed outside. He would be grilling and barbecuing ribs outside, but everything would be carried indoors. He felt that those arrangements would prove positive for moving people throughout the grounds and house. I gave him full control over the menus—both liquid and solid. He was thrilled.

I finished cleaning the remainder of lunch and found myself drawn to the kitchen window that looked out to the north. The entrance to the cemetery glared at me like an open wound. A sense of terrific sorrow washed over me as I stared at the dark, gaping hole. It was most disturbing because in my heart I believed I should be rejoicing the discovery, almost as if the discovery was freeing some souls lost for decades when no one visited them, cared for their graves, or thought about their lives. And yet I could not shake the depression that engulfed me.

I turned away from the window and as I did, I saw Emmaline standing at the far end of the kitchen, away from the window.

Emmaline. I almost felt guilty that I could not bring joy to the discovery for her.

Joy? She said, as if she read my mind. Of course. She didn't read my mind, she lived in it.

Were you aware that these graves were here? I asked, pointing toward the gaping hole in the woods.

How would I know such a thing? Both Ellen and John died after me. I'd have no way of knowing where they were put.

I was startled by her use of the word 'put' as opposed to buried, or laid to rest, or some other, gentler term. *Well, no, of course you could not have known...* I stumbled over my words, confused that I was becoming involved in such a conversation with someone who did not exist, but I was at the same time disconcerted by her tone. The sometimes-amusing tenor she placed on her words, her coy sense of curiosity, was gone, replaced by dark tones bordering on anger. I sensed she experienced no joy at having found John's grave. I could understand, perhaps, her lack of compassion for Ellen, but then again, *John married Ellen after Emmaline's death. And what the hell difference would it make anyway?* I did not realize that my words had become part of our mysterious conversation until Emmaline commented.

I have no compassion for Ellen. She had none for me when she took my husband to her bed long before I died!

I felt my eyebrows fly up to the top of my forehead. If they were not attached, I am sure they would have just left my face completely. My mouth formed a small 'o', and my eyes grew wide. I was unable to speak either out loud, or to Emmaline. I just stared.

Did I surprise you? She asked. *Of course, you would not have known. There would be no reason for you to know. It was important for John to have an heir, and when I could not satisfy that need, he sought comfort elsewhere.*

Words, questions, comments—all raced through my head as I tried to pull my thoughts together. *But surely, he could not have made an affair work. He was still married to you, and to produce a child with a woman who was not his wife—that may be okay in Hollywood today, but really? Maine in the 1870s? He would never have been able to explain that. And being Catholic?* Inadvertently I threw my hand to my face as I tried to consider the ramifications of such an act at that time. *The very idea defies comprehension.*

Yes, there was the marriage, and the church, wasn't there?

Well, divorce was certainly not an option unless he could get the church to somehow agree to annul your marriage. My head throbbed with questions.

My father would never have allowed that. Besides, although our child did not live, the fact remained that there had been a child and the church could hardly ignore that fact. And John was not one to hide his promiscuous behavior. He had the power and the money to do as he pleased, and people just turned their heads.

I shook my head as if to rid myself of these thoughts but could not. Emmaline's anger seemed to grow with every word, every thought.

Death was the only convenient answer, she said, as if to focus my mind in one direction.

Emmaline, what are you implying? Are you saying John murdered you?

I have absolutely no idea, she replied. *But my death was, nonetheless, convenient.*

My mind raced back to discovering John and Ellen's graves earlier in the day, and one fact came to mind. *If John did kill you in order to marry Ellen, it certainly did not turn out to his advantage. We never found any other graves. If they had no children, then his line still stopped with Ellen. She died childless as well. She died in 1876, only a year after you. Any children left behind would certainly have been known to the townspeople. So, no children with Ellen either.*

Emmaline did not reply. I came out of my deep thoughts and looked at her. She pursed her lips and just stared at me.

Hmmm, was all she said as she turned and left the kitchen, wandering toward the cliff. I moved to the windows and watched as her essence moved slowly, as if carrying a heavy weight. I leaned back against the counter and saw her turn and nod to me, when a thought came to mind. *For someone claiming not to have a memory of her life, she seems to know many convenient circumstances.* I refocused my attention to her and watched her disappear. I wondered if she was still in my mind.

At ten o'clock I felt a weariness wash over me, and I put away all thoughts of menus and guest lists. But my mind clouded with the discoveries of the past several days. Our failure to discover Emmaline's grave haunted me. When I first saw John and Ellen's graves, I was certain that there would be another nearby, but the disturbing fact was that she remained lost.

I opened the French doors and walked out onto the balcony. My glance turned toward the north and I considered the curiosity that had risen in the past few weeks for that lighthouse. Old, and deteriorating, it sat above the very edge of the grounds where the steps went down to the beach and river below. I wondered if Tom's insistence that there was something in the lighthouse held any truth. My one trip up there had not turned over anything that would confirm or deny his claim about ownership, and certainly my conversation with George reconfirmed my own position.

I looked for the glow that would tell me Emmaline was nearby but saw nothing more. The full moon shone upon the yard and I scanned the grounds, expanding my line of sight from the trees across the grounds to the north then sweeping back to the south. But it was clear that I was alone that night.

Chapter Twenty-One

Time moved quickly, although sadness hung over the house. I spoke to Charlie several times and he told me he was making progress with the hutch, although it required more attention and repair work than he originally anticipated. He was not sure if it would be finished in time for the open house, but he would try. I told him not to worry. If it wasn't finished, I could just show it off at the next open house, a comment that drew laughter from both of us. It was the first time laughter rang through the manor in several days.

Emmaline's visits had shrunk to nothing, and with each passing moment, she retreated further and further into my own memory. There was no mysterious movement of robes and slippers; no mysterious glow from the lighthouse; the gaping entrance to the Varcoe cemetery became nothing more than a hole in the woods. Although my life began to form a shell of normalcy, a pall remained that I could not shake.

The day before the open house I was reviewing the final menu from Lucius Bartels, when the phone rang. I answered and immediately heard the serious tone in Charlie's greeting. Our phone calls had taken on a warm quality—perhaps one that neither of us openly admitted to, but a warmth, nonetheless. Today was different.

"Charlie, is something wrong?" I asked.

He hesitated for a moment then said, "I have almost finished the hutch."

I laughed. "You sound like you broke it into a hundred pieces. Does it look that bad?"

He took a deep breath. "No, not really. It's a well constructed piece and cleaned up to be a beauty."

"So? What's the problem?"

"Well, I think I need to show you. I'd like to bring it out this afternoon if that's okay with you. I had to do some substitutions in a few places, but with the medium blue paint, you can't tell the difference unless you get really close to examine it. Actually, for the most part it turned out quite well."

"'For the most part,'" I repeated. "What does that mean?"

"I had to replace the carving board. It's just a temporary fix—at least I think so..." his sentence dribbled out of the telephone and dissipated into mid air.

"Okay," I responded. It was obvious that he chose not to go into detail over the phone. "This afternoon will be just fine. I'm going over the final plans for tomorrow, so I'll be here all day. Bring it out whenever."

"We'll be there this afternoon."

"Your team coming to help?" I asked.

"Yes, and Lorelei Tuttle will be joining us. I'll explain when we arrive. Sorry to sound so mysterious, but I'll see you then." He did not wait for any answer on my part, but hung up leaving me with dead air and an unanswered question...*Lorelei Tuttle? What is the world is the sheriff coming out for?*

* * *

The next ninety minutes dragged on and the ability to concentrate deserted me as I wandered through the house fluffing pillows, adjusting pictures, tidying up magazines. At one o'clock I found myself standing on the front porch, scanning the distance, and waiting for Charlie's arrival. I looked at my watch just as I heard the telltale sound of wheels on the dry ground of the driveway. Charlie's van rambled slowly up the drive toward me through the arch of trees. He drove around the circular drive and came to a halt in front of the porch. But the sound did not stop as a State Police car followed slowly behind, weaving around to avoid ruts in the path.

Charlie, Tom, and Frank emerged from the van and I watched as a tall, sinewy woman exited the State Police vehicle. She seemed almost to unfold from the car, placed the official police hat on her head of short, golden brown hair, and adjusted her gun belt. My eyes remained glued to her while my peripheral vision caught movement to my right. I turned and watched Charlie climb the steps toward me. Over his shoulder I saw Frank and Tom open the side van door and prepare to move the hutch.

I watched as Charlie approached with Sheriff Tuttle close behind.

"Charlotte, this is Lorelei Tuttle—Sheriff Tuttle." He turned to the woman who walked up to the steps.

She put her hand out, and a large smile, full lips, and perfectly formed teeth covered what appeared to be an otherwise somber face. I reached out, grabbed her hand, and smiled. I hoped my smile looked genuine. I was anxious to know more about this meeting. Sheriff Tuttle did not strike me as someone to fool around with.

"How do you do?" I asked.

She nodded. "Just fine, Charlotte—may I call you Charlotte?" she asked.

My smile grew. I sensed I would like her. "Please, do. Although I'm a little unsure of why the sheriff is accompanying my hutch."

"Perhaps we should talk inside?" she said.

I stepped aside and motioned for Sheriff Tuttle to come in. Charlie returned to the van and he and his men began to remove the hutch as I led Sheriff Tuttle into the kitchen. We both remained silent while the hutch was pushed and prodded and nudged from the van and up the front steps as they carried it into the house. They placed it on a large dolly and rolled it into the kitchen. As they passed me and moved it to the far wall in the kitchen, I was stunned by its beauty. The blueberry blue Charlie had chosen was the perfect contrast to the stark white wall it sat against. I knew I could not have purchased a new piece of furniture that would meet this standard.

They nestled it precisely in the middle of the wall, on the far side of the kitchen between the small dividing wall next to the storage cabinet and the windows.

"There, that should do it," Charlie said, wiping sweat from his brow with the sleeve of his tee. "What do you think?" he asked.

"It's perfect. Other than the new carving board, which I'm sure no one else would notice, it is exactly what I had hoped for."

Sheriff Tuttle broke into my thoughts. "Well, Charlotte, it's that carving board we want to talk about."

My head swiveled from Lorelei to Charlie and back again. A frown crinkled my brow and I asked, "What about the carving board?"

"Charlotte," Charlie said, "maybe we should sit down for this conversation."

We all sat at the table and I waited for someone to make the first move. Charlie did not disappoint.

"Charlotte, do you remember when I told you that Lorelei wanted to use that carving board to test some new equipment in the lab?"

I nodded. "I think you said she wanted to see if they could determine what kinds of animals were put on the board." I shivered at the thought.

Charlie nodded. "Yes, that's right."

Lorelei interrupted. "I was only hoping we could become familiar with this equipment; you know, get some experience in using it. Learn the ins and outs of how it operates; what it will tell us, that sort of thing."

I sat silent, my glance once again moving from Lorelei to Charlie, and back. "And?" I asked.

I saw a look pass between Lorelei and Charlie. "We got more than we anticipated. We did learn a lot about the blood on the carving board."

"So, how many animals? Were you able to determine what animals were carved on that board?"

A second look passed between Lorelei and Charlie. Tom and Frank stood in the kitchen doorway; eerily quiet, curiosity creased their faces.

Lorelei folded her hands and placed them on the table. Her gray eyes locked with mine. "There's no easy way to say this, but the blood was human."

I blinked my eyes. "Human?" As the concept of what they were saying began to sink in, I repeated, with the volume inched up, "Human??? What are you saying?"

"Someone was murdered on that carving board."

My mind did not focus. My eyes darted around the room, unable to settle until I reached Tom's face. His jaw clamped tight, the muscles working back and forth; his eyes narrowed into small slits. I saw what I interpreted as a mixture of anger and fear, but I had no idea why. His eyes met mine and he quickly moved his glance to the tabletop.

"Do you know whose blood?" I asked, returning my attention to Lorelei.

Lorelei shook her head. "No, we only know the blood is quite old. But I understand from Charlie here that you've recently found two graves on the property?"

"Yes. Are you saying that you think that blood may have come from one of the people buried there?"

A cold breeze blew through the room although no one else seemed to react. *I think I'll be getting a visit,* I thought to myself. But I got no response.

Lorelei answered, "We don't know, but would like to take a look at those bones—rule them out or rule them in."

I looked at Charlie and he just shrugged. I looked back at Lorelei. "Well, they're not family, and if it helps you then I have no problem with it. I don't know what you have to do to make that truly legal, but if you need my permission, you have it."

"Okay then, I'll make the arrangements. We won't be able to get the paperwork settled for several days...probably sometime next week. And since you're having your open house tomorrow, well, let's not disrupt that. Oh, and thank you for the invitation."

My answer was weak. "Of course, you're more than welcome. I hope you'll enjoy yourself." My voice became a whisper as my mind flooded with thoughts of rabbits and humans and blood—lots and lots of blood.

"Well, I'll be on my way. We'll process the exhumation order and move forward. I'm sorry about the disruption."

"It's really not a problem," I muttered. "The exhumation, I mean. I do find it disturbing that there is human blood on the carving board."

Lorelei placed her official hat on her head, nodded, and left.

Charlie scraped the floor as he moved his chair back to rise. "Tom, Frank, meet me in the truck. I need a minute with Charlotte."

Both men had been quiet through the entire discussion, and I found it curious that Tom had made no comment; I wondered if he considered this worthy of his claim about my ownership. I could not determine how that would figure in, but at this point, nothing escaped me.

When they left, Charlie turned to me. "Charlotte, I'm really sorry about this. I didn't think this would turn out this way at all. I really thought I was just doing Lorelei a favor."

I nodded my head. "I understand, Charlie. I hope Lorelei can find out something about this mystery. I do hate to disturb the two graves, but if it's necessary, then it's necessary. Honestly, I can't image what anyone expects to find if the blood is quite old."

"Yeah, me too. On another note, is there anything I can do to help tomorrow?"

"Moral support will be just about all I need."

"I can do that!" He leaned in and gave me a quick kiss on the cheek.

"That's becoming a habit, Mr. Beasley!" I saw a light pink hue climb up from under his tee shirt.

"Yeah, I guess it is."

I sensed heat rising above my own collar.

"I'll be here early in case you need any help. Maybe I can be a tour guide. I am, after all, familiar with this building."

I threw my head back and laughed for the first time in the day. "The party starts at 2:00. You're welcome any time, just let me know when.

"I'll be here at 1:00."

We left the kitchen and at the front door, Charlie took the steps two at a time and hurried around to the driver's side of the van.

I spent the rest of the day looking over my shoulder, expecting to see Emmaline appear out of the dust, but nothing. I went to bed early, tired and anxious, with a new series of questions that I felt were likely to go unanswered. I laid my head on the pillow, still expecting to roll over and find Emmaline sitting on the chair, but I was alone, and my eyes slid closed.

Chapter Twenty-Two

I slept well that night with no visitors, although dreams of forests and graves and groaning board tables overflowing with food and drink seemed to embed themselves in my subconscious, with no organized flow.

When I rolled over and looked at the clock, the blue digital numbers displayed 7:30. I sat up in bed and looked around. The windows over the balcony remained open and a breeze drifted through the room. I stretched and again looked at the chair, but still no Emmaline.

I brushed the fog out of my head and thoughts of today's open house began rushing through my mind. I hurried into the bathroom, washed my face and brushed my teeth, then threw on a pair of cargo pants and a light sweatshirt. I glanced again at the clock—8:15 a.m. Lucius Bartels would arrive at 11:00 with his staff to set the stage. I rushed downstairs to the kitchen and made a cup of coffee. Any other breakfast would have to wait, or I would just skip it altogether.

At the kitchen door I looked toward the lighthouse but saw nothing other than the cliff and the house, the river beyond, and the light fog that had not yet burned off the water. I wondered what had happened to Emmaline. She had made no appearance since the discovery of the graves, and for a brief moment I considered that perhaps she got the answer to her questions. Something in the back of my mind, however, told me that was not entirely accurate. As quickly as this thought passed out of my mind, the phone rang.

"Hope I didn't wake you?" Charlie said.

I smiled. "Not at all. I've been up for about an hour. Mr. Bartels is arriving at 11:00 to start setting up everything. The house is as ready as it could be so I'm just hovering." I laughed.

Charlie did not laugh. "Well, I think you should know something—"

The unease in his voice caught me off guard. I took a deep breath. "And what would that be?" I asked as a flurry of possible answers rolled around in my head.

"Apparently several of my workers could not wait to get home after finding those graves and, well, word spread rapidly. I suspect there will be a lot of curiosity about the graves. Unless you want people traipsing all over that area, I thought I might come out early and see if I could tape it off to keep intruders out."

"Oh, dear!" I said. "If you wouldn't mind doing that, it would be very helpful. I really don't want anyone wandering into that area, and I suspect Sheriff Tuttle wouldn't be crazy about it either."

"Yeah, I've already talked to her and she'll probably arrive a little early as well just to make sure it is clearly marked as a 'no trespass' zone. I'm really sorry about that, Charlotte. I had no idea these guys would chatter the way they did."

"That's okay, Charlie. Sooner or later that discovery would have come out with the same results. I just happen to be having an open house, which I'm sure several guests will consider literally 'open grounds.' Come out anytime that's convenient for you and we'll get this done."

"Can I impose upon you further? I'll wear some work clothes but would like to be able to shower and change there. Otherwise, I'll have to come back into town."

I cut him off. "Not a problem. I have baths in the spare bedrooms, and you're welcome to use any one of them."

"Thanks. I'll be out within the hour. Not sure when Lorelei will be arriving, but she'll probably show up around one o'clock. Since this thing starts at two, you can count on people just happening to arrive early. The sooner we get this taken care of, the better." Then he laughed. "I got some crime tape from Lorelei. It was the only thing either of us had handy on the spur of the moment. So, I'll bring out a few posts and we'll just spread the tape across the opening, and I'll make it as obvious as I can that this is not an area where anyone is welcome to wander through."

"I don't know what I'd do without you. I guess I didn't think that anyone would know about these graves. Actually, I haven't given them a lot of thought either."

We ended the call, and I went to one of the spare bedrooms and placed some towels on the bed. I placed soap and shampoo in the shower and gave a quick thought about Charlie showering in my house. I hovered over that though longer than I should have!

I spent the next hour busying myself with non-work; I walked through the house straightening afghans, removing a wayward speck of dust from a shelf, and generally just passing time.

As I considered the outcome ahead of me, I heard the sound of a vehicle rumbling up the driveway and looked out the library window to see Charlie's van. He drove to the north side of the house and I met him as he parked near the graveyard entrance.

"Hi, how can I help?" I asked. My voice quivered.

He opened the side door and retrieved three rolls of yellow tape that read 'CRIME SCENE' across the middle in large black capital letters. He handed them to me. I took them, stared at them briefly then looked at Charlie. We both broke into loud peals of laughter. My anxiety lessened and I felt a strong jolt of gratitude for Charlie's help. He turned back to the van and removed two tall metal poles and a rubber mallet then closed the truck and we walked down the path to the graves.

"Might as well get this done as quickly as possible. I can't promise this will keep the die-hard curiosity seekers out, but it should at least deter them. Between me and Lorelei, we'll keep an eye on the area and redirect anyone who is snooping too much."

"Do you really think people would do that? I mean, this isn't their property."

Charlie stopped and placed the poles on the ground. He picked up one pole and the mallet, walked to the left edge of the entrance to the clearing. "Charlotte, you have to understand something," he said as he began pounding the pole into the ground. "At this point, and probably for the rest of your life, you are a squatter on this property."

I opened my eyes wide at this comment and Charlie laughed.

"I don't mean that to insult you, and I realize you've put a lot into making this place a home, but you're an outsider. You may have been born here, but you have no family here, and you're not involved with anyone here in any way. The manor has been here since 1870. The manor belongs to the people of Portsborough...or at least that's how they see it—you're a squatter—you just occupy space. People don't need to be told that this is your property. They know you inherited it, but it's still theirs. At least, that's how a lot of people think."

I stood quietly, trying to digest this information. "Do you think that?" I asked, waiting for the next slap in my face.

He stopped pounding and took one of the rolls of tape out of my hand. "No, of course not. I like you; you know—more than a little." He looked at the tape and avoided looking at me. "It's just that I've had the opportunity to get to know you. Many of these people have only *heard* of you. This is their first chance to see the manor, as it should look, and the new mistress of the manor, so to speak. They're excited and they probably won't think anything of checking it out completely. We have a second situation that no one other than you, Lorelei, Tom, Frank and I know about and that's the blood on the carving board. I've made it quite clear to Tom and Frank that there will be no discussion of that topic. We're not about to make that knowledge public or we would have a full-blown stampede on our hands. This is the best way to keep these folks at bay."

I looked at the roll of tape in his hand and I started to laugh again. "Right. We're going to keep them at bay with 'CRIME SCENE' tape."

A wide grin crept across Charlie's face as he began winding the tape around the pole close to the ground to secure it. "Well, that's going to be our challenge, isn't it?"

He picked up the second pole, walked across the face of the opening, and pounded it into the ground. He took the tape and wound it around the second pole then walked back and forth, crisscrossing the distance between the poles and moving from the ground up toward the top. After twenty minutes of wrapping and rewrapping, the opening was almost completely covered as though it were a closed door, preventing access to anyone who might think to journey there. We both knew that it would be a deterrent at best, but it was better than nothing.

We stepped back and stood next to each other admiring his work when the sound of a vehicle approaching caught our attention. We turned to see Lucius Bartels' catering van arrive at the house. I brushed my hand over Charlie's arm then hurried over to greet Lucius.

"Charlotte, my dear, how nice to see you again. Thought I'd get an early start. We have to set up the grill and get it going; that will take a little time, then of course the cooking and laying out of everything." He leaned sideways slightly and peered over my shoulder and nodded his head. "I see you are preparing for the onslaught."

"I see you've heard also."

"Oh, my dear. You are absolutely the talk of the town. We don't have much to chatter about other than whose children shoplifted from the drugstore or who is sleeping with whose spouse. You've absolutely stopped all gossip in its tracks. I guess there'll be some disappointed guests today, eh? No grave observations?" He laughed at his own comment.

"We just recently found these graves, and until I can get my head around what to do next, I really don't want a horde of people trampling over everything. I don't even know for sure if we've found everything there is to find."

Lucius patted my arm. "I fully understand. You're doing the right thing."

Charlie came around from the side of the house where he finished packing up the van and greeted Lucius. "Hey, Lucius. Good to see you."

Lucius raised his eyebrows as Charlie approached. "Charles, good to see you. I see you're helping our new neighbor. How nice."

Charlie just nodded his head then turned to me. "Think I can get that shower now?"

My peripheral vision observed the look of interest on Lucius's face. I grabbed Charlie by the arm and redirected him toward the house. "Absolutely. Follow me. I have to take my shower as well." I looked over my shoulder. "Lucius, you know the way around. Just let yourself in and I'll be back in about thirty minutes." A wide grin draped across Lucius Bartels' face.

I turned back to Charlie and whispered. "That should keep him wondering."

Charlie rolled his head back and barked out a loud laugh.

Chapter Twenty-Three

I dressed for the open house and when I left my room, I locked the door. Uninvited guests were not on my welcome list. As I passed the guest room I stopped for a brief moment and listened but did not hear the shower running and assumed that Charlie was either dressing or already finished and downstairs.

Charlie was seated at the kitchen table and he rose as I entered. A faint smell of shea butter and cocoanut shampoo curled around me as he bent over and kissed my cheek. His hair, still damp from the shower, glistened in the bright light that shone through the windows.

I took a chair across from him and for a moment we had an awkward silence.

"Sorry about the kiss – just wanted to thank you for allowing me to use the shower."

"Not at all. It's the least I could do. You are more help than you know!"

An uncomfortable pregnant pause landed on the table between us and it was several seconds before either of us spoke. I turned and looked at the island in the middle of the kitchen. A bounty of fresh cut fruits surrounded by Swiss, Havarti, cheddar, and provolone cheeses clustered throughout the trays made my mouth water.

Lucius entered the kitchen from the deck. "Would either of you care for an early glass of wine? I have several whites and reds to choose from. The whites are cooling—I got a wonderful sparkling zinfandel that I think you'll enjoy."

I looked at Charlie, then back at Lucius. "I'll have the pinot gris. You Charlie?"

"I'll have the same."

Lucius poured our drinks and returned to the grill on the lawn, where he directed his staff through a multitude of exercises to prepare for the onslaught of guests. The faint smell of barbecue sauce floated through the open door.

"He's really quite good at this, isn't he?" I said.

Charlie nodded. "He's got a good business going here. Everyone seems to like his service and his food is excellent. He's a good choice."

We avoided anything more detailed. Finally, Charlie looked at me and asked, "Are you nervous?"

I shrugged. "A little, I guess. There have been so many things happening over the past several weeks that I'm having trouble getting my head around them."

"I guess that's right. You seem to have moved from one thing to another—an unknown inheritance, discovering the hutch, discovering the pictures, learning that the one picture is of Emmaline, the blood on the carving board, the graves—it feels like it's just an ongoing game."

I sensed that there was something left unsaid in that sentence but wasn't sure how to ask. I had not told him about Emmaline's visits and since she had not reappeared recently, I thought it was not the time to bring Charlie into my mind.

"Well, these weeks have certainly been eye-opening. I wonder what's next." Then the thought crossed my mind, and I asked, "Speaking of next, what about that other picture?"

"I'll get it from the attic after the guests have gone. My apologies for the delay. I'll probably find some time this week. I'm anxious to see how it cleans up and who's behind that glass." He finished his glass of wine and as he set the glass on the table, the sound of a vehicle approaching rumbled through the open windows.

"That must be Lorelei. I'll show her what we did and see if she wants to make any changes."

"And I'll check on Lucius and make sure he has everything he needs. I'll meet you out by the 'Crime Scene' tape!"

We both laughed and went our separate ways. I wandered across the lawn and met Lucius as he waved directions through the warm air to his staff. I knew I was out of my league, I just smiled, turned, and walked back toward the cemetery. I noticed that Lucius had not set any tables or chairs in that area, to discourage people from migrating there. *He really is a gem,* I thought.

I rounded the corner and saw Charlie and Lorelei inspecting the 'gate' that Charlie had erected. As I approached, they both turned.

Lorelei put out her hand in greeting. "Hi Charlotte. I was just inspecting Charlie's handiwork. I think it sends the proper message. Sorry about this, but once the word about something like this gets out, the curious seem to flock toward it like moths toward the proverbial flame! Charlie and I will take turns keeping an eye on the area."

"Lorelei, thanks for coming and thanks for the tape. I don't want you two to spend your entire time here watching for trespassers. If anyone asks about this, I'll just tell them that we're still excavating the area and don't know yet what exactly is there. So maybe I can deflect some traffic as well."

At that moment, the sounds of movement carried across the still afternoon air. We walked around to the front of the house to see a caravan of vehicles meandering up the drive.

"I think your guests are arriving," Charlie said. We watched a trail of vehicles that seemed never-ending.

"Jeez! It's like they all met at some place and decided to arrive together," I said.

Charlie laughed. "I think they probably did!"

Belinda Stapleford and Tom Greene arrived in the first car. She parked directly at the front door and exited with Tom trailing just behind her.

"Charlotte, I wanted to get here early and thought maybe I could walk people through the house and give them some history of the place. Thought I'd get here before the rush, but I guess everyone had the same idea." She pushed past me and hurried up the steps into the hallway.

I followed close behind not sure what to say. I was annoyed at her presumption; I sensed that she just wanted to go through and see what I had done, but as I turned and watched several other guests arriving in close pursuit, I realized the curiosity of my guests was at a boiling point, and I agreed. "Belinda, perhaps that would be helpful. I've just locked off my bedroom for privacy, and please avoid the attic, but the rest of the house is open."

"And the grounds?" she asked.

"All but the area north of the house, Belinda. We're working on that and we don't want it disturbed."

"Oh, yes...the graves..."

I turned Belinda's attention away from that area. "Come with me. I want to show you some things that we've done and perhaps you can add them to your tour."

Charlie stood in the doorway watching the volley between me and Belinda. He nodded to me, turned, and left.

We.

I jumped as the word whispered through my ear. I turned my head but saw no one. Nonetheless, I was sure Emmaline had come to the party.

Belinda, Tom, and I walked from the hallway into the sitting room. I had made many changes since my first days at the manor, adding several touches of my own. Of course, the most dramatic change was hanging over the fireplace. Emmaline's picture looked down from its place of honor and I heard Belinda gasp.

"Why, that's Emmaline Varcoe!" she exclaimed and pointed to the picture.

I smiled. "Yes, it is. I found the picture in the attic. We didn't know who it was at first, but now know it's Emmaline. Charlie cleaned the frame. It's perfect there, don't you think?"

Belinda stared at me; a curious look crossed her face. "Who told you this was Emmaline?"

I realized then that if I said anything about Madelyn that could set off fireworks, and I was not about to tell her of my newfound relationship with the previous lady of the manor, so I resorted to the next best thing. I lied. "I'm sure you remember—I was in the library and Claudia Cooper leant me that book from their reference desk. I picked up the name from there. I made the assumption when I found the picture. This was, after all, her home." *Vague,* I said to myself, *just remain vague.*

It must have worked because Belinda turned her glance back to the picture and nodded. I could hear her mind working like coins dropping into a metal box.

"You know, Charlotte, that picture really ought to be on display in the Historical Society. I could collect it tomorrow. I have just the right place for it."

I stared at her for a moment, dumbfounded. "No, Belinda, that remains right here where it belongs. I found it in the attic and since she is the mistress of the house, she stays." As I listened to my voice rise, I realized my tone carried a tinge of anger, but I was not about to let Emmaline's photo sit in some dreary building.

"Not very pretty, was she?" Tom's rude comment stopped me. It was more a statement than a question. His tone fell flat with a marked contempt rather than curiosity. I watched him as he stared at the picture, transfixed. His face clouded with disrespect.

I felt combative; a need to disagree and defend Emmaline. "I actually think she was quite attractive." I turned away from Tom toward Belinda. "Charlie found another picture in an identical frame when he moved a piece of furniture from the attic. We're not sure who it is a picture of, but I believe it could be John Varcoe."

A dark silence fell across the room and a murky shadow passed over Tom's face as he continued to stare at the picture. He made a brief move away from the sitting room and I wondered why he felt so antagonistic toward this picture.

"Another picture? How very interesting. I don't know that anyone has ever seen a picture of John Varcoe. Does Charlie have the picture at his office?" Belinda asked.

Her question made me think about the damage done to Emmaline's picture. I thought her tone became more than curious—it wandered into prodding. "No, he's not taken it yet. We left it in the attic. He'll gather it this evening after the guests leave."

Again, her tone changed. "Well, I'm sure we will all be curious to see who's in the frame." She laughed. "I appreciate you letting me guide people through the house. I'm going to use Tom's research on the history of the manor and the grounds. I'm sure everyone will be very interested."

"Of course, Belinda. Just remember, my room is locked, so it's out of bounds, and that includes the attic."

"I understand, Charlotte." She turned and walked through the house to the kitchen and out to the lawn. I noticed that Tom had disappeared from view. He had said nothing more during this entire exchange, but I sensed his interest in Emmaline just furthered his interest in the manor. I wondered how this would play into his quest for answers to the ownership of the manor.

I stepped out onto the deck and watched so many strangers greet each other with hugs and air kisses. I took a deep breath and prepared to meet my rapidly growing body of guests.

Chapter Twenty-Four

The initial introductions passed quickly, and people began to gather in their little cliques. Belinda gathered her tours together in groups of four and five while everyone else wandered the grounds chatting.

I took another glass of chilled pinot gris and watched Charlie and Lorelei redirect several curious visitors from the cemetery, when I heard a cough from behind. I turned around and saw two gentlemen approach me. It was obvious from his clothing that one was Father Peabody.

"Good afternoon, Ms. Sunday," he said as he greeted me. "I'm Father Peabody and I must say I'm quite excited about visiting this place. This is such a lovely day for your open house."

The other man stepped in front of Father Peabody. "And I'm Reverend Smithers, with the Methodist Church here in town." He stuck out his hand and grabbed mine.

"How do you do, Father Peabody, Reverend Smithers. I'm glad you could both come. I thought it would be appropriate to welcome my neighbors into the manor." I glanced around at the multitude of guests that wandered across the lawn toward the house as Belinda stood on the deck waving them forward.

"Yes, you've done quite a remarkable job with the renovations. I understand Charles Beasley did this work for you?" Father Peabody commented.

"Yes, that's right. And he did a marvelous job. I'm quite thankful to him. He's continued to work with me on a few things that still need attention."

Reverend Smithers, not to be left behind in the conversation interjected, "Ah yes, very helpful man. I've known him since he was young. I actually married him and his lovely wife. That must be about thirty-five years ago now; somewhere around that timeframe."

My neck went white hot. *Charlie is married?* I stumbled with my next words. "I've not met his wife." I let the sentence dribble off my lips.

Father Peabody stared at me for a brief moment before an awareness crossed his face. "Oh, my goodness, of course you wouldn't know. His wife, Laura, died just a few years after their marriage. Some kind of cancer. Very tragic." He bent his head down as if saying a quiet prayer.

"I had no idea," I mumbled. It was a vague and stupid comment but seemed to pass the priest without notice.

"He never remarried." Reverend Smithers leaned in close to me and whispered, "Of course, the women of this town tried to get him interested in various ladies, but all without success. Probably just as well. A loss like that at a young age can be difficult to handle."

"I'm sure you're right." I had no idea what to say to him. The air around me hung like a heavy metal chain.

Both men looked around as they spoke, and their eyes settled on the Crime Scene tape in the distance.

Thoughts raced through my mind in a hundred different directions. *Why wouldn't Charlie tell me? Am I being childish or worse still, jealous?*

Father Peabody leaned toward me as if to confide a secret. "Now, my dear, do tell about this recent discovery you've made."

"What?" My mind continued to dwell on Charlie.

Both men stared at me, anxious for details. "These graves that you've found. Are they really John and Emmaline Varcoe?" Reverend Smithers asked.

"Emmaline?" I repeated. "No, the stones read John Varcoe and Ellen Varcoe; nothing about Emmaline. She seems to be a lost soul." As I said the last words, I focused on Emmaline's search. "I understand that Emmaline's whereabouts are a mystery."

Disappointment scurried across Reverend Smither's face.

Father Peabody spoke up quickly. "Of course, it would be Ellen. After Emmaline's tragic death—a suicide, you know. Emmaline could not be buried in consecrated ground."

Anger flickered through Reverend's Smithers's eyes. "Really, Winston. She was a Methodist, not a heathen! And it wasn't against the church rules at that time to bury a suicide in consecrated ground. That went away years before."

"Well, Harvey, it wasn't *my* decision for heaven's sake. I'm just relaying what happened."

I watched the volley of words flick back and forth but remained on the fringes, preferring to observe rather than participate.

To diffuse the argument, Father Peabody turned back to me and asked, "Speaking of which, had you given any thought to possibly moving John and Ellen to the Catholic Cemetery in town?"

Reverend Smithers raised his eyes to heaven as if looking for help.

"No, I haven't had enough time to think about this. We only discovered the graves a few days ago and Charlie wants to spend a little more time to see if there are any other graves there," I answered.

"Well, the ground here is not consecrated but if you thought you would want to leave them where they are, I'd be happy to go through the process and bless the ground—or at least those two graves."

I blinked my eyes rapidly, trying to wrap my mind around his offer. I realized I had that exact thought when we found the graves. "I appreciate that, but I think it's a little premature for me to be making those decisions. I have no relationship to these people, so I have to give some thought to doing something like that."

"Of course, my dear. Just know that it is an open offer."

Father Peabody put his hand out and touched my arm. His withered fingers, cold and dry, rested for a moment too long on my arm. I shuddered, thinking about the offer, when a thought flitted through my mind.

"Father Peabody let me ask you a question. Does the church have any archives that might shed some light on those deaths and burials?"

"Oh my, there have been many people rummaging through the church papers over the years trying to find the answer to many family questions. I'm afraid we are not terribly organized. Other things seem to get in the way. Emmaline being a Methodist could be a stumbling block—although they *were* married in our church."

"Oh, for Heaven's sake, Winston!" Reverend Smithers said and took a deep breath.

Father Peabody shot a withering glance toward the good reverend then turned back to me. "But to the best of my knowledge, no one has ever found the answer. You might check with Belinda Stapleford. As the head of the Historical Society, she has spent a lot of time in our archives. Why, just a few weeks ago Tom Greene was moving books and looking for information."

Interesting, I thought. *It seems that Belinda takes her position at the society very seriously, as does Tom.* "Thanks, I'll do that," I responded.

Father Peabody turned and hurried away with Reverend Smithers. I suspected their conversation was not over. As the other guests mingled, I saw Peter Tidewater approach.

"Hi Peter." I said and waved.

"I must say, you've done a marvelous job with the manor. Remember my offer?

"Peter, of course. And remember my answer."

He exhaled a heavy sigh. "Charlie Beasley did a wonderful job. He is so successful with his business. Nobody like him in a 100-mile radius."

I smiled, although my mind continued to wrap around 'Charlie, the widower.'

Peter continued, "Charlie's family has a wonderful history in Portsborough. One of the first families to settle in the town."

I stared at him. Without asking one question, I was learning more about Charlie Beasley than I ever thought to know.

"Yes, indeed. Charlie's family has had a number of professions throughout the history of this town. His grandfather several times removed was the doctor here in Portsborough. Saw to all the births and deaths. He was the only doctor in the area for most of his professional life."

As we spoke, Belinda arrived behind Peter. "Oh, Charlotte, I see you've met our genealogy specialist. It is too bad your roots here are shallow, or Peter would be writing your story! Isn't that true Peter?"

I sensed a bit of antagonism in her voice but wasn't sure what it meant. I hesitated to tell her how close I was to having roots here and Peter just gave me a knowing smile.

"Really, Belinda. I just try to do my best to keep the families alive." He forced a smile through thin lips; he squinted his eyes to nearly closing.

"What's he been telling you?" she turned to me and asked.

"Oh, just talking about the various family histories of the area." *I think I'll keep my conversations with Peter to myself.*

Peter joined in, "I was telling her about Charlie's great-great-great-great-grandfather being the doctor here. He was the one who tended to poor Emmaline's death. They found her at the base of the cliff, you know."

I straightened up and my interest level rose. "Do you have information about Emmaline's death?" My mind went back to Simeon's book and the family tradition.

Sheepishly he lowered his head and said, "Well, only the town lore I've already shared with you. We don't have anything in writing about it."

I stepped closer and looked at both of them. "Do you mean there are no official town records about her death?"

Belinda chimed in. "No, at least nothing we can find. There was only a brief piece in the newspaper of the time saying she died when she threw herself off the cliff. It was right over there."

"They say she climbed to the lighthouse and that's where it happened." Peter joined in, pointing toward the lighthouse steps.

You must see the lighthouse. I recalled a brief comment from several weeks ago. Stunned by this revelation, I turned and looked at the decrepit old building. I thought I saw Emmaline, but when I looked at Belinda and Peter, I saw no recognition of such a sight from either of them.

"Well, hello everyone." I turned to see Charlie arriving with two glasses of wine. He handed one to me. "This looks like a serious conversation. What's so interesting over by the cliff?" he asked.

Peter responded, "We were just talking about Emmaline's suicide back in 1875. I mentioned how Doc Beasley tended to that tragic event."

Charlie's demeanor changed, his face tightened, but before he could say anything, Belinda sidled up next to him.

"Charlie, do you have any records from Doctor Beasley that might have been handed down to you? We'd love to have them at the Historical Society. That type of information really should be archived with us."

Peter jumped in, "No actually, if there is any such information like that, it's 'family' data and the Genealogical Society should house it. We do, after all, trace family histories. You only trace the town and county history, not families."

She spun around toward him and snarled. "Peter, the Historical Society handles all historical data, and anything that Charlie has should come to us—"

Charlie threw a hand in the air to stop the discussion. "I don't know if such documentation exists, and if it does, it belongs to me and will stay with me. So, you can both close those arguments."

The air grew thick with silence. Peter and Belinda both stepped back at Charlie's retort.

I wonder if there IS information about Emmaline's death, I thought.

Peter was first to respond. "I understand, Charlie. Parting with family records can be difficult. Perhaps we can talk about this at another time." He turned and hurried back to the bar.

Belinda wrinkled her brow. "I really do think you should give those records to us." She remained stuck in place with her right hand on her right hip.

"Belinda, as I said before, if there are any records, I'm not aware of them, but *if* they exist, they will remain with me. Do you understand?"

She took a deep breath, pursed her lips in frustration, spun around, and left without saying anything more. Charlie turned to me and grinned. I turned and walked away, but I could feel him following me.

"Did I say or do something wrong?"

I wasn't sure how to respond but turned back to him. "This day has been an amazing eye-opener for me. You were married? You're a widower? Some distant ancestor tended to Emmaline after she committed suicide? And the day isn't even over!"

"Yes, most of that is true. Not sure about the Doc's role. So?"

He stared at me, and I realized how stupid I sounded and that none of this was important to Charlie today. Of course, it's none of my business if he was married some thirty-odd years ago as long as he's not married today. I took a deep breath.

"Well, don't I look stupid! I guess finding out these things from total strangers is a little unnerving." I turned and stared out toward the river. I felt a heavy blanket of embarrassment settle on me. I knew the color was rising quickly. "I'm sorry, I didn't mean to jump on you."

Charlie gently took my arm and turned me around. "You didn't jump on me. I just didn't know where our friendship was going, and I felt my life's history was something we would or could get into down the road when the time was right. There's really nothing to it. Laura and I were married thirty-four years ago; she succumbed to cancer thirty-two years ago. We hardly had a chance to get to know each other before she was gone."

"I'm sorry. Of course, you are right. I can't tell you how embarrassing it is to be jealous at my age."

Charlie put his arm around my waist and laughed. "Jealous?" he asked. "Okay, so we both learned something new."

We turned and looked toward the graveyard and saw several inquisitive guests, not quite ready to leave without the final tour, confront Lorelei in a large group.

Charlie stepped away from me. "Looks like Lorelei needs some help. We'll talk more later." He brushed a kiss on my cheek and warm air surrounded me.

Chapter Twenty-Five

For several hours I met and talked with people whose names I would probably forget until the next time we met. The town officials and business leaders expressed gratitude that Varcoe Manor had been placed in my care. As the afternoon faded into early evening, the crowd began to thin. I smiled and nodded, knowing I had already forgotten many of their names. I watched the last guest leave and saw Lucius redirecting traffic for his staff.

I turned back toward the house in time to see Peter hurrying toward me, carrying a briefcase. He grabbed my arm and redirected me toward one of the tables where he looked around, then motioned me to sit. He sat and opened the briefcase.

I smiled. "What in the world, Peter? You look like you have the secrets of the world with you."

"You have no idea. At least I have the secrets of your world."

I leaned in closer to him "What do you mean?" I asked.

"Remember when you asked me to do your genealogy?"

"Yessss," I stretched out the word for several seconds wondering why he asked me this.

"Well, here's what I found!" He pulled a small scroll out of the briefcase and unrolled it to show a genealogical chart with my name at the bottom. I leaned in close to the chart and followed his finger as he read.

"You asked that I focus on your mother's family, and that's what I have here. I didn't want to talk about this in front of Belinda, but based on the information you gave me, I learned that your mother, Lyda Converse was the daughter of Abigail Burlingame and Chambers Converse; Abigail was the daughter of Silence Grimes and Horace

Burlingame; Silence was the daughter of Simeon Grimes and Caroline Farmer; Simeon was, of course, the son of Emmaline Grime's sister!"

Peter broke out into a grand smile. "So, you see, Charlotte, not only are you a Maine daughter—a few times removed— but you are the niece of Emmaline Grimes Varcoe…let me see, that would be about five times removed if I figured it right." He pushed the chart closer to me.

I was stunned. "Are you absolutely certain about this?" I could not take my eyes off the flow of the chart.

"Charlotte! I am hurt." He said with just a tinge of sarcasm. "I may fail in many respects, but my genealogy research is unquestionable. I also looked into Simeon Barkley." This was followed by a long moment of silence.

"Yes. What about him?"

He coughed. "Well, yes, he was Emmaline's nephew. Her younger sister married shortly after she did and began her family right away. He grew up with the stories about his aunt's death. Apparently, no one in the family thought it was quite right—the story, I mean. But the Varcoes in this area had died off by the time Simeon grew up, so he decided to write what he thought was her story. One news article I found indicated that Emmaline and her sister were very close, and the death hit her hard." He let the sentence hang in the air.

"And why do I feel there is something more coming?" I asked.

"Because I think there is. Now, this is just a coincidence, I'm sure, but I found it curious. Do you know what Emmaline's sister's name was? Her name was Lyda."

"Yes, I did, and my mother's name was Lyda."

"But that's not all," Peter continued. "Emmaline's sister's middle name? Charlotte."

I remained quiet as I wrapped my mind around the information. And yet, the chart seemed to confirm Peter's findings.

"Yes, you are definitely related to the original lady of this fine manor. And you may have the chart and I will leave you to it. I prepared it just for you. Read it carefully and let me know if you have any questions."

"Thank you, Peter. This is another piece of an ever-unfolding puzzle and I'm grateful. I may be calling on you again soon."

Peter nodded his head and rose. "Until then." And he turned and left.

I rolled up the chart and carried it back into the house where I placed it on the kitchen table. I returned to the lawn to see a few stragglers, reluctant to leave. I wandered toward the side of the cliff as I thought about everything that happened today and expressed silent gratitude for a stunning day when I heard the creaking of wood to my left.

I turned around to see Tom marching up the steps toward the lighthouse. I called to him to come away.

When he did not respond but kept on marching up the steps, I chased after him.

As I reached him, halfway up, I grabbed his arm and he spun around and whipped his right hand across the air as he grabbed my wrist.

I stared into his face; his eyes wide with rage, he was in a drunken stupor.

I wrenched my wrist free and glared at him. "Tom," I shouted. "Where do you think you're going? We've had this discussion, and no one is to go up these steps; it's far too dangerous."

"Who do you think you are?" he demanded in a hoarse whisper as spittle flew from his mouth. "Nobody tells me where I can and can't go on my own property." He teetered two steps above me and hovered close to my face.

A blast of fear shot through me and I attempted to back away, but he wrapped my wrist in a tight grip and yanked me toward him. I felt myself falling and as I struggled to free myself his grasp grew tighter. We began to tumble, and I screamed as the ground rose to meet us.

We twisted in a grotesque dance. Startled, Tom released me but not before we landed on the ground, me on top of him. The sound of bone-on-stone resonated across the quiet air.

I pushed away and turned to see Tom on the ground next to a large rock, a nasty gash across his temple. The sound of voices raced toward us and through foggy peripheral vision I saw Charlie and Lorelei dashing across the lawn.

Lorelei arrived first. "What the hell is going on here?" she demanded.

I rose on unsteady legs and turned toward an unconscious Tom; I stared, both astounded and alarmed, at his still figure.

"I hardly even know where to begin," I said. I reached into my foggy mind to recall everything that happened. "Tom was going up to the lighthouse and when I called him back, he didn't return. I chased him up the steps and then he reached out and grabbed me. He said he had the right to go anywhere he wanted to, and I couldn't stop him from being on his own property. I reached for his arm, and that's when everything moved at warp speed." I brushed a stray hair away from my face and winced at the pain in my right wrist.

Charlie remained quiet. Across the lawn I saw Lucius staring in awe at the picture that unfolded. He saw Tom at the base of the steps, grabbed an ice bucket, and rushed toward us. In the crush of events, it appeared that Tom's injuries were substantial. Sheriff Tuttle spoke into the radio on her shoulder and called for an ambulance.

Lorelei asked, "Do you have any idea what he was after?"

I offered a vague answer. "Several days ago, I found him here attempting to go up to the lighthouse. When I confronted him, he said he was doing research about the true ownership of this property. I assured him that there was no question as to my right of ownership, but apparently, he chose not to believe me. I have no idea why he was trying again to go up there, but I don't need someone falling down these stairs, injuring themselves." I turned my attention to the stairs and the lighthouse above.

"Do you want me to keep an eye on him?" she asked.

"No, I don't think that will be necessary. I suppose he was just plain drunk."

Lorelei nodded. "I'll do some follow-up just in case." She turned to Charlie and said, "You better get her attended to."

"I twisted my wrist, but I don't believe anything is broken. I'll probably have some major aches for the next few days, but otherwise I think I'm fine."

Charlie walked me back to the kitchen and sat me at the table. Lucius followed several minutes later with a bowl of ice. My wrist had begun to ache, and Charlie wrapped several cubes in a towel.

Charlie sat across from me and asked, "Are you okay?"

"I guess I'm not as young as I used to be." I answered with a half smile. "Should have been more careful."

Charlie looked at my wrist then back to my face. The questions tumbled out quickly. "Do you have any idea what he thought he was doing? And what in the world did he mean about ownership of the manor? And why didn't you tell me that you had that confrontation?"

"I haven't any idea why he thinks he owns this property. My lawyer has checked and rechecked the question of ownership. And there is no doubt in his mind, nor mine. And I'm sorry I didn't tell you. I think I felt that it was a resolved issue when he left."

We remained silent for several seconds before we heard the sound of an ambulance siren as it raced up the drive. From the window we watched quietly as the EMTs worked on Tom. It only took minutes before they departed, and I saw Belinda race after it.

I looked out the side window toward the 'Crime Scene' gate.

"Were there very many people who wanted to get into that area?" I asked, changing the subject.

"Not while I was there. Lorelei told me that she had to ward off a few! And Tom came over with Belinda and tried to gain access. He tried to say that because he worked in the area, he had the right to go in there. Belinda played the 'Historical Society' card, but Lorelei refused to give them entry. I guess Belinda got a little belligerent but still did not get in. Lorelei knows how to handle those situations. How did your day go? Well, except for Tom, that is?"

The sound of the ambulance siren whining down the drive brought the reality of the last 30 minutes to roost in my mind. *I hope he'll be alright.*

Charlie brought me back to the present. "Was the day a success?"

"For the most part, I'd say yes. People were curious about the house, but Belinda took them on the tour, and everyone seemed to be quite happy with the work and the state of the manor. I think they were impressed. You and your workers got a lot of compliments."

"Good, I can always use the business."

"Belinda got a little pushy about the picture of Emmaline over the fireplace. She wants it for the Historical Society. I said no. Emmaline remains where she is."

I placed my hand in the bowl of ice. We both remained lost in our thoughts and I hovered over a question, and finally just took the dive. "The information about your many-great-grandfather, Doctor Beasley, was that true? Was he called here when Emmaline died?"

"I honestly don't know. It's true that my family dates back to the founding of the town, and Doc Beasley is my ancestor, but the family never talked much about that time. Since he was the doctor at that time, I assume he did attend to them." He became quiet and stared across my shoulder deep in thought.

"What is it?" I asked.

"My house — our family has had it forever. I have the advantage of knowing about renovation, and I've done a lot to that house. There are a number of crates in the attic with different family heirlooms and boxes of papers, but I've never had the interest to go through them, so I don't know what's there.

"When Doc Beasley lived there, he used the parlor as his office, and when he died, all of his equipment and files were moved to the attic. I guess our family is a bunch of hoarders, because we don't seem to get rid of anything."

I leaned over the table close to him. "Do you think it's possible there could be any records from Emmaline's death?"

"I don't know, but I'll make a point of starting a search. Who knows, I might discover a fortune hidden up there."

"I'd be happy with just some answers. If he did tend to her body, he might have recorded where she was buried."

Charlie scratched his head. "Want to climb through over 145 years worth of dust with me?"

"I'd love to!"

"If you're available tomorrow, come over and we'll start our search. In the meantime, I'll go get that frame and photograph from the attic and I can start that clean up project this week."

I removed my hand from the bowl of ice and wiped it. The swelling had gone down, but the pain remained. I heard him walk up the stairs toward the attic and after several minutes of silence he returned.

"Charlotte, did you move the picture? It's not in the attic."

I looked at him and frowned. "I haven't done anything with that frame. I haven't even been back to the attic. It would have had no place here while guests were wandering the house."

"Well, it's not there now."

We returned to the attic and Charlie pointed to where he had left the picture. It had disappeared—frame, glass, and photo—all were gone. We turned over boxes, looked behind other pieces of furniture, searched the entire attic and we found no trace of the photograph.

"Are you sure you didn't take it by accident?" I asked.

Charlie looked at me and raised one eyebrow. He did not have to answer the question. Of course, he did not take it.

"Well, this is extraordinary. I can't imagine where it could be."

We both stopped and turned to face each other at exactly the same moment. Like a Greek chorus, we both spoke at the same time. "Belinda!"

We agreed that Charlie would confront Belinda. Although we had no proof, Charlie felt he could maneuver her around into a confession and I agreed. We also changed the attic date to Monday.

After Charlie left, I saw the rolled-up chart on the kitchen counter. I had not told him about Peter's discovery.

Chapter Twenty-Six

A wet, heavy fog rolled in Sunday morning. I was grateful it hadn't happened on Saturday or the entire open house could have been a disaster—not that dealing with property being stolen, Tom's curious behavior and his ownership claim, my genealogy, and Charlie's history weren't enough.

Several times I wandered over to the kitchen window and looked out at the Crime Scene tape and I felt electricity in the air crackle at the idea that soon those bodies would be exhumed and examined. I took Peter's chart into the sitting room and stared at the information.

Time won't move any faster if you worry about it.

The whispered words surrounded me, and I turned to see Emmaline sitting in one of the Queen Anne wingback chairs across the room. There seemed to be a clarity to her appearance that came and went without noticed before.

I put down the chart and asked, *Where have you been?*

She smiled and waited for a few moments before responding. *I haven't been anywhere, Charlotte,* she answered as if to a petulant child. *You should know that by now. I'm always here, unable to leave. I watched your party from a distance. John and I never had guests to the house. I'm glad you did that; the house needed that.*

A pang of pity rushed through my body at her words. *I'm sorry; I didn't mean to be unkind.*

I know. Did you learn anything more? Her question was fraught with anxiety.

I don't want to get your hopes up, but there are some odd things happening. You know about the two graves but there seems to be more. Tom seems believe he is the true owner of the property. I stopped, waiting for a reaction, a question, evidence of excitement—any emotional response— but received only a question

Who is Tom?

Well, surely, you've seen him around here. He is some kind of handyman around town. He's not been here long, perhaps a few months, but he's helping Belinda with research on the manor. He's been helping Charlie with some of the work around here.

She remained quiet for several moments, a frown crossing her brow. *I don't recall seeing him. Why does he think he is the owner of this home?*

I haven't any idea. We never got that far in our conversation. We had a bit of a row at the open house and I ended up with a sprained wrist, but I suspect he got the worst of it. I assume you were in the lighthouse. Didn't you see that row?

She stared beyond me, still frowning. *No. I was watching Charlie and that lady. I don't think I like this Tom.*

I thought it time to change the subject. *Charlie refurbished the hutch.* At the mention of the hutch, I felt the air crackle and the temperature in the room drop several degrees. Emmaline straightened her back and leaned forward slightly but said nothing. My conversation stumbled forward; I wondered if I had chosen a bad path to take. *Charlie learned that the carving board had human blood on it and apparently the blood is quite old. The sheriff, Lorelei Tuttle—*I suddenly felt foolish. Why would this matter to her?

She sat back quietly and nodded her head. *Yes?*

Well, the sheriff is going to exhume the bodies to see if there is any kind of DNA match.

DNA?

I was not about to go into a scientific explanation of something I barely understood myself. *It's a scientific evaluation of the blood.* I stopped short of further embarrassing myself with a high level of stupidity.

The room became quiet and I sensed Emmaline was evaluating this new information. *When is this to happen?*

I'm not sure, sometime this week.

Do you think he could have murdered her?

I sucked in air at her comment. *He who? You mean John—kill Ellen? Why would you think that?* I suddenly leaned forward toward her, even though we were separated by about twenty feet.

I watched her expression change to one of curiosity. *I don't think that. It was just a question. I really have no idea. But this should be an interesting exercise. Does your sheriff do this experiment here?*

No. She will take the bodies away. It will probably take several days, if not weeks, to learn anything.

Then we still wait, don't we?

There is one other thing. I wasn't sure how she would take this. *I had our local genealogist run my family history. We learned that my ancestor-grandmother was Lyda Grimes.*

She sat up straight in the chair. *My sister? My Lyda?* A tear wandered down her cheek. Then she smiled. *You see, I was right. I knew your mother was the right person to help me, and now that falls to you.*

And we might have another opportunity in that respect. Did you know Doctor Beasley?

Her gaze wandered around the room as if struggling to pull a memory from somewhere deep inside. *Doctor Beasley? A familiar name. I believe he came to the manor on a few occasions. Not often. Why?*

Someone mentioned that he was the doctor in Portsborough during your life.

The room suddenly warmed. *Do you think he would know what happened to me? Where I am?*

Well, Emmaline, it's not like we can question him. He died over a hundred years ago. Apparently, Charlie is a descendant of his. I'm going to Charlie's house tomorrow and we're going to go through old family papers and files to see if we can find anything. I felt a sadness wash over me. I did not want to disappoint Emmaline, but I had to follow the trail of crumbs that lay before me regardless of how meager. *We really don't know if we'll find anything at all. But we'll try.*

We. That's good. Say hello to Charles for me.

Suddenly Emmaline was gone as quickly as she had appeared. "Say hello for you?" I said out loud. "It's not as if he has participated in these discussions. He would think I had lost my mind." I laughed to myself and recalled mother's same words in her diary.

I turned back to the chart as the phone rang.

"Hey, Charlotte. I just got back from the Historical Society. I have our wandering photograph," Charlie said.

"And what was her excuse?"

"She said she wanted it for the Historical Society's main museum room. When she could not convince you to give her Emmaline's photo, she decided she would see what this one held. It might be a duplicate or it might be something else, but regardless she felt it had significance to the society and she wanted it before Peter Tidewater could get it for the Genealogical Society."

"This town is full of crazies!" I mumbled.

Charlie laughed. "I'm going to work on it this afternoon and see what I can find. Oh, and Belinda told me that Tom remained in the hospital over night Saturday. He sustained a concussion, but he's been released."

"Well, I'm sorry about the concussion, but I'm grateful it was nothing worse than that."

Thankfully, he changed the subject.

Are you still up for tomorrow—wandering through my family history?"

"More than ever." I did not want to go into my conversation with Emmaline, or my newfound relationship to her, but my interest was piqued even more. I would be ready for whatever fell into our laps.

"Good. Come over in the morning, maybe around 8:30? I'll fix breakfast and then we'll see what the attic holds. Wear old clothes or something you don't mind getting dusty."

Charlie rattled off his address and directions, "I'll be there." I hung up and thought I'd wear my old jeans and my new *Welcome to Portsborough* tee. I could always brush the dust off.

As I prepared my mind for tomorrow's historical search, my phone rang again, and the ID was George Breckenridge. I answered it immediately. "George, how good to hear from you—well, it is good, right?"

George laughed. "Well, let's say it's interesting information. I'm not sure it will help you, but you have certainly raised my level of interest. I realize you don't have a biological relationship to John Varcoe, but I decided to do a little more investigating. As you know, John's older brother, Thomas, inherited the manor when John died. Thomas only had a daughter, Ann Nancy; no sons to carry on the name. We haven't found anything out about his younger brother, so although the genes may still be around, the name is history for this limb of the tree. Just doing follow up on this ownership thing."

Another piece to the puzzle. I asked George to keep looking but not spend a great deal of time on this. It was apparent that family connections along this line were a dead end.

Chapter Twenty-Seven

When the alarm rang at seven o'clock on Monday morning, I rolled over, reached across the nightstand, and slammed down the alarm button. Ninety minutes to get dressed and to Charlie's.

I arrived at Charlie's house and spent several moments just looking at it. Clearly an older building, the modifications were minor, mostly structural, but they enriched its appearance. Light blue shutters against bright white cedar shingle siding. Three stories tall, the house and the property sprawled over two large plots of land. Behind the house I noticed neatly trimmed woods that led into a thick forest and I realized that Charlie fully understood the importance of keeping the growing roots at bay. At the top of the roof, I saw a widow's walk and wondered how far the line of sight went. I shaded my eyes and looked around the building when Charlie came out to greet me.

"Nice location, eh?" he said.

"This is lovely. I was just admiring your widow's walk. What's the view like?"

"Come on in for breakfast and I'll take you up there as soon as we're finished. It's one of my favorite spots."

We entered the house where the warmth of family enveloped me. He walked me around the first floor across narrow wood floorboards finished and polished to a high shine and covered with scatter rugs throughout. I did not see even one speck of dust. Charlie's choice in furniture was eclectic but for the most part he leaned toward colonial American.

"This is lovely, Charlie," I said as we returned to the kitchen. His rough-hewn oak table was set for two and the nutty smell of fresh cranberry-pistachio bread greeted me as I sat.

"Mostly family furniture that has been handed down through the generations. When it gets too old or dilapidated to even repair, I go on the hunt for something similar. But I like the feeling the furniture brings. That's one of the things I enjoyed most about working on the manor. Searching through the furniture in the attic and the possibilities they bring. I see you're wearing your new tee!" he teased.

I nodded and grinned. "I thought it appropriate since we're going to be diving into Portsborough's history."

"Well, I have to admit, I've done nothing to prepare for this. I took a flashlight upstairs yesterday although there is lighting there, but I really have not spent any time up in the attic in quite a while, so I'm not sure even where to begin. There's no defined order to how things have been placed up there, although I may be able to navigate to the right years a little bit."

"That's fine. We'll just see what we can find. Anything more on the picture that you retrieved from Belinda?"

He took a deep sip of coffee then said, "I've given it to Frank to work on. He's good with wood and he said he was intrigued by the piece. From my close look, it seemed as if the glass was dirtier, covered with more grime than Emmaline's picture. Frank said he didn't think it would take much to clean up the wood frame. Not sure when he'll have that done. He's my office manager, so he'll work on it between jobs. I trust him to do a good job."

I finished my coffee and stood. "Well, shall we take this on?"

"First the widow's walk, then the attic." He opened a door to a small deck off the back of the second-floor office, and a rush of warm humid air wrapped around me. We stepped onto the deck and he led me to a narrow, enclosed stairwell that led up to the widow's walk. When we arrived at the top a strong wind blew across my face.

Charlie organized my tour and turned me toward the back of the house first, where I saw nothing but forest. I slowly turned right toward the north and saw the town laid out in a grid format with streets and avenues crisscrossing at ninety-degree angles. A defined historic district nestled in the middle of town with several historic buildings crowded next to one another. I sensed a change in the architecture as the town expanded and grew, although the sense of history hovered over the town.

"Here, take these." Charlie reached into a built-in cabinet and retrieved a pair of binoculars. "You can make out most of the town from here. I frequently come up here just to observe."

I raised the binoculars up and stared further north beyond the town borders.

Charlie read my mind. "Yes, you can see the edge of your property, but the manor and lawns are basically not visible. Too far even for binoculars and hidden behind heavy wooded growth."

I smiled and Charlie turned me around to look toward the south. There were no houses beyond Charlie's property. The forest crawled around from the west to the south, blocking any further development. Charlie saved the best for last, and I knew he had done that on purpose. He turned me toward the front of the house where I faced the river. Basically, Charlie's house was an island with a view unobstructed by anything but nature.

The view took my breath away. The river waters roiled rough that morning, driven by the stiff breeze. White caps rolled toward shore, lapped against the rocks, then retreated to the depths of the river, only to repeat the movement several moments later. I breathed deep the air filled with the vanilla scented heliotrope. I raised the binoculars and stared across the river to the far shore, although nothing was distinguishable. I lowered the glasses and looked at Charlie. Even his close-cropped hair riffled in the breeze.

"Pretty amazing, isn't it?"

I exhaled the breath that I had been holding. "I'm not sure I even know of a word that would describe this feeling."

He looked out across the river. "I find solace here. When I think of Laura, I find that this is the best place for me to be. I seem to set her free when I'm up here."

I fidgeted at his remark. My mind went blank and I did not respond. As quickly as the moment came, it went and Charlie took the binoculars and put them back into the cabinet, then turned me back toward the stairs.

"I think it's time for us to begin our search."

I nodded, still holding onto his comments.

Back in the house, he led me to a small door at the end of the hall to the opposite side of the office. When he opened it, the musty smell of old air curled out of the stairwell. Dust motes swirled out to greet us and Charlie wafted his hand around to move them.

"Sorry about that, Charlotte. As I said, other than a short visit yesterday, I've not been up here in a while."

He flipped a switch and lights turned on, showing us the way up the narrow, steep stairwell. In spite of the musty smell and the dust motes that initially greeted us, I was surprised to see a completely refinished storage room.

"This is not what I expected," I said as I turned a full circle.

"I don't like to leave things unfinished. But as you can see, this is definitely a storage space. I've never considered finishing it any further because no one would be living up here. At least it makes for a clean storage area."

I looked to Charlie for some guidance. "Any idea where to start?" My eyes swept across the room at the mass of boxes, desks, cabinets, and other pieces of furniture.

"I think we should look over here first." He walked to a corner of the attic and began moving boxes. "Everything on the other side of the room is more recent...things I've put up here in the past twenty or thirty years." He pointed to storage boxes at the back of the room as he spoke.

"Over there, across from this pile of boxes and cabinets, probably dates back about ninety to 100 years, maybe more. I'm pretty sure the stuff in this area is where we'll find anything. That is, if there is anything to find."

"Oh, Charlie, please don't say that. I'm counting on finding something."

He looked at me and took a deep sigh. "Just don't be disappointed if there's nothing here. I've never seen anything that would refer to Doc Beasley. Of course, I've never had a reason to look."

He moved a little deeper into the dim corner and pulled out four boxes stacked one on top of the other. We dug in and began our search.

* * *

After an hour and a half of finding old recipes and dressmaking patterns, I felt my enthusiasm begin to dwindle. Charlie found three books of old photographs that dated back to the turn of the last century. He commented that maybe he should see if Belinda wanted any of them—might smooth some ruffled feathers.

"Here, look at this," he said as he motioned me toward him and held out an old photograph. "This is my grandfather. That would have been Doc Beasley's grandson. I recall my mother telling me there had been a rift between Doc and my great-grandfather because my great-grandfather would not follow in his grandfather's steps to be a doctor. He became an accountant instead. Ha—family lore. I had completely forgotten that story."

I was crouching close to the floor and when I rose, I momentarily lost my balance. I righted myself and as I did, I backed against a low wall.

"Ouch," I said as I bumped my head.

Charlie looked away from the picture in his hand and asked, "Are you okay?"

I turned and looked at the wall and the low slanted ceiling. "Yeah, I'm okay. I should be more careful. The ceiling here in this corner is slanted low." I rubbed my head, and as I did, I noticed something tucked back far against the wall. "What's that?" I asked, pointing toward a dark corner.

Charlie put the photos down and came over to me. We both stooped down and stared into the darkness under the eave.

"Can you hand me that flashlight from over there?"

I turned in the direction he pointed and retrieved an industrial-sized flashlight from the floor. "Here, help me move these boxes." We moved several boxes, and he shined the beam of the flashlight through a narrow space.

We pushed and shoved more boxes across the floor and when Charlie shined the light again, we saw what appeared to be a low, wooden two-drawer filing cabinet and several other heavy trunks.

"Hold this for me," he said as he handed me the flashlight.

He crawled into the small area and began to nudge and pull the cabinet toward us. It took several minutes before he could get it into a position where we could both look into it. He reached for a cloth and wiped the cabinet of decades of dust. He shined the light onto the cabinet and a small, tarnished plaque on the front corner of the cabinet reflected the words 'Beasley, M.D.' He looked at me and wiggled his eyebrows.

"Shall we see what's here?" he asked the rhetorical question.

He wiped the front of the cabinet and when he pulled open the top drawer that stale old-paper smell blossomed out and swirled around us. I stretched forward as close as I could as he shined the light on the cabinet's contents. Journals lay inside, some standing on their sides, others laying on their back and front. Charlie reached in and removed one. There was little dust, but the odor was the same.

He sat back and propped himself against the wall next to the cabinet and patted the floor. I didn't need a second invitation before I plopped down next to him. He propped the flashlight on the top of the cabinet facing us and held the journal up and read the first page. The dates reflected records from 1865 to 1868. The paper was brittle and yellowed with age and Charlie gently turned to the last page.

"The last entry is December 1868." He put the book aside and retrieved the next. It was obvious there was no order to how these books were stored as the next book reflected appointments from 1900 to 1902.

"How long did he practice? Do you know?" I asked.

Charlie looked toward the ceiling, as though calculating something in his head. "I believe he died in 1905, so this book would be the last, or one of the last, books of records. I believe he practiced until his death."

I remained silent for a moment. "Didn't John's grave marker indicate that he died in 1902?"

Charlie began thumbing through the pages looking for information but found nothing. He put the book down and removed the next. It was dated 1902 to 1905. A quick check of the book showed information listed for John Varcoe in March of 1902, but it was about a visit for bronchitis.

"There must be more here. Hold this—" and he handed me the journal. He began to fish out other journals with different dates written on them. He wiped his brow with the back of his hand, then said, "I think we should just take all of these downstairs and see what we've got."

"I agree."

There were ten journals of different sizes with various dates written on them. Charlie took six, I took four and we returned to the first floor. As we piled the journals on the kitchen table, the phone rang.

"Hello? Damn! Okay Frank, I'll come over right away. Try to calm him down and let him know that I'm on my way." He hung up and looked at me with a sheepish grin. "Peter Tidewater hired us to do some work at the Genealogical Society – they've had trouble with their foundation, and we've been working on it. It appears that we're not working fast enough to satisfy Peter, so I'm going to have to go and smooth some ruffled feathers. Can I give you these to take home? I'll call you later to see if there is anything of interest."

I smiled. "If you didn't offer to let me take these, I'd have found some way to steal them!"

"I'm really sorry about this, but I'll call you as soon as I figure out what's going on. Okay?"

"Of course. Oh, by the way," I said as I loaded the journals in the back of my car. "Speaking of Peter Tidewater, he created a genealogy chart of my family history on my mother's side. Found out I'm a five-generation niece of Emmaline Varcoe."

I smiled as I left Charlie standing in the driveway staring after me.

Chapter Twenty-Eight

I took the journals into the kitchen and set them on the table across from the windows. My first task was to put them in some order. I knew the dates I was interested in, and once I found them, I set the other journals aside.

I located the journal dated with records for 1875 and I coughed at the smell of old paper and stale air. The brittle journal pages crackled as I gently turned each to avoid crumbling the fragile paper. I did not know Emmaline's exact death date, only the year, so my task became clear: read every entry in every page. The information about the town and its citizens fascinated me and the good doctor had a knack for adding flavor to his notes—flavor that brought movement to his words, life to his characters.

Surnames appeared in front of me and I recognized some from my open house. The births and deaths were written in a strong, left-handed slant and I thought about how different we are today, as cursive writing is not taught, and barely practiced. Doctor Beasley's handwriting was as clear today as it had been almost 150 years ago, in spite of the faded ink and paper.

Time slipped away as the ailments, the joys, and the anguish of the town's inhabitants bubbled to the surface. Each page I turned led me down a new path of acquaintance with people long dead. Doctor Beasley was precise with his records. He did not abbreviate and went into deep detail about even the most minor events. I had just finished reading about how Willard Tuttle broke his arm falling out of a tree when I turned to a page dated June 3, 1875. My mind had almost left the thoughts of Emmaline's death in the background as I had become so interested in the mundane lives of the people of Portsborough when the name John Varcoe rose off the page. I focused on every letter of every word.

June 3, 1875. 9:30 p.m. John Varcoe arrived at my doorstep this evening, requesting that I return to Varcoe Manor with him. When I asked what was wrong, he only said there had been an accident. I asked why he did not send his man to fetch me, but John said the servants had the night off and were not expected back until tomorrow.

John gave me no details about this accident, although I prodded several times. I sensed that with each question, he became more peevish. I was rather surprised that we did not rush back to the manor, but he kept his horse and buggy at a slow gait.

When we arrived, John did not take me to the manor house, but walked with a determined step around the house and through the yard toward the edge of the cliff below the lighthouse. The sky was dark with spotty clouds looming overhead, blocking out what little moonlight shone through.

In the darkness I could hear the sounds of the river as the water roiled against the rocks below, and I was surprised when John began to climb down the steps. I asked him where he was taking me, but he said nothing, just motioned for me to follow.

At the bottom of the stairway, I did not need a lot of light to see where he pointed. Emmaline lay crumpled in the sand at the base of the steps, water lapping at the hem of her dress. I rushed to her side, but even a cursory examination told me what I already knew. She was dead and had been for some time. Blood coagulated around several cuts in her head and face. I gently rolled her over and saw an extremely deep gash on the right side of her head behind her ear. The right side of her upper body appeared crushed; I assumed from the fall.

I looked at John, several questions racing through my mind but before I could ask them, he spoke and told me that she had committed suicide. He looked up toward the lighthouse and expressed his belief that she threw herself from the light, in a state of desperation. He blamed her state of mind on losing the child. I was startled at his statement, but more so at his calm demeanor. I told him I would have to examine her before I could determine truly what happened.

The stairway between the top of the cliff and the rocks below is steep and narrow, and moving Emmaline's body was a difficult task even with both of us taking it on. It took about ten minutes before we reached the top, where we placed her body on the ground beneath the lighthouse. I was just grateful that the weather cooperated with us. John walked to the manor and in five minutes I saw the flicker of candlelight first on the first floor then gradually move to the second and into one of the rooms. I remained alone for what seemed like an eternity until about twenty minutes later John returned. He picked up Emmaline's body and stumbled silently back to the house.

I followed him as he took her up the stairs to the second floor. I noted that although her clothes were damp, dribbling water and sand across the floor, the blood on her head had clotted to a dried mess, clumping her hair and leaving no blood trail across the floors.

I removed her clothing and hung it on the clothes tree next to the bed and spent the next hour cleaning and examining her body but found nothing that would change John's declaration about her death. I told John that her body should be brought to my office the next day for a more thorough exam and he refused, saying it was not necessary since this was a death by her own hand.

John thanked me and brought me back to the house. He asked me to expedite the death certificate. When I asked him about her burial, he said he would take care of it, and he asked me not to make this public.

I began to argue that the proper authorities would have to know about this, and he assured me that he would take care of that.

I prepared the certificate after he brought me home, but I am not comfortable that I did not get a chance to do a more thorough examination.

I flipped the next page back and forth, but the entry ended at that point. I sat back and stared through the windows next to me. My gaze settled on the cliff and lighthouse and I wondered about its role in Emmaline's death. I quickly scanned the dates of the other journals and picked up the two dated 1876 and the two for 1902. I began to read when the phone rang.

"Hey. Thought I'd call and see if you found anything of interest. Oh, and thanks for that last bombshell you dropped before leaving my house!"

I laughed. I was glad to hear Charlie's voice, which brought me out of the reverie of Emmaline's death. "More about that later, but I certainly have found something of interest."

"Oh?" A curious tone slipped into his question. "How about dinner? I can pick you up in about an hour if that's okay with you. We have a nice diner in town with pretty good family dinners. We can talk."

"Diner?" I asked. I wondered briefly if this was the same diner my parents had eaten at just a few days before my mother's death. A chill raced up my spine. I looked at my watch and it was 6:00 p.m. I realized I had spent the entire afternoon learning about the aches and pains of Portsborough's residents, not to mention the doctor's account of Emmaline's curious death. "An hour would be fine. I have something to show you."

"Good! A mystery. I like that. I have some information for you also, about the exhumation."

"I'll see you at 7:00," I said. We hung up and I had just enough time for a quick shower. I grabbed the journals and took them to the bedroom with me. When I entered the room, I wondered if this was the same room where the doctor had examined Emmaline. A small chill raced up my spine as I remained still for a moment. I placed the journals on the floor next to the bed and took my shower.

At seven o'clock exactly I looked out the library window and saw a black Lexus moving up the driveway. Charlie emerged and I realized I had never seen him drive anything but one of his trucks.

I hurried to the front door to greet him. "I must admit I'm surprised at your arrival. I've never thought about you and a car!" I laughed.

He walked toward me smiling. "Never use the good stuff during working hours. But I thought a date was entitled to ride in something nice."

A date, the comment echoed through my mind. I had not thought of this as a date and I rather liked the idea.

* * *

The diner was small and comfortable, and a favorite of the locals. Eyes followed us as we walked back to a table in a small alcove where we had some privacy, although not much. It was obvious that Charlie had made arrangements with the proprietor for something with at least a small semblance of isolation.

Several people walked past us and nodded. Two women at another table glared at me, or so it seemed. Charlie must have also noticed. He seated me then took his own seat but did not acknowledge the two women. A small chuckle emerged through his throat.

"This has been a problem ever since Laura died. The women of this town don't think a man should be without a woman for any length of time. I've had more women trying to mate me with a friend or relative, or worse still, just trying to mate with me."

"Without success, I see."

He flushed red. "I don't mean to sound so arrogant. It's not like I'm the catch of the world. It's just a dance they all do. After almost thirty-five years, you would think they'd have given up and moved on."

"I suspect you *are* quite a catch, Charlie." I was not embarrassed by my comment. I meant it.

"Well, thanks, but probably not. I keep my own life personal and who I see is my business."

"Anyone special?" I asked. The words were out of my mouth before I even considered how intrusive I was being.

He looked directly at me. "Yes, there is. And she's sitting across from me. I hope that's not too forward. You're just the first woman I've been comfortable with since Laura, and that is a very long time to be uncomfortable."

"Not forward at all. The feeling is mutual." I could not believe that I was saying this. After almost four decades of men wandering through my life with nothing set in concrete by any of them, I thought I was perfectly happy with my life. Now I wondered.

The waitress came over with menus. "Hi Charlie," she said and smiled at him. She did not look at me. "Something to drink?"

He looked at me, and I just asked for water with lemon. He took the same.

"So, let me go first," he said, "because I suspect you're going to have more to talk about. Lorelei Tuttle stopped by after I finished my discussion with Peter. She told me that the paperwork was all finished and the exhumation order was approved. That will be done tomorrow. We're rather short on city workers, so since my crew was all there when she announced it, they volunteered to help." He hesitated for a moment then added, "Oh, and I talked to Tom—he heard about the exhumation from one of my guys and he asked if he could help with the it. I'm really short on people so I said okay as long as he stayed away from the lighthouse. I made it clear that a revisit to his behavior at the open house would result in legal action. I hope you don't mind.

I thought for a moment, then shook my head. "I have no problem with that. I'll just steer clear of him."

He continued, "Lorelei agreed provided no one brought along any extras to observe. I think she was directing that comment about Tom and Belinda. Anyway, I told them I was going to take you to dinner to talk about some information we found, and I'd let you know about tomorrow. You don't really have to be there if you don't want to, but it's important that you know it's going to happen."

"I'd like to be there. I'm as curious as Belinda and Peter would be."

Our meals arrived and the waitress smiled at Charlie, but still did not look at me.

"So, what's your news?" Charlie asked.

I told him about the journal entry and Doctor Beasley's doubts, or at the least his curiosity, about Emmaline's death.

"I got so engrossed with the health of the citizens that it was late by the time I found this entry. I put it aside for a few minutes and that's when you called to ask me to dinner. I've not had a chance to look for anything else. I also put aside the journals for 1876 and 1902 to see if there is anything else about Ellen and John's deaths. I don't know that either will have any connection to Emmaline, but my curiosity is certainly raised."

"Was there anything else?" He was obviously interested in my family's genealogy.

"Ah, yes—my family. Well, Peter charted my family ancestry and discovered that I am related to Emmaline through five generations. On my mother's side I go back to Emmaline's sister, Lyda, which by the way, was my mother's name. And Emmaline's sister's middle name was Charlotte! Peter was thrilled that I am officially, as he put it, a 'Maine daughter.'"

Charlie nodded his head. "I should have known!" He thought for another moment then said, "Why don't we finish dinner then have coffee at your place? I'd like to see this entry and maybe see if we can find anything more." I relished the idea of Charlie coming back to the manor and had to admit that I also wanted to get back into searching through the journals.

We arrived back at the house by 8:30 and as Charlie pulled up to the steps at the front of the house, we both stopped and stared. He grabbed my arm and said, "Wait here. Something doesn't look right."

I saw that the front door was slightly ajar.

"No way," I said.

We both emerged from the car at the same time. Charlie rushed around the front and took the steps two at a time. I was right behind him when he stopped in his tracks. He held his hand up to stop me and then moved forward very slowly. The door has been forced and he quietly pushed it open and poked his head around. There was no one in the hallway and we nudged our way further into the house, crawling at a snail's pace.

He edged over to the door to the sitting room and switched on the light, but the room was empty, and nothing was out of place.

"Maybe I just didn't close the door tight when we left," I whispered.

He turned to me and whispered back, "No," he said, and pointed to the damage on the door. "But we'll not take any chances."

We crossed the hallway to the library. The pocket doors were not closed, but I knew I had not closed them when I took the journals up to my bedroom that afternoon. The lights were not on and the room was bathed in the twilight of the evening. Charlie reached in and switched on the lights.

We remained still. The room was a mess. Books pulled out of the bookshelves lay scattered across the floor; cushions were pulled off the sofa and Queen Anne's chairs, the throw rug was crumpled in a corner and the drawers in the desk had been pulled out and emptied.

"Oh my God!" I cried. "The journals!"

I ran to the far side of the coffee table and saw several journals strewn across floor. I turned and stared at Charlie. Without saying a word, I raced up the stairs to the bedroom. I flicked on the light switch and saw that everything was in order as I had left it. I ran over to the side of the bed where the journals lay on the floor where I placed them. I picked them up and rushed back to the first floor where I met Charlie in the library. He had not straightened the furniture and or put the books back on the shelves.

"I've called Lorelei and she's on her way out here. I thought it better that we not touch anything until she gets here."

"Do you really think that was necessary? Whoever was here didn't get what they wanted." I held up the journals that I retrieved from my bedroom.

"Yes, Charlotte. This is necessary. What if you were here when this person broke in? What would we be finding then?" His anger rose with each question.

My grasp on the journals lightened. "But I *wasn't* here. Whoever did this probably was watching the place and would have waited until I went to bed. The ones I left down here had nothing to do with John, Ellen, or Emmaline—at least I don't think they did. Certainly, they had nothing to do with their deaths. If there is any record about those events, this is where we will find them."

Many thoughts raced through my mind in no significant order. For some oblique reason, I thought they were after the journals. I had no real basis for believing anyone would look for them because they were important only to me and maybe Charlie, and yet I could not shake the idea that they were at the root of the break-in."

"Well, I'm not leaving until Lorelei gets here. Maybe I should just stay."

"That won't be necessary, Charlie. We'll give Lorelei the information and then you can both leave. I'll be perfectly fine. No one is going to return at this point in time. Besides, I'd never be able to explain that to the women at the diner!"

The mood lightened and we both laughed. At that moment, the sound of a siren grew as we went to the door and watched the State Sheriff's patrol car approach. The car screeched to a halt and Lorelei jumped out of the car and ran up to the door.

"So, Charlie, what happened here?" Lorelei took one look at the shambles of the room and whistled. "Anything stolen?" she asked.

"No, I don't believe so," I answered. I was still carrying the journals and held them up to her. "I believe whoever did this was after these."

Lorelei looked from me to Charlie and back to me. "And these are what?"

Charlie spoke up. "These are journals from Doc Beasley. He was the only doctor here when Emmaline and John Varcoe lived here, and he tended to Emmaline when she died. Apparently, he also tended to Ellen Varcoe, John's second wife and possibly John himself."

"Why would this information be of any interest to anyone?"

Charlie and I looked at each other then back to her. I said, "When I first moved here, I began hearing stories about unusual deaths here at the manor and I started looking into them. Morbid curiosity, I guess. Anyway, I became especially interested in Emmaline Varcoe's death." I did not mention mother's role in the story or my new-found relationship with Emmaline.

"I've heard all those stories," she said. "They're old news. Why would someone suddenly take enough of an interest to break into your home? And if they're your property, Charlie, why would someone be searching for them here?"

"That's a good question," he answered. "I'm not sure I have an answer for it.

"Who else knew you had these, Charlotte?" she asked me.

I shook my head. "No one but Charlie. We just found them at his house earlier today. I've not spoken to anyone about them."

"Hmmmm," Charlie mumbled under his breath.

Lorelei and I both turned to him.

"Charlie?" Lorelei asked. "Something?"

"When you stopped by today to let me know about the exhumation tomorrow, I mentioned to the men that Charlotte and I would be going to dinner tonight. I believe I did mention the fact that we found some journals. I think I mentioned something about discussing some information Charlotte found in some of Doc Beasley's journals. I don't think I said anything more specific than that." He turned to me. "I'm sorry Charlotte. I wasn't thinking..."

I took a deep breath, not sure if I was angry at him for sharing that information or relieved that we were both out of the house when this occurred. "Don't worry about it. What's done is done."

My response was sharper than I intended, but I felt Charlie got the message. I stooped over to look at the journals on the floor and Lorelei pulled me back. "Don't touch anything. I've got a team coming out. They'll take pictures and we'll see if there are any fingerprints. Can you tell just by looking at them if they're all here?"

I bent over, careful not to touch anything. "From the dates on the covers, it looks like the ones I left here are still here. These," I pointed to the ones still in my hands, "are the ones that have the information we were looking for. At least this one does. I've not had a chance to go through the others."

"Where were those?" she asked.

"I had taken them upstairs. They were in my room where I had left them."

"So, no one was upstairs? Nothing out of order there?"

I shook my head. "No, nothing out of order there at all."

"Okay. You can keep those. Put them somewhere away from this room."

I left Charlie and Lorelei in the library and carried the journals into the kitchen. I didn't put them down.

"Charlie! Lorelei! You'd better come here."

They rushed into the kitchen and I pointed to the kitchen door. It was open and the screen was open. As we moved closer to the doors, we were greeted by the sound of a police siren as the patrol car roared up the driveway.

"That'll be my team. Don't touch anything." Lorelei left the kitchen to meet her officers and direct them into the library.

"We might have just missed the culprit. Still think I shouldn't stay?"

"No, I don't think you should stay. Who knows how long these people will be here, and I'll be perfectly safe with them."

Charlie stood his ground. "Okay, make some coffee. You can show me what you found in that journal, and maybe we'll have time to check the others as well. And I still want to see this genealogy chart."

Lorelei returned to the kitchen. "I've got them going through the library. Will probably take at least an hour before you can get back in there and clean everything up. I'll have my fingerprint guy come in here and see if we can find anything on these doors. Does anything else look out of place?" she asked.

I looked around but everything was neat and where it should be. "No, nothing. Charlie and I are going to go over these journals. I'm making some coffee; can I make some for you and your officers?"

"That would be nice. Thanks." Lorelei turned and walked back to the library. I could hear her in the distance growling orders and demanding answers.

"She seems quite capable, doesn't she?" I asked.

"She does indeed."

I made the coffee while Charlie took the journals and laid them out on the kitchen table. I called over my shoulder, "Start with the journal for 1875. That's where I found the doctor's notes about Emmaline's death. It was in June of that year."

He ruffled through the journal until he got to the month of June and then he slowed down and moved page by page. "Here it is—" He stopped talking and began to read the entry. When he finished, he looked up at me. I held two cups of coffee and set one down in front of him.

"Interesting, isn't it?" I asked.

He whistled quietly. "I should say so. But why would Doc believe it was anything but a suicide?"

I sat down next to him and sipped my coffee. "No idea. But he must have seen something that led him to believe it. John's behavior alone would have sent a message that something was wrong. That's the only entry I got to. I wonder if there is anything further along that might explain his concerns?"

We spent the next hour skimming through the journal, revisiting Portsborough's citizens but found no further entries about Emmaline. At eleven o'clock Lorelei returned to the kitchen.

"We've got all we can get from the scene. I'll need your and Charlie's fingerprints just to compare against what we took, but I'm not sure we'll find much. The room is yours again. You can clean it up." She looked at her watch as one of her team took our fingerprints. "Charlie, what time can you have your people here tomorrow to help with the exhumation?"

"What time do you need us? For the most part they show up around 9:00 a.m. to start work."

"Okay, let's meet here at ten. Do you have the equipment necessary for this job?"

"Well, we're not professional grave diggers, but I'll have my pickup truck and we'll probably dig by hand or with small tools, considering the fragility of what I expect we'll find."

Lorelei turned to me. "Charlotte, I realize this is an imposition, but I really want to learn more about the blood is on that block."

"It's not a problem for me, Lorelei. Let's discuss the status of the remains when you're finished. Father Peabody offered to bless the ground. I'm not a religious person, but that was a nice gesture and I guess I have a sense of putting things right for them. He really wants to move them to the Catholic Cemetery, so I have some options to think about."

She smiled and nodded her head in agreement. "Sounds right to me. Not sure how long this'll take, but you will get them back." She turned to Charlie and said, "See you tomorrow morning."

As she left, Charlie turned to me but before he could say anything, I held my hand up. "No. Go home. I'll be just fine. I'll barricade the door!"

"I'll fix the door tomorrow when we get here. Lock everything else!"

"I will, I promise."

We walked to the front door in time to see Lorelei and her caravan departing down the drive. Charlie forced the door back into place and left shortly behind them. I closed the door and leaned against it and the activities of the day washed over me.

Charles!

I stood up straight and looked around but remained alone. I spent an hour cleaning the library and kitchen door of fingerprint dust before retiring. We had not looked at the family chart.

Chapter Twenty-Nine

I did not sleep well that night. Visions repeated through my mind of Emmaline throwing herself from the lighthouse and Doc Beasley and John Varcoe struggling to move her body up a steep set of stairs to the lawn above. Several times I awoke and rolled over to look at the chair, but it remained vacant. Time seemed to wander through thick mud, with the clock ticking off minutes as if they were hours.

Finally, at 6:00 a.m., when I could no longer fight the dreams I rose and walked to the French doors and out onto the balcony where the sight of Queen Anne's lace blooming across the garden below greeted me. My breath slowed and I wished I could remain there for the rest of the day but knew I could not. I wondered if Emmaline was nearby and would join us for the exhumation. A cold chill scuttled up my spine.

The warm summer air wrapped around me, and I moved quickly, knowing that Charlie would probably arrive by 9:00 a.m. to fix the door. I felt numbness at the nape of my neck as I thought about the deed to be performed this morning. It should not have concerned me other than what it would do to the lawn; after all, these people were not relatives or friends, and yet I felt a sadness knowing that something truly bad had happened here over 145 years ago and I could not wrap my mind around it. I did not believe in any afterlife, but if *they* did, then perhaps it was best to try and resolve this.

I finished dressing and went to the kitchen and was startled to see Emmaline sitting at the kitchen table, her hand on the journal. She gently touched the book, and I felt a sadness for her situation. Sorrow shaded her eyes and I sensed that something was there, within her grasp, and she needed to know what it was. She looked up at me. *You're getting close, aren't you?*

I walked over and sat across from her. *I'm honestly not sure, Emmaline. I'm learning more about your life here, but I'm not sure it leads me anywhere that you want to go.* I still was not sure if her memory was weak or just convenient and I did not know how to tell her about what we found.

She looked down at the journal. *What is this?* she asked.

It's one of Doctor Beasley's journals. We thought it might shed some light on— well— events.

Did it?

I knew there was no getting around that question. *I'm not entirely sure, but there is an entry about your death.* The temperature in the room went frigid. A line of frost formed at the base the windows that looked out on the graveyard.

Emmaline turned and looked at the windows. *What information was that?* She asked. Her question carried no emotion, just mild curiosity.

I took a deep breath. *It was June 3, 1875. John arrived at Doc Beasley's house and said there had been an accident and he brought the doctor back here. Your body was lying at the base of the cliff. John said you had committed suicide by throwing yourself from the lighthouse.*

Why would I do that? Her question was not indignant or angry. Again, just more curiosity.

There was a vague explanation in the journal, although we got the impression that the doctor was not comfortable with that explanation–he just didn't have a better one. John said you were depressed about losing the baby and that accounted for your actions—" I did not know how to finish the sentence.

How bad was I?

Emmaline, why do you want to go over this? It's very uncomfortable.

She looked down at the book then back up into my eyes. *It's part of what I need to know.*

I wasn't sure I understood that answer, but it did not matter. I felt compelled to tell her. *There was a lot of damage to your body and especially your head. Falling from that height would have caused irreparable damage.*

I see. Did you learn where I was put?

For a second time I was uncomfortable with her choice of the word 'put.' *We've not found anything to indicate that Doctor Beasley had any further interaction with John about your death. Your body was not examined any further than that evening, just long enough to be able to issue a death certificate.*

So, my place is still a mystery.

Is it possible that your remains could be in the lighthouse? If that's...where... the sentence was becoming difficult to continue...

What are you talking about? I lost the child many months before I died. I was no longer despondent! And there is no possibility that I would be there!"

I felt as well as saw Emmaline's anger and was not sure about going forward. But I needed answers as much as she did. *What about your desire to have another child, and your inability to conceive?*

My inability to conceive had nothing to do with despondency. My husband left my bed long before the child died.

My thoughts became muddled regarding what she remembered and what she did not. A deep quiet settled between us. I felt helpless that there was nothing more I could share with her, and I wasn't even sure there was more to learn. Out of the quiet the sound of heavy vehicles rumbling up the driveway drew our attention back to the present. We both looked out the window as Charlie's large pickup truck drove up to the opening to the graveyard.

Emmaline looked at me and frowned. *What is that?*

The bodies are being exhumed today. That's the truck that will be used to take them to be examined.

Oh yes, something about blood and science. I'm not sure I understand that.

At that moment, I watched as Charlie raced up the porch steps and into the kitchen. I expected Emmaline to have disappeared, but she remained seated, looking out the window. I looked at Charlie, not sure what to expect but he said nothing about her. He held out a bag and said, "I got a new lock to put on the door. I'll check and see what kind of repairs need to be done to the door itself, if any. Otherwise at least we'll get a new secure lock put in."

"Thanks," I said, a tentative tone in my voice. Emmaline's visage began to disperse.

He turned around and went to the front door and began his repair work. A crowd of workers and police gathered at the graveyard. Tom, his head wrapped in a bandage, and Frank began to unravel the 'Crime Scene' tape and I was glad to see it go. Eddie, one of Charlie's employees, measured off the opening and he determined that it needed to be widened to get the truck through it. He threw out directions and the rest of the team began cutting more shrubbery away until they had expanded the opening by another five feet on each side.

"All done," Charlie said.

I jumped. I had not heard him return to the kitchen. I looked at the table, and Emmaline was gone.

"The door is fixed," Charlie said. "I don't think you'll need a new door. I'll sand it down and repaint it and it should be as good as new."

"Thanks," I said. "Am I allowed to go out and watch this exercise? Will Lorelei mind?" I asked.

"Sure, if you really want to. I don't think she'll mind. It is, after all, your property."

We left the kitchen and walked over to the graveyard entrance where Eddie was maneuvering the pickup truck to back it into the graveyard. Tom had accompanied Charlie's team, and as I approached, he avoided my eyes.

"Wanted to apologize for my behavior," he whispered, looking at the ground. "Too much to drink." I sensed he did not want to apologize as much as he knew he needed to.

"I'm not sure you should be here after your accident, but since you are, please be careful." I nodded toward the bandage on his head, but I was not convinced about his sincerity.

Frank was already in place behind the truck, directing traffic and Tom quickly joined him. Eddie positioned the truck, and it took about ten minutes to slowly back it into place and to avoid coming too close to the graves.

Lorelei was already in the glen directing her officers and two of Charlie's employees on where to dig and how to avoid doing any damage. Charlie and I could hear her barking orders although we could not see her. We followed her voice into the graveyard.

"You don't have to be here, you know," he whispered to me.

"Charlie, I'm not a weakling. I actually find this interesting."

"Sorry, didn't mean to imply—" but his sentence dropped off as the sound of dirt being shoveled reached our ears.

We walked closer to watch the activity and gradually the holes widened and deepened until we heard a thud of metal hitting something. We all crowded around the graves and Lorelei warned everyone to go easy. Knowing the age of these graves caused me to worry about destruction of what would certainly have been wooden coffins and no burial vaults. The time seemed to slow until Frank laid his shovel down on the ground and lowered himself into the grave marked for John Varcoe.

The density of the surrounding trees and shrubs turned the entire area into a dark gray hole. Charlie grabbed a flashlight from the truck and shined the light into the grave where Frank stood. Frank removed a large paintbrush from his back pocket and gently began to sweep away at the damp earth. It became a painstaking process and Tom soon followed Frank's direction and lowered himself into Ellen's grave.

It was a full hour before either coffin was cleaned.

"I'm rather surprised at the condition of these coffins," Charlie said. "I would have thought they would have disintegrated by now."

Lorelei watched the entire process with a careful eye. "That may still be the case," she said. "Once we begin to move them and put them on the truck, they may well crumble in our hands."

I stood silently watching as she directed their movements, motioning Eddie to edge the truck closer to the graves. Two of her police officers stood on either side of the truck and directed his move. The truck inched backward, and I was amazed at Eddie's skill with a vehicle so large in an area so small.

With the truck in place, Lorelei directed two men to either side of John's grave. They wrestled with the coffin and placed a wide flat strap a foot under the front end and wrapped it around the coffin to secured it. The other men repeated the movement at the far end of the grave. Once convinced the coffin could be lifted, the men raised themselves from the grave and began to slowly shuffle the casket wrapped with the straps.

I stood back and watched as their precarious movements gently lifted the delicate box. Eddie had lowered the lift on the back of the truck and after fifteen minutes, the coffin was on the lift and had been edged up toward the front of the bed of the truck. The coffin, although rough and coated with mud, remained intact.

"I hope we have the same luck with Ellen's coffin," I said, looking at Ellen's grave.

Charlie's glance followed my stare and he looked at the second grave. "We'll keep our fingers crossed."

Tom had remained in Ellen's grave, gently brushing dirt and cleaning the coffin. The team removed the straps from John's coffin and walked to the second grave. Tom remained where he was and moved into position to help. The process proved more difficult. Ellen's coffin had seen some deterioration at the center bottom and once the straps were in place and the men began to shuffle and nudge, I heard a loud, groaning sound. Before anyone could do anything, the coffin began to split. Everyone scrambled to keep it from falling and disintegrating entirely.

I held my breath. The men stopped and looked at one another, not sure what to do next. Charlie stepped up to the grave and began directing traffic.

"Tom, you move toward the front; Frank and Harry, you two on the side close to Tom." He turned and looked at the others, his eyes darting around as his mind engineered the next move. "Eddie, if you can inch the truck back just another foot. Charlotte, see if you can help direct him. Lorelei, I'll need two of your men to help as well."

I stood to one side of the truck and slowly waved my hand for Eddie's benefit. Charlie directed each man to take the straps that remained under the coffin and tie them on top then drape the straps around the coffin one more time. They did the same thing to the strap at the opposite end of the coffin. "Lorelei, fetch me another strap from the flatbed. It's in one of the toolboxes."

I looked at Charlie and silently asked him if I could do anything more. He understood my facial expressions and just shook his head. Lorelei returned with two more straps. Charlie directed the men to gently tilt the coffin while he lowered himself into the grave, grabbed one of the straps, and strung it lengthwise along the ground underneath the coffin. The men laid the box back onto the strap while Charlie grabbed one end and Tom the other. They drew the strap across the top, weaving it around the other two straps and securing it.

Charlie wiped his forehead with the back of his hand and looked at the men around him. "I don't know if this jury-rig will work, but I think you all get the drift. We're not going to be able to lift it, but if we can shovel enough dirt out this end of the grave into a slope, perhaps we can pull and push it without doing much more damage.

It took Charlie, his men, and Lorelei's officers all nudging and prodding it, but after twenty minutes, they had the coffin on the truck's lift. Charlie and Tom both jumped up on the bed of the truck and moved the coffin tight against one side of the pickup next to John's coffin.

"Lorelei, tell us where you want these things to go. Tom, Frank, Van, and Harry, you need to ride in the back of the truck and make sure these things don't shuffle around. I'll ride in the front with Eddie."

"Charlie, if you'll follow me, we'll take them to the offices in Bangor. They're waiting for everything," Lorelei said.

Charlie turned to me. "Sorry, but no sense in you coming along. I'll call you when we get there and let you know how things go."

"I understand." I turned to Lorelei and asked, "Do you know how long this will take? I'm just curious."

"I'm not sure. This is new to us, but I suspect a week. We just need to get DNA from each body to compare to the carving board blood. I'll stay in touch with you and Charlie and as soon as we know anything, I'll share it with you."

"Thanks," I said.

I walked out of the graveyard and as I approached the manor, I looked up at the kitchen windows. I saw Emmaline staring out at us and I raced into the kitchen.

Anger raced across her face as she asked, *who is that?* She pointed to the pickup truck where the men stood.

I leaned forward to see who she was referring to and realized that she was pointing at Tom. *Oh, that's Tom Greene. He's the man I told you about from the open house.*

Why is he here—at my house?

I was startled by her anger. *He's helping Charlie; he's been here several times, but I guess you didn't—*I did not get to finish my sentence when she turned and stared at me.

Get him out of here. He is not to be in my house or on my grounds!

I stared out the window to see if anyone else had seen her but saw no recognition on anyone's face. Charlie had finished securing everything and gotten into the cab of the truck. He looked at me, smiled, and waved.

I whirled back around, and Emmaline remained at the window. Her face was contorted and angry. She stood with her arms folded across her midsection and it appeared as if she was tapping her left arm with the fingers on her right hand. I looked back to Charlie but saw no recognition from him and when I turned back to Emmaline, I was alone.

Chapter Thirty

I paced through the house for the remainder of the day with no call from Charlie and no further appearance of Emmaline. I grew annoyed, as if I were being intentionally left out of the network. I realized that was ridiculous, but still a flutter of anxiety settled within me.

After a light dinner, I sat back down at the kitchen table and began a deeper search through the 1875 journal. I did not expect to find anything but happened upon an entry dated Thursday, June 17, 1875.

I had an unusual conversation this morning with Father O'Brien. He was preparing for Sunday services and had fallen at the altar. He sprained his wrist and needed attention. We sat at his table and as I wrapped his wrist, he mentioned how saddened he was to learn of Emmaline's death. My days had been busy the previous two weeks and I had not given another thought to that awful evening until he mentioned it.

I nodded my head and told him that I had not heard anything of Emmaline's arrangements. I assumed John took her back to Portsmouth for burial. Father O'Brien raised his eyebrows and said that could not be. Since she committed suicide, she could not be buried in consecrated ground. John would not have taken her back there and could not bury her here in our cemetery.

I was stunned at the good father's comment and asked him where she was buried. He said he did not know. Then he told me that John asked him to come out to the manor. He thought it had something to do with Emmaline's death, but when he got there, John said he wanted him to perform a marriage ceremony. I could barely believe what he was saying and asked who in the world was getting married. Well, it was John and Ellen Harrison, a young woman from a family back in Portsmouth. Father O'Brien performed the ceremony and that was that.

I reread the passage in disbelief. He married Ellen only two weeks after Emmaline died. I thought back to my conversation with Emmaline and how angry she was about Ellen. Now I understood why. I suddenly thought there was more to John Varcoe than any of us knew. A question ran through my mind as I wondered if the local town families were aware of this turn of events or if they even cared.

My thoughts wandered to Peter and Belinda and I wondered who thought they had more of a claim on the doctor's journals. Was this town history or family history? As I ran these thoughts through my mind, the phone rang and brought me back to reality.

"Did everything go alright?" I asked.

"Getting the coffins out of the truck proved to be a challenge, but we were able to do it," Charlie said. "The authorities in Bangor are really looking forward to learning more about their new equipment and our old bodies. From what Lorelei tells me, they're going to be working night and day to get the information. Not that it's going to matter to anyone around here—after all, every one of these people has been dead for decades. But now I'm as curious as you are."

"Yes, well now I'm even more curious."

"Oh?" Charlie said. He must have read the odd tone in my voice. "What's happened?"

"I read some more of the journal. It seems that only two weeks after Emmaline died, John married Ellen. Apparently, they did not socialize a lot, or the doctor would have known. Of course, with such a short turnaround between wives, it's no wonder John didn't want to parade his new wife around town."

Charlie let out a low whistle. "Anything else surface?" he asked.

"Not yet. I still have more to read."

"Are you available tomorrow? Thought I'd come out and check the door and lock. And maybe we can read some more in the journals."

"That sounds fine to me. How about lunch?"

"I'll be there at noon."

As I hung up the phone I heard, *Our bodies!*

I spun around and saw Emmaline sitting at the kitchen table.

I saw you at the window, I said. *You looked angry.*

I cannot control my emotions. They wash over me at the most unexpected moments. She looked at me but continued to caress the journal. *And you? What have you learned?*

I sat across from her and pulled the journal toward me and opened to the page dated two weeks after her death. I did not read the passage but paraphrased it. *It seems that John and Ellen married only two weeks after your death.*

I told you. She reminded me of our earlier conversation about Ellen and John.

Yes, you did, but two weeks? What must he have been thinking? Was there anything else?

She did not answer my question and I did not pursue it. *Only that the doctor seemed to have been taken aback. That type of behavior would still be scandalous today; I'm sure it was beyond infamy 145-some years ago.*

I suppose so, she said noncommittally. She changed the subject and asked, *What about your science exam?*

We won't get the result for several days, if even that quickly. I hope to hear by the end of the week.

I see. As she spoke these last words, she turned her attention toward the lighthouse, and I followed her glance but saw nothing. I wondered if she was recalling her death. When I turned back, I watched her disappear.

I returned to the journal and scanned the rest of 1875 for any more information, but found nothing more about John, Ellen, or Emmaline. I placed the journal in a drawer of the hutch and turned to the journal year of John's death, 1902. I noticed that Doctor Beasley's handwriting had begun to deteriorate with his age, and the entries were shorter with less information. He had also developed a shorthand of sorts that took some thought on my part to translate.

He remained the only doctor in town, but his own comments showed that he was looking to bring in someone who could gradually take over his practice. He understood the resistance from the citizens— many of whom he had brought into this world, many whose family members were under his care for their entire lives. Only dire emergencies and procedures such as surgeries were conducted at the hospital in Bangor, and even then, the doctor accompanied the patient for support.

* * *

The next day, Charlie walked in the front door carrying a sander, paint, brushes, cleaner, dropcloth, and all of the necessary paraphernalia he needed to repair the door.

"Hi," he said, giving the door a quick examination. "I think the door is going to be okay; that is, you won't need to replace it, but let me do some sanding and painting to clean it up."

"Fine." My response was subdued. "I'll make some sandwiches with chips. Let me know when you're ready."

"Something wrong?" he asked.

"Just a disturbing night." Emmaline's visit and her anger had remained with me throughout the night, but I thought better than to share it.

"Yeah. It was a tough day yesterday." He laid out the dropcloth and removed the electric sander from its box. "Did you read any more in the journals?"

"Yes, as a matter of fact I did."

Charlie had started sanding the door and he stopped, turned off the sander and turned to me.

I continued, "As I mentioned, two weeks after Emmaline died, John married Ellen."

He thought for a moment. "Two weeks!" Charlie said, echoing my comment, almost in a whisper. "You know, I noticed the date of Ellen's death was just the year following Emmaline's and I thought it odd, but two weeks! Apparently, John didn't like living without a woman around."

"He must have been having something to do with her while he was married to Emmaline." My thoughts returned to my conversation with Emmaline.

"What did the journal say?" he asked.

"It was just a short entry." I explained the entry about Doc meeting with Father O'Brien and the confused issue of Emmaline's death and the following marriage.

"So, did John take Emmaline's body somewhere else? Do we need to look further in the graveyard?" he said, pointing a hand in the direction of the glen.

"According to the journal, the priest said John would not have taken her home to Portsmouth, although who knows what he did in that two-week period between Emmaline's death and his remarriage."

We both fell silent, wrapped in our own thoughts.

"Well, let me get this door done then we can talk more about this."

"I started looking at one of the 1902 journals to see if the doctor wrote anything about John's death. Haven't found it yet but I'll let you know."

I left Charlie to his sanding and returned to the kitchen and the journal. Doc's handwriting continued to deteriorate, and reading was slow and cumbersome. I still had not found an entry when Charlie came into the kitchen.

"Door is sanded and ready for paint. I might wait until later to do that if that's okay with you. The door is totally usable, just bland."

I laughed. "I've always wanted a bland door. You can use the bathroom upstairs if you want to clean up. I'll get the sandwiches made."

"Good. Did you find anything about John's death?"

"No. It was apparent that Doc's age was catching up to him. His handwriting is becoming difficult to read and it's taking me longer than I anticipated. Maybe you can help decipher it."

Charlie turned and went up to the guest room while I made the sandwiches. When he returned, we sat next to each other and thumbed through the journal one page at a time. As we approached the end of the year, I felt disappointment at not having found anything.

"Maybe John had another doctor?" I asked.

"I doubt it. Doc was pretty much established in town, at least with the long-time residents. Unless, of course, John had some kind of major illness that Doc could not take care of."

As he made his comment, I turned the page to December 18, 1902. "Look, here," I cried. "John's name."

We hovered close to one another and read silently:

December 18, 1902. John Varcoe's brother, Thomas, came to the house today to fetch me to the manor. He said that John was suffering and needed help. We rushed back to the manor and I found John in bed in the master suite with a fire burning in the fireplace. The room was intolerably hot.

John wheezed with each breath. It was apparent to me that he was not long for this world. A quick exam and I realized he was suffering from bronchitis, most likely complicated by pneumonia. He was agitated and delirious and I was at a loss to know why, other than he was at death's door. Enough to upset even the strongest of men. But John's delirium expressed itself through his ramblings. He called out to Ellen and Emmaline begging their forgiveness. I thought that his callous act of marrying Ellen just two short weeks after Emmaline's tragic death—well, he should be asking for forgiveness, but then it was not my call to make.

I remained with him through the night and he died that following morning. Thomas had not remained with John—I thought that rather callous, but again, not my business. The butler had taken my things downstairs and as I turned to leave, I felt John's spirit lift and leave the room. I met Thomas in the library and told him. I asked if he needed any help and he said other than the death certificate, no, he would take care of everything before he left to return to Boston. I found him to be a rather cold person; there were no tears, no remorse. John's butler had the carriage ready to take me back home.

As I left, I could not help but think about those three lives and the sadness that wrapped around the house.

Charlie and I finished reading the passage at almost the same moment and we both sat back in silence.

"Well, that doesn't really tell us much, except he apparently regretted his fast remarriage and wanted forgiveness on his deathbed," I said.

"Still doesn't answer the question about the blood on the carving board."

I laughed. "What did you expect, that he was a serial killer who did away with his victims in the kitchen at the hutch with an axe? It sounds like something from the game of CLUE."

We both laughed at the image that presented.

"Okay, I guess we'll have to let this sit for a while." He looked back at the journal and thumbed through the few remaining days of 1902. "Nothing more here about John. As I recall, Doc did not last many more years himself. Looking at his handwriting, I suspect he was failing on all fronts."

I touched Charlie's shoulder. "But look at the impact he had on this community. He gave a lot."

"That he did," he replied and closed the book.

Chapter Thirty-One

I am not a patient person. I found myself becoming anxious about the blood tests. One week had passed since the bodies had been taken to Lorelei's laboratory, and that evening I found myself pacing the floor when Charlie called.

"Lorelei called and she said the blood tests were finished. She wouldn't give me anything over the phone but said I should meet her at the manor. She'll update us tomorrow afternoon if that's okay with you. Also, she's going to want to know about returning the bodies and what you want to do."

I realized I had given no thought to their return at all. Now I wondered what exactly that would involve. I returned my thoughts to Charlie. "Of course. Tomorrow is fine."

"Oh, and Frank said he was almost finished with the other frame. I've not seen it yet, but I'll bring it with me tomorrow."

"Any idea who it is?"

"No, he just said it's a man. I'm going to assume it's probably John. Do you think you'll want to hang him with Emmaline?"

The question disturbed me. I had become accustomed to having Emmaline in the sitting room alone; I considered that her room, and I wasn't sure I wanted John to share her space. "I don't know. Let's wait until tomorrow and see."

We ended our conversation and I wandered back into the kitchen where a hundred thoughts crisscrossed my mind. I removed the journals from the hutch drawer, opened the 1876 journals, and began to flip through the one that covered the last half of the year. Again, I did not know Ellen's exact death date, so I began the cumbersome task of looking through each page.

The afternoon moved quickly into evening as I once again became engrossed with the healthcare of Portsborough's citizens. At times I found myself so rapt with the doctor's reports that my search for information on Ellen lapsed.

Several times I looked up expecting to see Emmaline, but she did not appear, and I was left alone with my own thoughts. By the time nine o'clock arrived, I realized I had almost reached the end of the year and still found nothing about Ellen. Then I remembered that there were two 1876 journals, so I began my journey again.

I had hardly opened the book when January 19, 1876 appeared, and I saw the name Ellen Varcoe. I stopped and focused on the entry.

January 19, 1876 – I find myself becoming weary of my journeys to Varcoe Manor. There is nothing but gloom and death with every trip. John sent his butler, Arthur, to bring me back to the manor and to tend to Ellen. Ellen and John had become quite reclusive and my few encounters with her indicated she was a healthy young woman, alone in the world with no family for support.

When I arrived, Arthur left the horse and carriage in front of the house, leading me to believe this would not be a long visit. Again, this did not prove true.

Upon entering the house there was a noticeable pall that blanketed the manor. A house the size of the manor with the number of servants John employed should have buzzed with activity but I was hard-pressed to find anyone—maids, manservants, anyone. I heard noise in the distance that I assumed to be from the lower kitchen. The only person I saw was Arthur, who silently guided me to the second floor. I thought I would be going to the master bedroom, but Arthur directed me to one of the smaller guest rooms where the loud wails of crying greeted me.

I entered the room to find John standing in front of the window, his back to the bed where Ellen lay writhing in pain. Another man who I later learned was John's older brother, Thomas, sat in a chair not far from John. He had a churlish frown upon his face. Neither man paid any attention to Ellen. I recognized immediately that Ellen was in the throes of childbirth. There was one female at her side, but clearly waiting for further instructions. I was not familiar with this woman but by her behavior it was clear to me that she was a midwife. I can only assume she came with John's brother.

I stopped reading immediately and my head shot up; I stared out the window toward the graveyard. "Oh my God!" I said out loud. "There *was* a baby!" My eyes returned to the journal.

The birth was difficult. The baby was turned the wrong way, presenting its buttocks first in the breech position. My experience with this type of birth is limited and I feared for both the baby and the mother. Ellen struggled in pain, while John remained staring out the window, immobile. He was totally useless.

In the end, death was imminent and there was nothing I could do to prevent it.

I expressed my condolences to John and was returned to my home by Arthur.

I scanned the next few pages but saw nothing else about Ellen or John, or how Ellen and the baby were to be disposed of. I thought about calling Charlie to let him know what I learned but decided I would just wait until he and Lorelei arrived tomorrow. I was anxious about the DNA search and wanted some advice about reinterring the bodies. I also looked forward to seeing this other picture.

* * *

I fell into a deep sleep and awoke at eight o'clock, later than I usually sleep, but the rest was welcome. I sensed perhaps an end to this search and more important, some answers for Emmaline. She had been conspicuously absent, and I wondered if she would appear during the flurry of information that we would all be sharing.

As I stood in the kitchen wondering about Emmaline's disappearance, I was distracted by a knock at the door. I opened it to find Peter Tidewater and his briefcase standing in front of me.

"I am terribly sorry to bother you on this morning, but I do have more information that I thought might interest you. Now, granted, it is about John's brother, but still…" He let the sentence fade.

"Actually, I'm very interested in information about John and Ellen. Please, come in."

We went into the kitchen, where Peter opened his briefcase and retrieved another notebook.

"I followed a trail with John's older brother, Thomas, who lived in Boston. As I mentioned previously, his only child was a daughter, Ann Nancy, so the 'heir' line ended for Thomas Varcoe when she and her husband, Mathias Greene, had only daughters. But there was something unusual here. There is a church record in Boston of Ann and her husband having a baptism for a male child in 1876. There is no record of the child's birth. Don't know if that means anything, I just thought it was odd. I know this is a stretch, but the family lore being what it is, I just thought this would interest you."

"Peter, you are absolutely correct. I am interested in this. May I keep the notebook?"

"Well, of course, although I would be grateful for any information you might find as well. The Varcoes were a formidable family in Portsborough and it would be a shot in the arm for the Genealogical Society if we could map out their existence."

I was not sure exactly how much information Peter thought would be a shot in the arm for the society, but I promised to keep him apprised. I put the notebook with the journals to show to Charlie when he arrived.

"And by the way, any more information on the graves?" He turned and looked out the kitchen window. "Oh my, it looks like there has been something going on." He pointed to the massive trail carved out during the exhumation.

"Well, yes. We're trying to put some things together. Father Peabody offered to inter John and Ellen in the Catholic cemetery and I'm considering that."

"Oh, what a very Christian thing to do."

I showed Peter to the door with the promise that he would be the first to get any new information about the Varcoe family as it surfaced.

No longer had I tucked my thoughts back into my head than I heard the sound of a car roaring up the drive. I looked out the window and saw Charlie's Lexus slam to a halt in front of the house. I opened the library French door as he ran around to the side of the car and retrieved the framed photo. I beckoned him to come in through the library doors and he raced up the steps.

"You are not going to believe this!" we both chimed at once.

"You first," he offered and leaned the frame against the side of the desk.

I shared Peter's discovery with Charlie.

"I don't get it. What's this about John's niece having a son baptized? Why is that news?"

Now it was my turn to grin. I handed him the journal with the page for January 19, 1876 marked. "Here, read this and see what you make of it."

He scanned the page, then went back and reread it more closely. "Ellen was pregnant when they got married, two freakin' weeks after Emmaline's death? That's incredible…wait, there's a motive for getting rid of Emmaline. But the baby died…"

I turned him back to the computer. "Read the notebook again; and no death certificate for the baby is mentioned in Doc's journal." I laughed out loud. "This is quite a rabbit hole. The doctor's journal doesn't really say the child died, only that there was death. I suspect that the child lived and was taken back to Boston by the brother, where he gave the child to his daughter to raise. Now, it's your turn."

"Wait a minute, I think I know what's going on. Come with me." he said. Charlie picked up the picture and hurried into the kitchen and placed the picture on the table. I leaned over and looked at it and I felt my eyes grow wide. I turned and looked at Charlie and a wide grin shot across his face.

I looked back at the picture. "That looks enough like Tom Greene to be his twin. A few nuances of difference, but this is amazing."

"I think it's the eyes. Tom has those incredibly long eyelashes that all the women in town would kill for. Similar shaped nose and lips — not quite thin but not quite plump, just somewhere in between," he added. He continued to grin. "Ann Nancy Greene, Mathias Greene…and Tom Greene? Too much of a coincidence for me."

A knock on the door drew us back to the front hall to find Lorelei Tuttle standing waiting for us.

"Greetings, all," she said with a wave of her hand.

I stood back and beckoned her to come in. My curiosity about the blood tests raced forward to the front of my mind, tucking Tom Greene and the Varcoe genes in the background. "Any information about the DNA tests?" I asked.

"Nothing conclusive. We got DNA from their teeth, but the blood on the carving board didn't match either John or Ellen Varcoe. We know it's human, but don't know of any other deaths that could have caused it. Of course, there were a few other more recent deaths on this property, but we don't have any way of getting samples. I'm sorry I don't have more for you. Since we now have those samples, we'll keep them on file, but I don't hold out much hope for getting an answer. Oh, there was one other thing. We learned that Ellen had given birth to a child. When we return their bodies, you might let us know if you find another grave."

Charlie and I both grinned at her. "That probably won't happen. Let us show you what we found. Charlie, take Lorelei into the kitchen and I'll get the journal." I ran into the library and grabbed the journal and rushed back to the kitchen where Charlie was just showing Lorelei the picture.

"Recognize anyone?" he asked.

She looked closely at the photograph then at Charlie then at me, then back at the photograph. "Sure, looks a lot like Tom Greene, but—"

I handed her the notebook. "This is why we don't think there is a baby's body anywhere. Doctor Beasley's journal indicated that Ellen died in childbirth, but there is no mention of what happened to the baby. The only death certificate was apparently for Ellen—nothing for a baby. Peter Tidewater has been doing some research on the Varcoe family for me, and he learned that Thomas Varcoe, John's older brother, had a daughter who one day shows up with a baby boy that she and her husband raised as their own. There is no record of a male birth for them or any adoption papers. I suspect that in 1876 the laws were not so strict on adoption, so this is just an assumption. If the woman who was at the birth was a midwife as the doctor assumed, then Thomas must have planned ahead. He must have known something was not right with Ellen's pregnancy."

Lorelei scrunched up her face and looked from me to Charlie. "So, what does that have to do with anything?"

"Thomas Varcoe's daughter married a man by the name of Mathias Greene. They lived in Boston." I let the thought linger.

Lorelei slowly nodded her head. "No baby's body in the coffin," Lorelei added. "And Tom Greene moved here a few months ago…from Massachusetts. Boston? I'll be damned."

"Of course," I added, "I have no idea what this means to our situation. Regardless of his heritage, Tom would have had nothing to do with deaths that long ago."

Charlie had remained silent then quietly mumbled, "Hmmmm."

"What?" I asked.

"I wonder if he could have had something to do with Belinda taking this photograph on the day of your open house."

Lorelei pursed her lips. "I think I need to chat with Belinda and Tom."

"Do you think you could hold off on that for a few days?" I asked. "After all, we got the photo back. I'd like to think about this for a bit." I bit the inside of my cheek. I wasn't sure where I was going with this, but thought I'd like to keep it just between the three of us.

"Okay, but I'm not going to wait too long. So, you let me know. Now, what do you want to do about the bodies? I have to get them out of the offices in Bangor, and relatives or not, they belong to you."

"I have no idea what to do with them. Let me think about this and I'll call you tomorrow."

Charlie looked at me and asked, "Didn't Father Peabody offer to reinter them in the Catholic Cemetery? You already have the headstones, perhaps he'd be willing to take them and their markers."

I thought for a moment. Based on my journal readings, and my conversations with Emmaline, I had not developed a strong bond with either John or Ellen Varcoe. "That's not a bad idea. Lorelei, I'll call the church tomorrow and see if the offer still stands."

"Sounds like a plan to me. I'll let you know about Tom and Belinda. If nothing else, they both need to know we have questions." She turned and left, and Charlie and I watched as she drove off.

I turned back into the hallway and sighed. "We may know the secret about John and Ellen Varcoe, but we're no closer to the mystery of the carving board, or where Emmaline is buried." I turned to Charlie and frowned.

"Well, Charlotte, we may never have those answers." He seemed to recognize my disappointment and changed the subject. "But we still have work to do here. I'll get the men out here tomorrow and we'll look at doing some more work on that forest area, and I'll have Frank start to look at the driveway. If we work on both areas, we should be able to finish everything before the end of fall." Then it was his turn to frown.

"What's the matter?" I asked.

"If I get all this work done, I won't have a reason to come around anymore." He grinned.

I laughed. "I don't think I'd worry about that."

"So, what do you want to do about John's photograph?" he asked.

I did not take long to answer. "Put it back in the attic."

Chapter Thirty-Two

The next morning, I called Father Peabody. My thoughts were unsettled about the whole interment process. These bodies had been buried for well over a hundred years in one place, lost to the rest of the world. No one had come looking for them or even cared enough to inquire. Now I was preparing to just move them aside, unsettled thoughts, indeed.

I found the phone number for St. Aubin's Catholic Church online and dialed. I did not have to wait long before a woman answered.

"May I speak to Father Peabody, please?" I asked.

A moment of silence followed my question. "May I ask who's calling?"

"Yes, my name is Charlotte Sunday."

"And what is this about?"

I became annoyed by the inquisitive tone of her voice, and I responded in kind. "It's a private matter."

"Father Peabody is busy with Sunday's sermon. If you want to leave your phone number, I'll see if he has the time to talk to you."

"It's about a burial. Perhaps I should just call the Methodist church and see if they have someone who is not quite so busy." I knew I was being unkind, but my mood was such that I just did not care.

Suddenly, her tone changed. "Oh, no, we don't want that. Just a moment, let me see if I can disturb him."

She placed the phone down and then I heard the clattering of rapid steps moving away from the phone. In the distance I heard mumbled voices, and then the sound of shoes on another hard surface getting louder as someone approached the phone.

"Hello? Ms. Sunday? This is Father Peabody." Then he whispered, "Pardon my housekeeper, she's somewhat fusty about disturbing me."

I laughed. "I understand."

"What can I do for you?"

"I'm not sure if you will recall this or not, but at the open house we talked about finding the bodies of John and Ellen Varcoe. You asked about removing their bodies to the St. Aubin's Cemetery?"

"Oh, yes, I certainly do recall that conversation. Have you made a decision?"

I heard hope in his voice. "Yes. The police have concluded their work and are going to return the bodies. I have given this some thought and believe it would be proper to move them away from all of this undergrowth and perhaps give them a more appropriate burial place. There are also grave markers with their names and birth and death dates. If you are willing to take the bodies, the only stipulation I have is that you also accept these markers."

"Oh, Ms. Sunday, yes, we would love to be able to lay them to rest in consecrated ground. Can you tell me where they are right now?" The hope in his voice grew to jubilation.

"They are still with the police department in Bangor, but I need to call Lorelei Tuttle and let her know where to take them."

"I see, I see," he mumbled. "Every year in August we have an annual blessing for those departed in the prior year—that's still several weeks away…"

I did not sense that he was talking directly to me, rather counting on his fingers the number of weeks before this event.

"I'm sure we could include them in that ceremony, if that would be all right with you," he said.

"Father Peabody, it doesn't matter to me one way or the other. I'm sure that would be a lovely way to return them to the earth, and certainly in consecrated ground. I appreciate you agreeing to do this. I just have to figure out what I'll do with them…" I too began counting on my fingers.

"Oh, my dear, we can 'house' them for you. I will contact the funeral home and see what arrangements can be made. The church will assume the cost of the facilities. I'm sure we will get some donations to help with that. Our congregation is quite generous that way. I will have some paperwork that you'll need to sign. Even though you have no relationship, they *are* still your property."

I cringed at the thought of John and Ellen being my property, but at the same time I understood what he meant.

"If you'll let me know when and where you want the bodies delivered, I'll make arrangements with Lorelei and I can come to the church at the same time and complete whatever paperwork you need."

"Let me contact Kimberly at the funeral home and I'll get back to you. Should have an answer by the end of the day."

"That sounds great. I'll wait for your call."

My spirits lifted knowing that John and Ellen would be taken off my hands. And yet in the back of my mind an ominous shadow remained.

* * *

I went into the library and walked out onto the front deck, when I heard the sound of Charlie's van drive up toward the manor. He and his team emerged, and I noticed that Tom Greene was among the workers.

"Hi," Charlie greeted me. "I thought we'd come up and take another look at this area and try to figure out what to do with it. Also, I want Frank to start looking at the driveway. As we get closer to fall and winter people want to start using their fireplaces again. Lots of old homes that have chimneys that need shoring up or tuck-pointing, or just plain replacement. So, this is a good time for us to start."

"I see Tom is with you. I'm not sure I'm comfortable with him being here. Have you talked to him at all?" I asked.

Charlie fidgeted. "No, not yet. Not sure how to approach him, but I'll get to it before Lorelei has a fit."

"Please do. I'm becoming more concerned about his claim to the manor."

"You don't really think he has a legitimate claim, do you?" Charlie asked.

"No, I don't, but do you think Tom has changed his mind? I doubt it. Anyway, I understand you need the extra hands, just keep him away from me." I realized my voice was rising and I needed to get away from the conversation. "I talked to Father Peabody this morning. He said the church would be glad to take the bodies and inter them in the church's cemetery. Something about a ceremony he referred to as the blessing of the dead?"

"Ah, yes, that's a fundraiser for the church."

I opened my eyes wide. "A fundraiser? Blessing the dead?"

Charlie laughed. "Yes. They've done that every summer since I can remember. It started out decades ago as a religious service but over the years it's become a festival of sorts. Supposed to bring joy as well as solace to the people who have lost someone over the past year. I never quite got it, but it's good for the church and for the community and brings in visitors from around the area."

"I told him I had to let Lorelei know so she could take care of returning the bodies." I shuddered as I spoke. "Father Peabody seemed genuinely pleased to give John and Ellen a final resting place for eternity."

Charlie pursed his lips. "I think there's more to it. As the festival nears, you'll probably see something in the local papers about the burial of members of Portsborough's founding family. That will draw a crowd for sure."

I frowned and remained silent for a moment. "It sounds like something P. T. Barnum would do!"

Charlie nodded in agreement. "Probably but think about your alternative. We could rebury them here."

I sighed. "No, I don't want to do that."

"You've taken a dislike to John, haven't you?"

"To both of them, actually. Although they did nothing more than others have done for millennia, I think I'm just in Emmaline's corner on this. These two adulterers get to be buried in a nice, cozy little plot in their churchyard cemetery, and Emmaline is still missing." I turned toward the graveyard. "Do you think there's a possibility that she might really be buried there, in some kind of unmarked grave?"

"I don't know, but we'll be careful as we go through it. I've given some thought to this and I believe it would be best to just pull the roots out and cut all of this growth back to the denser forest line. That would be about a hundred feet further north. That could be leveled out to a really nice lawn. Probably add to the value of the house and property."

"What about—"

"Emmaline? We don't know where she is, or if she is even on this property. Again, we'll be very careful as we go through and cut the trees and shrubs down and pull up their roots. I think it's the best thing to do, Charlotte."

Before I could answer, a voice from behind called out. Frank approached us and said, "Charlie, I looked at this driveway and I think we can do a pretty good job of redesigning it. I found some bricks poking up through the ground and they seem to be in pretty good shape. I picked a few places and dug down and just kept finding more bricks. Apparently, it was originally a brick driveway. The brick drive seems to come all the way up from the road to the manor. I think three or four of us can uncover them pretty quickly."

He continued, "If you want to reuse them for a new drive, we'll have to lift them, lay down some base of support, and then relay the bricks. It shouldn't be a difficult task, just time consuming. What do you think?"

He looked at Charlie and they both turned and looked at me. "It sounds fine to me," I said. "I know nothing about these things, so I just have to rely on you, Charlie."

"I'll go with Frank and take a look, but I would follow his judgment on this."

My mind drifted for a moment. "You don't think it's possible that—"

"What? That Emmaline is buried in the driveway? Good God, Charlotte, where is your mind going?" He held his hands up as if to stop the thought, then continued. "I don't believe that we'll find her buried under the driveway, but I'll make sure the men are cautioned to be on the lookout for any wayward body as they're pulling up the bricks."

I turned and walked away without a further comment. From behind me I heard Charlie whimper, "I'm sorry—didn't mean…"

Chapter Thirty-Three

Later that afternoon I sat in the library looking through the journals when Father Peabody called to tell me that Kimberly had agreed, and she could either bring the bodies down from Bangor or I could ask Lorelei to do that. I wasn't sure of any steps that the police would need to take, so I told him I'd call her and find out how to proceed.

The conversation with Lorelei was uncomplicated. They had completed all the tests they needed to make and if the funeral home wanted to come for them, that was fine with the police. I got the impression that the sooner, the better. She asked me about any new bodies we may have found—they *did* still have a bloody carving board, after all; but I assured her we were clean on this end. Unless I wanted it back, they would store it for the time being and that was fine with me.

I called Father Peabody and gave him Lorelei's phone number to make the necessary arrangements. He told me he would take care of everything, and he would let me know when I should come to the church and complete the necessary paperwork. He was absolutely delighted about the prospect of burying John and Ellen in the churchyard.

As I finished the calls, I sensed a presence and knew that Emmaline had joined me. I turned toward the windows and I found her standing with her back to the room, gazing out at the work being done.

So? Any word? she asked without looking at me.

The blood on the carving board was not Ellen's or John's.

Did you expect it to be?

I joined her at the window. *I don't know what I expected. I'm not even sure I want to know. I just have a curious mind. Whatever happened, it occurred a long time ago and we have no way of pinning down who or when. So, it's a dead end. You should know that John and Ellen's bodies are going to be interred in the St. Aubin's churchyard cemetery.* I waited for a rush of anger, but the room remained eerily quiet. Through my peripheral vision I thought I saw her smile.

Well now, isn't that just how it should be?

You're not angry or upset? I asked.

Certainly not. Why should they be buried on the manor grounds, while I'm lost in some shallow hole, who-knows-where? Let them be reburied in the cemetery and I hope their souls mourn the move.

I was startled by her controlled vehemence and the conversation stopped in an uncomfortable end. Her attention turned to the movement outside. She seemed to watch the work in the graveyard with interest.

What are they doing? she asked as Charlie's team pulled shrubbery out of the area.

*Charlie wants to finish cleaning out this area. He has his men doing just that. Charlie has assured me he would direct them to be careful while digging around in there—just in case—well...*I was at a loss as to how to proceed.

Charles, she said. *Yes, he would watch out for me.* I detected a small smile grace her lips. Then she leaned forward, looking for something. *Where is he?*

I rolled my eyes and thinly disguised my jealousy. *He's working with some of the other team on the driveway. It's been a mess since before I moved in, and I asked him to see if they could clear out that messy hedgerow and thin out the trees. They found an old brick driveway buried under some dirt and think they can reconstruct it to look like it did when the manor was first built.* I felt like I was babbling, just to move further away from the discussion of Charlie's whereabouts.

Suddenly the air in the room became frigid. Emmaline leaned forward and placed her hands on the glass frames of the windows. They immediately frosted.

Why is that man here again? Emmaline demanded.

I stared out the window and saw Tom Greene working on the shrubs. *I'm sorry Emmaline. I'll see to it that he leaves. But there is something you should know.*

She swung around and stared into my eyes. I had never been this close to her in the past and I was surprised at the clarity I saw in her face. Her dark hair was just as it appeared in the photograph above the fireplace. Her nose had that same upward tilt, but her lips cut across her face in a thin, angry line and her eyes pinched almost closed.

And what is it I should know?

I took a deep breath. *We believe that Tom is a descendant of John's. It seems that Ellen died in childbirth, and apparently John either did not want the baby, or knew he could not raise it. Regardless, John's older brother, Thomas, was present when Ellen died, and he showed up in Boston with a mysterious male baby not long after Ellen's death, and the baby was given to Thomas's married daughter to raise as her own. That's a supposition. We can't prove that's what happened, but all the pieces fit. And when Charlie got the second photograph cleaned up and we saw John's picture, well, the resemblance between John and Tom is remarkable and we just made some assumptions.*

She swung back around and looked out the window again. *Of course, that's what happened!*

And before I could answer, she was gone. I had no idea how I was going to explain this to Charlie when a knock on the door carried me away from my conversation with Emmaline and I found Charlie standing before me, his pants coated to the knee in mud, streaks of dirt decorating his face.

"Look, Charlotte, I'm sorry about what I said earlier. It was crass and uncalled for."

I took a deep breath. "Don't worry about it, Charlie. I've let this thing about Emmaline crawl under my skin. I shouldn't have been so prickly about it."

He smiled and nodded his head. "Anything from Father Peabody?"

"Oh, yes. He did call and told me the funeral home was willing to go pick up the bodies and he said he would make all the arrangements. All I have to do is come in and complete some paperwork. He sounded almost flighty."

"It's like I told you. The festival is coming up in August and the fact that John and Ellen will be buried at the church is bound to draw a crowd."

"Oh, you don't think they'll prop up the bodies—"

Charlie held up his hand and dipped his head down toward his chest. "No, that won't happen. It will all be quite respectful as well as very profitable."

"Well, I'll be glad to get this over with," I said. "Oh, by the way. When I spoke with Father Peabody, I told him the whole deal was incumbent upon him also taking the grave markers. Between you and me, I don't care what they do with them; I just want them out of here. Would you take then to the church?"

"Be happy to." He looked at his watch and said, "It's getting late and I need to get home and try to chip some of this mud off! We're going to leave but we'll be back next week if that's okay. How about Tuesday?"

"Of course, it is." Then I recalled Emmaline's last demand. "When you come back, do you think you could put Tom down at the driveway to work and move one of the other men up here?"

"Why? Did he do something inappropriate?" Charlie's face became blotchy.

"No, I'd just be more comfortable with him there."

He eyed me with suspicion but agreed. "Okay, but you're sure everything is okay?"

"Yes." I said nothing more except, "I'll see you next week."

Charlie went to his van and directed the men to retrieve the grave markers. As they drove away, he waved.

I turned and walked back into the hallway and saw Emmaline's silhouette in the kitchen doorway. *Thank you,* she whispered, and disappeared.

As I walked through the hallway to the kitchen, the phone rang.

"Miss Sunday? This is Father Peabody. I spoke with Sheriff Tuttle and we've arranged to pick up John and Ellen on Wednesday, the 26th. And Kimberly will take care of them until the blessing in August. We have plenty of time between now and then, so there's no rush on the paperwork. Just let me know what works for you."

"I'll plan to come in on Tuesday," I said. I'm anxious to get this taken care of as soon as possible. Oh, and I gave Charlie the grave markers and asked him to take them to you."

"That's wonderful. We'll make sure they're all cleaned up. The Blessing Committee is looking at the cemetery grounds to find the most appropriate place for them."

I started at the term 'Blessing Committee' but decided not to make any comments. "I'm sure you'll find a nice place to lay them to rest." My thoughts went back to Emmaline's comment about their mourning souls, but thought it not fitting to share.

"Good. Then I'll look forward to seeing you Tuesday. Shall we say ten o'clock in the morning?"

"Ten is fine. I'll see you then." I ended the call and looked around, expecting to see Emmaline, but instead remained in a quiet, lonely kitchen. I looked out toward the cliff but saw nothing. I briefly wondered where Emmaline retreated to when she left me.

Chapter Thirty-Four

I followed through the weekend with a sense of anxiety wondering if the work on the manor would ever be completed. Charlie called me on Saturday just to talk. I would have liked to have seen him, but problems with work kept his weekend full of activity.

Before I went to bed Saturday evening I sat in the library and wondered where Emmaline had disappeared to. Her visits had an infrequency to them that I found disturbing. Or perhaps it was my own inability to find her physical body and put her spirit to rest that gnawed at me. But one way or the other I wished she would come and talk to me. *We have so many more things to talk about.*

I did not sleep well, tossing and turning with fitful dreams of digging up some bodies and burying others. On Monday, at 7:30 a.m., I rolled over and looked at the clock. Given half a chance I would have just rolled to the other side, pulled the blanket over my head, and slept for a month. Unfortunately, I knew that could not happen.

At nine o'clock the knock at the front door informed me that Charlie and his team had arrived to continue work on the driveway and the graveyard. I realized if they did not find Emmaline's body, I'd have to start thinking of that area as something other than a graveyard, but for now, it fit the bill.

"Good morning," I said as I opened the door. I eyed him from top to bottom and back up. "You cleaned up nicely."

Charlie was in fresh jeans and his *Welcome to Portsborough* tee. He looked down at the writing and grinned. "I'm supervising today, so I thought I'd clean myself up."

I invited him in for coffee. "What's the plan for today?"

"Well, first, Tom will be working at the driveway and Eddie will be up here. I didn't make up any excuses, just gave the order. I reminded everyone up here to be careful about pulling up the shrubs and thinning out the trees. I thought a few of the trees should remain—they give the place some dimension."

We walked to the north side of the kitchen and looked at the area. "I like that. And thanks for asking the men to be careful."

"You don't really expect that we'll find her, do you?"

I detected a note of worry in his question. "No," I sighed. "I guess I really don't. I just can't imagine what in the world John did with her body. You don't think he threw her in the river, do you?" The very idea of such blatant disregard roiled my stomach.

My thoughts traveled back to a comment that Emmaline had made about her dislike for Father O'Brien when Charlie interrupted my reflections.

"I wouldn't speculate about what someone might have done 145-plus years ago. But if she were thrown into the water, her body would have eventually floated up and been discovered—so no, I don't believe the river was an option. It's pretty clear that Emmaline stood in his way, or maybe she stood in Ellen's way."

I had not considered that Ellen could be responsible for Emmaline's death until Charlie mentioned it, and now that opened a whole new rabbit hole to fall down.

Charlie must have read my mind, as he quickly added, "Don't even think about that, Charlotte. It was just a reflection, and even if it was a possibility, we have no way of proving its validity. Let it go."

Of course, he was right, and I drove it out of my mind. "So, what are you taking on today?" I asked.

"As I said, today I'm only going to direct traffic, so to speak. I want to make sure Eddie and his men are being careful, but also want to see what kinds of problems we're up against here. I've got Frank planning the driveway renovation. I want to see what condition those bricks are in. I can't imagine why anyone would cover over them, but that might just have saved them. What about you? What are you doing?"

"I'm going to see Father Peabody tomorrow at 10 a.m. to do this paperwork that he needs—some kind of release, I suppose. Will I be able to get out of the driveway?"

"It may be tricky, but I'll have the truck pulled off to the side and I'll talk with Frank to see if we can work on one side of the drive, leaving the other side open. Most of the work will be thinning out the undergrowth. We won't really get to the drive itself until that stuff is removed. There are a number of smaller trees that have sprung up and we'll see what it takes to get them out. One way or another, we'll not trap you here!" He grinned.

I took a deep breath and exhaled. "Thanks, Charlie." He leaned over and kissed my cheek. "That *is* becoming a habit," I said.

"I just couldn't resist."

* * *

I spent the rest of the day in the library scanning the journals, when the computer beeped the arrival of an email. It was from Peter.

Charlotte, I spent some more time researching John's second wife, Ellen. Found some genealogy sites that referenced her and based on time and location, I figured this was the same person. One site had a lot of notes attached to various people, and one comment was a lengthy note about her less-than-stellar reputation. It refers to her loose morals and low reputation among the people of *Portsmouth*. Now, that's not Portsborough, and we found it interesting that both Ellen and Emmaline were from the same town. Of course, Portsmouth was a substantial city and there's no indication that they knew each other. Just thought this was interesting. No details on how Ellen came to be in Portsborough. The site was started by someone named Donna Grimes, with comments from both families. Don't know if this helps any. I'll keep looking. - Peter

Grimes, I thought, looking back at the email. *That was Emmaline's maiden name. That little book was written by Simeon Barkley, the son of Lyda Grimes. Rabbit hole, indeed.* Now I wondered if Ellen really could have had something to do with Emmaline's death. I shook my head to clear the thoughts.

The clock on the mantle chimed 8:30 p.m. I stretched and yawned. My mind was now filled with many new possibilities, including the work on the grounds. At nine o'clock I dragged myself up the stairs, not realizing how tired I was; sleep came to me quickly, and Emmaline did not appear.

* * *

A quiet noise wrapped itself around me, and at first, I thought my dreams were entering my reality. Then I heard it again—a slight squeak on a distant step.

I threw the blankets off the bed and ran to the bedroom door. I cautiously poked my head out the door and looked into the dark hallway, but I saw nothing.

I returned to my bedroom and when the muffled sound reappeared, I realized it was coming from outside.

I ran onto the balcony. Moonlight hid behind the overcast sky, making its presence known only when a break occurred. Brief shadows appeared and swayed across the lawn, buffeted by the breeze that cut through the trees below. I saw nothing directly below me and wondered if I had dreamed the noise.

Then a slight ruffling from the north drifted up to me, cutting through the silence.

I ran to the north end of the balcony. In the dim light of the very early morning, I heard the sound of creaking wood again. The grounds remained overrun with shrubs and trees and I could not be sure of what my eyes thought they saw, but I was certain the sound came from the cliff and the lighthouse.

I hurried back into the bedroom, threw on my jeans and tee, and began turning on lights. Every room I entered, I flipped the switch and bright lights bathed each room. I saw nothing out of the ordinary. Light spilled out of four bedrooms and the hallway, and yet I still saw nothing strange.

Then I saw the attic door just slightly ajar.

Charlie had been the last person in the attic when he'd returned John's picture. Two options raced through my thoughts: I could grab something large and heavy and race up the stairs into the attic, swinging at anything that moved; or I could not be stupid and just lock the door.

I opted for the second choice and threw myself against the door, turned the key in the lock, and raced back into my bedroom. I closed the door behind me and locked it just as a precaution, then hurried to the phone and dialed Charlie's number.

His gravelly voice seemed deeper and groggier in the middle of the night. "Hullo?"

My melodramatic stage whisper sounded ridiculous even to me. I'm sure it must have sounded twice that to Charlie.

"Charlie—it's Charlotte. Someone was just in the house."

"DON'T LEAVE YOUR ROOM. I'M ON MY WAY." He slammed the phone down and I was surrounded by silence.

Disregarding Charlie's orders, I raced downstairs into the library and stood next to the French doors, and within fifteen minutes I saw headlights speeding up the drive. I ripped open the door just as Charlie's pickup truck screeched to a halt. He jumped out of the cab and took the stairs two at a time.

He grabbed me and pulled me into him, while looking over my head into the dark room behind. "What the hell happened?" he asked.

"It all happened so quickly. I was awakened by a noise—at first, I thought maybe it was part of a dream. Then I heard it again. The second time I investigated and when I went out onto the balcony, I thought I saw something move across the yard toward the cliff. But the night is so dark, and I could not distinguish anything. When I returned to the hallway, I noticed the attic door was slightly open—oh, I don't know—there might really not have been anything. Oh, Charlie, you must think I'm so stupid. The more I think about it, the more I think it was all the result of confusing dreams."

"What about the attic door? I know I closed it when I put John's picture back there. Have you been up there?"

"No. I had no reason to go up there."

He turned around and ran back to the truck. When he returned, he had a small revolver in his hand. I suddenly realized this was not a dream nor was it a game—this had suddenly become very serious

He hurried up the stairs and I followed close behind. By the time I reached the top, I could hear him turning the key in the lock to the attic door. I scurried up behind him. He turned and whispered, "You stay here. And I MEAN it! When I get to the top, I'll signal you to turn the lights on."

He turned back to the door and slowly opened it. There was no sound, no light. He stepped on each stair with the stealth of a cat. I squinted into the dark and watched as his shadow blurred into the darkness around him. He stopped and turned to me and I could barely see him, but he motioned to me and I quickly flipped the switch. I expected loud crashes as boxes and furniture overturned. But only silence greeted me.

"You can come up, Charlotte," he called.

I mounted the steps slowly, my eyes sweeping the room from corner to corner.

"Whoever was here is gone now," he said.

"Do you think there was really someone here?" I asked.

"Yes. There are several pieces out of place, and if you didn't move them, and I didn't move them, that means someone was here." He turned full circle as if looking for something, then noticed and pointed to a corner of the attic. "There."

"I don't see anything."

"My point exactly. Where's John's picture?"

Chapter Thirty-Five

Charlie tried to convince me to leave the house and return with him, but I refused. His second option was my guest bedroom. I assured him I was all right but agreed to his offer and although he agreed that whoever had been here was long gone, I was privately glad to have another person in the house.

I returned to my room at four o'clock but could still hear him roaming around the house checking doors and windows. I closed my eyes and fell into a deep sleep.

I didn't know how long I had slept but awoke to an odd sensation—the smell of bacon rose through the house. I realized I was extraordinarily hungry. I was still in my jeans and tee from earlier, and I hurried downstairs to find Charlie hovering over the stove, just finishing the bacon and eggs. The toaster dinged and I grabbed the toast while Charlie put the rest of breakfast on the table.

"I don't know how to work that coffee thing, and couldn't find a real coffee pot, so you'll have to do the coffee," he said as he scooped up the eggs onto each plate.

"I could get used to this!" I said. I looked sheepishly at him. "You know, I feel somewhat foolish about earlier this morning. I'm so sorry I called you."

He chewed on a piece of bacon and stared at me as he listened to my weak apology.

"Nope. No need to apologize. There was someone in the house, and I think we both know it was Tom Greene. If that picture weren't missing, then it would be a mystery, and I might even agree that nothing happened. But the picture is gone, and it was there when I took it up after getting it back from Belinda. Who else would take it?

Certainly not Belinda; not again! And I have trouble seeing her sneaking into your house in the dead of night." He barked out a loud laugh at the thought. "I called Lorelei to let her know. She's going to see if she can round Tom up."

"But how did he get into the house?"

Charlie got up and went to the front door, then returned. "The front door is fine. It's not been broken into." He turned to the kitchen door and opened it. "Hah! He must've come into the kitchen when you were in another part of the house—he put tape over the lock. You probably thought the door was locked if you hadn't used it, and you probably didn't think to check it before you went to bed."

I sat back in the chair and folded my arms. "How could I be so careless?" *Now I really do feel foolish!*

"Look, Charlotte, we don't have many burglaries in this town. People go out shopping and don't lock their doors. We all become careless. Don't beat yourself up over this." Then he wiggled his index finger close to my face. "Just don't make a habit of this."

I looked at the clock. Seven thirty. "I have to be at the church by ten, so I'm going to get a shower and dress."

"I've already called the men. They'll be out here in about thirty minutes. I don't expect Tom will show up, so I think I'm going to be one man short. I'm going to take another look in the graveyard and see if I can find anything. I suspect he went through there and found a way out through the woods. Kind of dense in the middle of the night, but who knows—maybe he already knew the way.

* * *

I arrived at St. Aubin's at exactly 9:45 a.m. I had no trouble finding the church or a parking place, but my lack of religious life left me a little unsettled. The church was small and surrounding it I saw a churchyard of gravestones; some tall, some small, everything from crosses to blocks of stone etched with names and dates. It was clear that the Catholic community thrived in this town, as the graveyard began close to the road and covered a vast swath of land beyond. A long, old stone wall, sagging from its own weight, drifted about fifty feet on both sides of a small path. Over the years the cemetery had grown but the stone fence had not. I wondered how far back this cemetery dated, and more important, if anyone visited the graves with any regularity. The grounds were well cared for, and I suspected Father Peabody had a lot to do with that.

My mind went to John and Ellen. They had no family here, and I wondered who would visit them. I knew I would not. A sign reading 'Rectory' on a small brick building behind the church blew around in a light breeze and caught my attention. I quickly walked around the church toward the sign. As I approached, the door opened, and Father Peabody smiled a warm welcome.

"Come in, Ms. Sunday. It's so nice to see you, and how prompt you are."

I suspected that the good father did not get many visitors beyond the protective woman who kept house for him and kept unwanted strangers from accosting him. He stood back and held the door open for me, beckoning me to enter. I smiled.

"Good morning, Father. I hope my early arrival isn't inconvenient."

"Not at all, not at all. Please, come in."

I stepped over the threshold into a small, cozy, dust-free room. I looked around at the many photographs and certificates hanging on the walls; the bookshelves from floor to ceiling packed with books and papers. The shelves were not neat, but not messy; they presented an organized chaos.

"This is a lovely room, Father Peabody. Very comfortable," I said, my eyes still glancing around.

"Mrs. Harrison keeps house for me, and I'm sure she was born with a dust cloth in her hand!" He chuckled at his joke. "My living quarters are down the hall. This is actually where we have our archives; all of the church history resides in this room. Our town was founded in 1795, just a few short years after Bangor, but of course we haven't seen the growth that Bangor has. We've remained a small community. Our church was built in 1815 and renovated in 1860 and we house all the records of activity in this room. We're quite proud of that." He exhaled a small sigh then continued. "I'm afraid the records of our early years are a little disorganized, but Mrs. Harrison and the board do the best they can. We focus more on current church history."

"I'm sure they take pride in keeping your history alive." I was at a loss as to what else to say.

"Yes, they do quite a good job in spite of some untoward moments."

My curiosity piqued. "Such as?"

"We had a break-in just last week. Well, I mean to tell you, Mrs. Harrison was beside herself."

I straightened up at the thought of a break-in at a church and my interest grew. "I can't imagine problems in a town this size." My thoughts went back to Charlie's comment about unlocked doors. "Especially not in one of the churches." I didn't mention my own problem with break-ins. "What happened?" I asked.

"Well, nothing was taken, and the only thing damaged was the door. It was just very unsettling to come into the archive room and find books and papers all thrown around. We're still in the process of cleaning up. But enough of our problems, you came here to sign some papers, so let's get to it. This is just a formality, you understand, but we do have to have permission to resettle John and Ellen and take the responsibility for their mortal souls."

I nodded my head slowly, wondering how much responsibility the good father would want if he knew their full story. I opted to remain quiet on that issue.

"Although they're not your relatives, you do own the property where they were buried and—well, I'm sure you understand."

I nodded in agreement, fully aware of my relationship with the deceased. He had begun a long string of explanations when I held my hand up to stop him. "I understand completely." I had stopped listening to him as my attention passed to the files and papers on the shelves behind him. "Father Peabody, may I ask you a question? Would it be possible for me to look through a few of your archival papers? I worked with a friend at the Historical Trust in Washington, DC for thirty years, and I'm fascinated by old documents." A lame excuse, not entirely true, but an excuse, nonetheless.

He waited for a moment, then said, "I can't see that it would be any problem. The recent history is more organized. A lot of people like to research their immediate past family members, so we've spent more time in these areas right behind me." He then pointed to several shelves in the far-left corner of the room. "Those shelves there have our distant past. I'm afraid my predecessors were not always careful about their records—both keeping and filing them—but the history starts there and moves up to these shelves directly behind me."

"I'm really grateful that you would let me look through here. Maybe I can put some organization to the earlier records."

He perked up at the thought. "Ms. Sunday, by all means, help yourself. You can start anywhere you'd like. I know this is a huge task, but we're grateful for anyone, especially with your background, who can help us." I said nothing more about my background. He turned and sighed at the disarray around him. "I'll go get the papers for you to sign and be right back."

He left the room and I immediately rushed to the bank of shelves that held the records from the early life of the church. To say they were disorganized and out of order was an understatement. I suspected that the only cleaning that occurred on these shelves was that of a wayward dust cloth! I grabbed the first book and was greeted by musty air that wafted out of the pages. The book had not been opened in years. It was dated 1818. I put it back at the beginning of the row. The next book was dated 1820, then 1815, 1825, and so on in no chronological order at all. I began replacing them by date until I had everything in order from 1860 to 1888. I read nothing, just shuffled books around. I was disappointed that I did not find 1875 or 1876.

In the distance I heard a telephone ring and a shrill woman's voice calling Father Peabody and telling him the call was about flowers for Sunday's service. The conversation was indistinguishable beyond that, but I knew I had been given a few more moments. My fingers quickly flipped from book to book, most still out of order, until I came across a bulk of books lying on their side on the bottom shelf. I pulled them out to see the dates when I saw a book shoved to the back of the shelf, hidden behind two other archives. I retrieved it and saw the date 1875.

The sound of footsteps shuffling down the hall grew louder and louder and I grabbed the book and raced over to where my purse sat on the desk. I shoved it into the bottom of my purse just as Father Peabody reentered the room carrying a manila folder. He opened it and looked at the paperwork inside, mumbling as he read each piece. He looked up and immediately saw I had organized at least one shelf of material.

"Oh, Ms. Sunday. I'm gone a few minutes and you've worked a miracle." He put the folder down on the desk and looked at my handiwork.

"It's really nothing. This information is too valuable not to archive it correctly. All I did was place these books in chronological order. They'll need more attention."

He turned back to me and the manila folder. "Let's get this taken care of, shall we?" he asked. "I'm extremely grateful that you're going to let us take on this immense responsibility."

I smiled and read the two pages of agreement simply stating that I was turning over the care of these bodies to St. Aubin's and that I would have no further claim on them. I signed the papers where he indicated. He had two copies and gave one to me for my files. I put it in my purse over the book lying on the bottom. I immediately zipped up the purse and turned to leave.

"I'd be happy to come back and help you with this project, if you like." I would need a way to return this book when I was finished with it.

"Why, that would be wonderful. I'll pass that offer on to the church board."

I tucked the purse under my left arm and Father Peabody led me to the door. I moved as quickly as I could and hoped it did not appear to the priest that I was speeding like lightning, but I wanted to get back to the manor and see if there was any valuable information. *Don't be disappointed,* I told myself. *This could be just a blind alley, but even a 'blind' alley is an alley. It might lead somewhere, even back to the beginning.*

Chapter Thirty-Six

As I turned onto the drive, I saw that about fifteen feet of the undergrowth at the top of the drive had been wrestled out of the ground and lay tucked in a tight pile against the taller trees, leaving the drive open to traffic. As I drove slowly, admiring the work, Charlie approached the car from behind a large pile of shrubs.

"Looks pretty good, eh? I'm anxious to see how this turns out once all this messy shrubbery is removed." He pointed toward the wrought iron gate behind me. "We've not opened that area yet; I think once we get that uncovered, it will draw attention to the gate. We'll get the dirt off the stone fence and clean it up; it should be a stunning entryway for the manor. Are John and Ellen now safely ensconced at the church?"

I laughed. "Well, their remains will be on ice at the funeral home until the festival, but the church now officially owns them, and I won't be taking them back. I thought it best not to share the information about the baby with the good father!"

Charlie raised his eyebrows. "Yeah, that would be a definite party crasher!"

"But I did find something—not sure if it will turn over any information, but while I was there Father Peabody and I talked about the history of the church and he mentioned that about a week ago, they had a break-in at the archives room where they keep all the church history."

Charlie leaned on the window ledge of the car. "Really? Anything taken?"

"Apparently not, but the place must have been ransacked. He said they were trying to reorganize everything. While he went to get the papers, I did a little snooping and found a journal dated 1875/1876."

Charlie wiggled his eyebrows. "Anything interesting in it?"

"I didn't have time to look." I let my eyes drift over to my purse on the passenger's seat.

"Charlotte! You didn't? Tell me you didn't steal from the church!"

"I didn't steal it, I borrowed it. I offered to help them organize their archives, and I can return the book under that pretext."

Charlie roared back with a laugh so loud it caused the men to stop working and look at us. Charlie just waved them back to work as he continued to laugh. After several moments he said, "What are we waiting for? Let's see if there's anything of value in the church archives. I'd like to do this before a lightning bolt streaks out of the blue killing both of us!"

"Get in and I'll drive us back to the manor."

Charlie raced around the car to the passenger side. Once back in the house, we hurried into the kitchen and sat side-by-side at the table. I opened the book's brittle, faded pages. The first page of the book read:

St. Aubin's Catholic Church
May 1, 1875 to May 31, 1876.
Marriage, birth, death, and baptism records for the members of
St. Aubin's Parish.
May God bless this book.
Father Joseph O'Brien

The tall letters appeared forced and cramped together, almost pretentious. They slanted to the left indicating a left-handed person. I gently picked up the lower right corner of the page and it crackled as I turned it and that now familiar earthy smell of old paper rose to my nostrils. I was beginning to like that odor. The ink in some places was smeared and the text difficult to read. A small black bug raced across the page.

Getting to the exact June date in 1875 was a laborious process. The paper was brittle. The priest had a creative bent to his writing, adding side comments after listing marriages, death, births, and baptisms. At moments he added his thoughts about events that occurred in the community and his writing was particularly difficult about the activities in and around the Methodist Church. *Competition for the souls of the city must have started early!*

There were no entries for June 3, 1875, and I began to wonder if John had not contacted the church. But when I turned the page to June 4, 1875, Charlie and I both stopped and stared. The room became cold and I wondered if Emmaline was present. I did not see her, but wondered, nonetheless.

Charlie placed his index finger on the date and began reading, *"I ask God's forgiveness for my actions, but anger leads me to write about what happened last night and I cannot but blame John Varcoe for his own troubles. If he had not married that Methodist in the first place, he would never have put me in this position. His wife, Emmaline, died last night, an apparent suicide. He said it was due to her being unable to conceive again and she was distraught at being childless. I questioned him in detail. His demeanor was not that of a mourning husband, but rather he seemed to have removed himself from any emotional entanglements relating to her death. I told him I could not bury her in the church graveyard because she never converted to the true faith. Although suicides have been treated with more respect since the early part of this century, I cannot bring myself to condone such behavior. It is against God's will to take one's own life, and I refused to allow her the respect of a true Catholic burial. Although I expected an argument, I got none. I could not baptize her after death, and when I turned him down on the burial question, he just shrugged. I have never seen such an expression of disregard for life, even though the death was such a reviled act.*

The one thing that agitated him was the disposal of her body. At first, I reiterated that I would not bury her in consecrated ground. He said he did not care about that. He did ask me to assist him in her removal. I was appalled that he was so noncommittal about where to bury her, and I began to repeat my disapproval when he removed his money pouch and placed an extremely large amount of money in my hand. He said it was his donation to the church, or to me specifically, for my help. God forgive me, I took the money.

John told me that the doctor had already been to the manor and would be providing a death certificate denoting 'suicide' as the cause. If John were to be asked, he would tell people that he moved her to some remote location. Her reason for suicide would satisfy even the most curious about her location. I agreed to help him, but under my direction. He agreed, and we took her body to the cross roads and buried it there under the stone fence. I have washed my hands of this matter and have asked John not to return to the church.

Charlie and I stopped reading and sat in silence, looking at one another. Suddenly, I jumped up and rushed to the library, calling for Charlie to follow. I booted up the computer and immediately began to search for Catholic churches and suicides and burials.

Charlie sat next me, and we went through a number of pages before we found one that discussed the treatment of suicides by Catholic churches. He read aloud from the screen, "At one time considered a crime against God, a person who committed suicide was refused burial in consecrated ground. Instead, they were buried outside the church graveyard at the entrance next to a cross roads. The meeting of the roads was considered a 'cross' road, symbolizing the religious cross; not giving the sinner access to God's land, but forcing their soul to wander outside its realm."

I turned to Charlie and said, "That's awful! What were they thinking?"

"Don't be too critical. Remember the times in which all of this happened. The church reigned and what its leaders said was taken as unequivocal truth."

My mind raced through possibilities. "Do you think Emmaline was buried outside of St. Aubin's cemetery? When I was there, I just got a look at the graveyard from a distance, and I noticed a long stone fence at the entry."

Charlie looked at me and a crooked grin crept across his face. "And just who is going to ask the good father if we can go and dig up the ground on a whim?"

I took a deep breath. "I just hate being this close and not being able to clinch the deal for Emmaline."

He looked at me with an odd question mark on his features. "You sound as if you actually know Emmaline."

This was as good a time as any. "Well, I sort of feel as if I do. I know you're not going to believe me, but ever since I first moved in here, I've had a feeling of her presence. I've often dreamed of conversations with her."

Charlie's face went solemn. "What were your conversations about?"

His was not a disparaging comment and he waited patiently for me to continue. I had started this conversation now, and it was too late to go back. "She indicated that she did not know where her remains were, and until she was found, she couldn't go forward."

"'Go forward?' So, you've been talking to a ghost?"

I became indignant at his flip attitude. "No, I don't believe she is a ghost. But there is an essence about her that lives in this house. This was *her* house, and her presence remains."

"So that's why you've been so adamant about this house. It's not the history of the house, it's her ongoing presence?"

"I know it sounds ridiculous, but yes, that about sums it up. I've come to like Emmaline a great deal, and the more I've learned about her life, the more I believe she got a raw deal. I'd like to set that right. This account confirms my thoughts."

I watched his reaction and expected him to roar back with his deep, throaty laugh, but he didn't. He remained still, looking into my eyes. "That's pretty much what she said to me, as well."

I stared, dumbfounded. "What?!"

"It started when we began our work here. I had the men in various parts of the house just investigating its structure, determining its safety. I was in the kitchen alone, looking at copies of the original house plans I had obtained from the county, when I felt a coldness draw through the room. At first, I wrote it off to drafts that would need attention, but then I looked up and through the window I saw what I can only describe as a vague presence moving toward me from the cliff."

"From the lighthouse?" I interrupted.

"Yes. That was the first time she approached me. She asked what I was doing to her house. I swear Charlotte, I thought I must have been hallucinating. But I also felt compelled to answer. I told her that someone would inherit it before too long. This was just after your father learned about how bad his health really was. I was there to maintain it and do any renovations needed. I don't know how I knew this, but she seemed happy the house was going to be cared for, and even happier to know that someone might live here."

"Did you see her often?"

"After that, only once or twice did I feel as if she were in the room or on the grounds while we worked. I drove my men to work harder and longer. I felt the importance of getting this place fixed and fixed right—as if I were doing it for her."

I suddenly understood Emmaline's attachment to Charlie. A cool breeze wrapped around us and we both turned to see Emmaline standing at the kitchen doorway.

Charlie pinched my arm and whispered, "Are you seeing what I'm seeing?"

Good day, Emmaline. I'm pleased to see you. I've missed you.

She did not immediately respond to my comments but remained still, looking at us. *Have you any news for me?* she asked, directing her attention to me. I looked at Charlie then back at Emmaline.

I'm not sure. We might be onto something, but we have to figure it out first. I wish I could be more positive, but I'm afraid we might be blocked against getting to the answer. But we're not giving up.

'We,' yes. Good day, Charles. She turned her attention away from me. Her smile teased a secret flirtation between them.

Good day, Emmaline. It's been a long time.

I was stunned that his thoughts entered my mind. I silently hoped it was only for conversations with Emmaline.

Yes, it has been too long. I have a sense that something will happen soon. I shall miss you both. A long, uncomfortable pause followed, until Emmaline said, *I should let you get back to your work.*

And she turned and vanished out the door. We both leaned forward and looked out the window toward the very lighthouse we had just discussed, watching her vision dissipate until it dissolved into a small cloud of mist.

Charlie leaned back in his chair and let out a long sigh. "Well, *that* was interesting."

"It's good to know that I'm not going slowly insane, unless you are too."

"Let's not talk about this to anyone; it's apparent that we both have the same goal in mind. Now, how about the cross roads at the church."

My mind suddenly became scrambled with information, and as it sorted itself out, I said, "Wait a minute. Maybe it isn't the church."

"What do you mean?" he asked.

"The sign…at the gate to this property."

He looked closely. I saw his eyes dart around the room. Then he smiled. "Of course, 'Varcoe Manor, 1875, The Crossroads.' I never got why he named the property The Crossroads…wait a minute."

He raced out to his truck and returned with a large number of papers rolled into a tight cylinder. He unrolled the papers and began shuffling through them.

"Here, I thought I remembered this. Look at this one." He lifted one of the papers and placed it on top of the others. The paper reflected a rendering of the property sign at the gate. He pointed to the words. "Look at this. It isn't 'The Crossroads,' it's 'The Cross Roads.' I remember when we had the sign in the workshop and Eddie worked on it. The writing on the sign was a mess. He must have corrected the spelling, not realizing it was right in the first place."

I stared at the paper then at Charlie. "Then the sign may have originally indicated something religious? You don't think Emmaline could be buried right here at that sign?"

Chapter Thirty-Seven

We sat for a moment in silence. *Could this really be the answer? Something so simple as this?* I wrapped my mind around the thought when Charlie interrupted me.

"Charlotte, I'd be willing to bet that's exactly where she is," Charlie said.

We sat for a moment of silence and then both rose at the same time and raced out the door. We flew down the driveway just as Eddie was getting into the CAT to begin the heavy task of uprooting more shrubs close to the gate. He started the engine, and it began its slow crawl toward the wrought iron fence. He approached the gate just as we arrived.

Charlie waved and shouted, with me right behind. The rest of the crew watched in stunned silence as Charlie raced up to Eddie and shouted over the roar of the engine. Eddie stopped the CAT and stared at Charlie as if he had lost his mind. Charlie leaned over and gulped in air, trying to catch his breath. As he did, he waved for the rest of the crew to come forward.

"Eddie, put the CAT away. We have another task to do. I need everyone to start working in these two areas." He walked over to the gate and began pulling layers of vines, clearing the stone wall that appeared underneath. "We need to uncover these two walls," he pointed to the part of the wall he had just uncovered and swung his arm around to point to the same location on the other side of the gate. "I want to know how long this wall is, and both sides of the wall need to be uncovered. Do not do anything else until this is cleared."

Everyone stared at him with curiosity written across their faces.

"I'm going to call for the men from the job up at the graveyard and bring them down here to help as well. Charlotte, I'll get you some work gloves. We need your help too."

Two men took a section and began pulling away the shrubs that grew tight against the wall. Two others began ripping away the many layers of vines that had crowded the other wall for decades. They remained silent; only the sounds of trowels and spades clawing against stone and large clumps of vines being thrust to the ground and an occasional grunt when a root proved to be particularly uncooperative echoed across the hot, still air.

"Charlotte," Charlie called as he rushed back with a pair of extra-large gloves. "The best I could do, sorry."

"That's okay, I'll make them work." I pulled on the gloves while Charlie redirected the other three men to the outside of the wall and gave them the same directions. I placed myself at the far end of one side of the wall and began the task of removing creeping weeds.

It took an hour before the two sections of wall were free of plants, vines, and any other type of creeper. The wall measured ten feet long on each side of the gate. Charlie and I looked at one another while the men waited for further directions. Their faces clearly reflected confusion, but they waited patiently.

"Okay guys, here's what we need to do next. Charlotte has been doing some research into the history of the manor and its grounds. In a nutshell, it appears that the wife of the original owner may have committed suicide and may be buried somewhere in this area. I want each of you to take a patch of land around this wall and begin digging. Be very careful and take as much time as you need. If she's buried here, it occurred 145 years ago, so there won't be much, but bone left, and we want to be very gentle. Any questions?"

There was a general murmur of 'no' and each man picked up a shovel and parked himself at a place next to the wall. I returned to the house and found a gardening spade and some old paintbrushes in the garden shed, turned, and rushed back to the wall.

Each man scooped dirt out of the ground in small shovelfuls. I was sure they must have thought us crazy, but they each approached their jobs with care. At four o'clock, the gate and both sides of the wall had been dug down two feet with nothing to show for the effort but more wall.

Charlie removed his gloves and wiped his forehead with the back of his hand. "Charlotte, this was a good effort, but I'm not sure we're going to have any success. Maybe the church gate was the right idea, but there's no way we're going to get them to dig up that area."

I exhaled a disappointing sign. "You're probably right. And I really thought we had something here."

He turned to the men and directed them to replace the dirt they had just dug up. He shuffled back and forth, stretching and pulling his tight muscles.

"Charlie!" I exclaimed. "Look where you're standing."

He looked down at his feet then back up at me. Curiosity spilled across his face and I realized he did not understand what I wanted him to look at. He wrinkled his brow and shrugged his shoulders.

"You're standing in the middle of the drive between the two stone walls."

"And?" he asked.

"You're standing at the cross of the roads...well, actually you're about four feet from the road, but it *is* at the crossing."

"Charlotte, that was referring to church cemeteries and their consecrated ground, not the driveway to a personal home."

"Well," I said, "let's stretch that. There is, after all, a cemetery up there." And I pointed toward the forest where the graves were found.

Charlie rolled his eyes at me. "That's a bit of a stretch...but...what the hell!" He looked at me for just a moment then dropped to his knees and started to dig. Eddie had finished filling in his dirt and he came over to help. As each man finished his task, he came over and began to dig. Within ten minutes, they had uncovered about ten inches of driveway, when Eddie stopped.

"Charlie," he said. "I think I struck something.

Charlie and I looked at where Eddie pointed. I took the spade out of my back pocket and began the arduous task of scooping out small amounts of dirt. As we worked the ground, I suddenly hit something hard. I took my fingers and brushed the dirt away to find a brick…then another, and another. My disappointment peaked, but then I felt something soft. I gave one of the brushes to Charlie and I took the other one and we gently brushed dirt away from the object until a piece of brown material appeared. Charlie looked up at me and we shared a moment of recognition.

"Emmaline's dress," We both said at the same time.

Charlie quickly directed the team to help uncover whatever it was we had found. Eddie took the spade, Charlie and I each used brushes, and the other men began to move small clumps of dirt with their hands.

More brown material appeared and disintegrated as we touched it and I felt a sharp intake of air force itself through my lungs.

Everyone leaned in close and Charlie brushed dirt away from something else hard, but not a brick. He lifted the object, and it was obvious that he had found a bony finger. Several quick flicks of the brush revealed a full skeletal hand. It only took moments for the rest of the team to kneel down around us and begin digging up more bricks. As they removed the bricks, a full skeleton, wrapped in dirty brown cloth, came into view. Charlie moved everyone away and finished uncovering it himself. I felt as though I were living through all eternity until he finally backed away and rose to his feet.

The skeleton was small and as I gently moved more dirt from around it, I clearly saw damage to the right shoulder—enough damage to almost separate the arm from the body. I had no way of knowing if that damage occurred before or after burial, but I my thoughts went back to Doc Beasley's journal and his visit to the manor on the night of Emmaline's death. The skull and right shoulder showed damage, but the amount of dirt and mud packed into it made it difficult to determine what, exactly, that damage was.

"Well?" he asked. "Do we think it's Emmaline?"

I looked at him, dumbfounded.

"Yeah, rightthe wrong question," he said. "Okay, Eddie, get some blankets out of the van and see if there is anything that we could use as a stretcher. We want to be particularly careful about moving this. It's extremely fragile."

Eddie found several lengths of plywood and he placed a blanket on top and set it next to the skeleton. It took four of the men, each jostling around the hole, to finally get the skeleton out and onto the blanket.

I remained off to the side, feeling useless, but knowing it would be best for me to just let them take care of this. I looked back into the hole from which the skeleton was removed, and something caught my eye. I leaned over for a closer look and saw what appeared to be a small chain. As I reached down and lifted it up, I felt the jab of a pin and quickly withdrew my hand. I leaned in and looked closer and saw the back of an object with a pin. I picked up one of the brushes and began sweeping dirt away until I uncovered the object. I placed both the chain and the pin in my hand when Charlie called to me.

"Okay Charlotte, I don't know who we have here – we both know who we think it is, but we need to know for sure. I'll call Lorelei and let her know that we're bringing something to her, and we need her help in identifying who this is."

"I know who it is," I said.

"Look, Charlotte, I know you want this to be Emmaline, but let's go by the rules."

"No, seriously Charlie, I mean it." I unfolded my hand to reveal the objects I had taken out of the hole. "Remember the picture of Emmaline? She was wearing this locket around her neck and this watch pinned to her bodice. I recognize them, but there's more." I raced back to the house and grabbed the small piece of cloth that I had discovered in the lighthouse. I ran back to the gate where everyone waited, unsure of what to do next. "I found this piece of material in the lighthouse and I'm sure it matches Emmaline's dress." Charlie did not take his eyes off me and I knew I was probably in trouble, but I continued. "I know, I know, I should never have gone up there, but my curiosity just dragged me by the shoulder. The point is, I found this stuck on a floorboard in the light room."

He nodded his head very slowly, but no smile graced his face. He took the piece of cloth and took a closer look. "I think you're right. We'll compare it to be sure. But let's get this taken care of first. We can't fill in the hole until Lorelei gives us the okay, so driving around it is going to be tricky, but I think we can do it." He turned back to me and said, "We'll have to talk about this later."

He sent his men home and told them to just go to the office tomorrow and we'd try to sort out our next moves. We returned to the manor, where Charlie phoned Lorelei and told her what we found. She told him to come right to the sheriff's office. We both cleaned up and within thirty minutes were on our way down the driveway again.

Charlie drove carefully around the trees lining the drive and as he did, I looked out the side window at the gaping hole in our path. I thought about 145 years of people walking and driving up and down that driveway, each time trampling across Emmaline's grave. I thought about John and Father O'Brien burying her then piling bricks on top of and around her body—why? To prevent animals from digging her up? To prevent her body from shifting in the ground? I felt tears well in my eyes at the idea of such cruelty.

Suddenly I felt Charlie's hand on mine. "Look, the good thing is that we've found her, and the search is over. But you cannot go back to that lighthouse. It is too dangerous."

He squeezed my hand and I silently wondered what that meant going forward.

We arrived at the sheriff's office to find Lorelei standing on the steps waiting for us.

"So," she asked, "what have we got?"

Charlie explained to her what we found and how we found it. I added that I was certain that this was Emmaline, and I showed her the locket and the watch that I retrieved from the hole where she had lain."

She took the locket and watch and turned them over in her hand. "And you're sure this was hers?"

"It's exactly like the one she is wearing in the picture in the sitting room," I said. "What are the chances that there would be an identical locket and watch, and would be found in a hole with this body if it weren't Emmaline?"

"Okay, that's a good case. I'll take the remains up to Bangor and well see what we can find out, if anything. If not, well, oh hell, we'll just declare her Emmaline and be done with it!"

Charlie and two of Lorelei's officers removed the remains and placed them on an official stretcher. As I watched them jockey around, I turned the locket over in my hand several times, not realizing that I was actually playing with the latch. I looked at the locket and when realized I had opened it; I raised my eyebrows high and sucked in a large mouthful of air.

As if in the distance I heard Lorelei's voice. "We'll take care of this. I've called the office in Bangor and they're ready to receive at any time. I'll have the officers take it up tonight. Not sure how long it'll take before we have any final word, probably several days. It seems the folks up in Bangor have taken an interest in this case and can't wait to get their hands on fresh evidence. As soon as I hear from them, I'll let you know what they find."

"Here, Lorelei," I said and handed her the open locket. "Maybe this will help." On one side of the locket sat Emmaline's picture, and on the other a small lock of hair. "Let's see if this hair is any help to you. I'm grateful for anything you can share with us. I'd like to put this to rest."

Charlie and I returned to the manor and enjoyed a glass of wine.

"You should be proud of yourself, Charlotte. You've solved this mystery, and you'll be setting Emmaline's 'essence' to rest and putting your own mind at ease."

I took a sip of my wine and stared out the kitchen window toward the lighthouse. "What mysteries does this settle for you?" I asked.

"For one, it tells me why all of those fine bricks that made up a good, solid driveway were buried under six inches of dirt. That made no sense to me when we first looked at it but now that we know Emmaline was buried under the driveway, John had to cover her body with more dirt to assure she remained where she was put."

And again, I shuddered at the word 'put.' "I guess that *does* make sense from his perspective. What a creep!" I exclaimed.

"There's one other thing that remains a mystery. Tom Greene. It's obvious he has a relationship somewhere in the past to the Varcoe family. From Doc Beasley's notes, it's all but a certainty that Ellen's baby was the one taken by John's brother, Thomas and given to his daughter to raise. I mean, that resemblance in the photograph to Tom is too close not to be a sure thing. But why would he steal John's picture?"

I put my elbows on the table and rested my chin in my hands. "The fact is, we don't know that it was Tom who did that. We've been making assumptions based on his resemblance to John Varcoe." I took a deep sigh. "I don't really care, Charlie. The picture is gone and whoever has it can keep it. I don't want it back. But I think we're at the end of this puzzle. I wonder when, or *if* Emmaline will return. If she knows we've found her, that may mean she's ready to move forward."

"Of course," Charlie added, "if she is still around, does that mean we have more work to do?"

"Oh, Charlie, don't even think that. I really want to see her on her way to—wherever!"

I was saddened by the idea that she would probably disappear from my life forever. I had grown quite fond of her. I didn't know how to call to her, to bring her to me so I could let her know, but then again, perhaps she already knew. As she'd said, she could not leave the property until her whereabouts were resolved, and she had an uncanny way of getting me to tell her things that I suspected she already knew.

Charlie looked at his watch. "Well, it's time for me to be on my way. I'll be back with the boys tomorrow and we can at least continue to clean up the graveyard, and we can pull some more of the shrubbery out of the driveway. We'll just avoid getting close to Emmaline's hole in case Lorelei needs to check it for something."

"Do you suppose we could stop calling it a 'hole' for now?"

Charlie laughed. "Okay, we'll call it her 'home.' How's that?"

"Well, it's better. Let me give you the good doctor's journals. I don't think we'll get anything more out of them, and they belong with you." I gathered up all of the journals and packed them in a box.

I followed Charlie out to his van and watched as he placed the box inside. He turned and came back up the steps. He smiled at me, and gently placed his lips on mine. Heat! He backed away and smiled. "See you tomorrow. And stay away from the lighthouse!"

Chapter Thirty-Eight

I had placed the watch that I retrieved from Emmaline's resting place on a paper towel on the kitchen table. A strong desire to know if it could be cleaned and put in working order embraced me.

I hobbled around the house the rest of the evening after Charlie left. My arms and back ached from the digging and kneeling and pulling that I did that afternoon. My mind raced with the excitement of finding Emmaline, although the official word still had to come down from Lorelei and the sheriff's office. I knew there was no way they could make that official call, but I was sure that once Emmaline knew, her memories would flood back.

A warm shower took much of the ache out of my body. When I walked back into the bedroom, I hoped to see her at the door of the balcony, or sitting in the chair next to the bed, but still, no Emmaline. I drew back the light summer sheet and thought of Charlie and his kiss. I smiled. I felt like a high school girl and laughed. I laid my head back on the pillow and a quiet sleep washed over me.

* * *

The noise surrounded me. At first very quiet, almost inaudible, just white enough to lift my unconscious to a state of awareness. I turned my head to the windows and stared out into a dark night. Another night of heavy clouds hovered high in the sky, blotting out any trace of moonlight.

The soft noise rose again but seemed to be at a distance. I got up and put on my jeans and tee shirt and went to the window. I looked at the grounds below and as my eyes adjusted to the dark morning, nothing out of the ordinary appeared. I returned to sit on the side of the bed and looked at the clock on the nightstand: 2:30 in the morning; I slid into my shoes and walked back to the French doors, peering slowly and deliberately to the ground below. Then I hear it again. The white noise increased very slightly, and I followed the direction to the lighthouse stairs. My eyes adjusted to the dim morning light and I saw the door to the lighthouse open. I hurried back into the bedroom and grabbed my cell phone and dialed Charlie's number.

"Hullo?" he answered, his voice lower than usual.

I cupped my hand around the phone and whispered, "Charlie, someone is in the lighthouse. I know, I know, this is like a repeat performance, but I can hear someone out there. I saw the door open."

"Do not leave your room. Lock yourself in. I'm on my way." He did not wait for goodbyes but hung up the phone and I once again listened to dead air.

My first inclination was to follow his directions, but my independent streak rose along with my anger. I felt intruded upon in my own house and was getting very tired of that. I grabbed my cell, left the room, and crept downstairs to the kitchen where I quietly opened the kitchen door and listened. For a moment I heard nothing, then a crackling sound accosted me as if something heavy was breaking wood. I tiptoed onto the deck and down the stairs, all the while listening for the noises of movement around me. The foreboding figure of the deserted lighthouse loomed high above me. I knew it was a mistake to continue, but I could not stop. After several agonizing minutes of a slow march up the old steps, the stairs creaking as I moved, I found myself near the top. As I approached the top steps, my head rose just level with the deck that encircled the prism room, and in the dark, I watched as an obscure shadow moved quickly across the room, unaware of my presence.

I continued to the top stair and stepped onto the deck that led around the lighthouse, where I tripped against a small piece of debris and sent it skittering across the floor. I watched in terror as the shadow rushed toward the door. I turned and raced down the stairs hearing the sounds of footsteps closing in with my pursuer just inches behind me. With just five steps to go to the bottom, he grabbed my hair, jerked me around and threw me backward toward the cliff, tumbling down those last few steps.

I fell and scuttled backward across the lawn like a crab, attempting to get further away into the safety of the yard, when he grabbed my leg. Adrenalin raced through my body as I fought his grip, but I felt my leg twist in the grasp of a much stronger hand. The dim light from the distant manor cast small shadows across the lawn, shedding enough light to clearly see my attacker.

"Tom!" I screamed. "What on earth are you doing?" I struggled to free myself but remained in his grasp.

He glared down at me, anger dancing across the shadows of his face. "You should have left after I sent you those messages on your walls. You don't belong here. This is MY house, not yours."

He continued to ramble about his house, his property, his inheritance—as much to himself as to me. I twisted free and jumped up, racing backward, trying to escape while watching him close in on me. My gaze wrapped around the grounds as I looked for a weapon—anything I could use to defend myself—but found nothing.

Tom slowed his approach; moving with purpose he waltzed around me in an ever-tightening circle, watching me, glaring at me. It was then that I saw a heavy piece of wood clutched in his hand. His body shook; his face twitched, and a grisly smile crossed his lips. He took a menacing step toward me, raising the hand that held the wood, and I had no place to go.

There must be some way to slow him down, some way to give me time. Can I talk him down? "Tom, I don't understand." *What a stupid thing to say,* but those were the first words that tumbled out of my mouth. "Why would you write such awful things?"

His hand trembled and the piece of wood shook. "You don't have to understand anything except you don't belong here. My ancestor built this place for his family and all of his descendants. Do you really think he wanted some stranger living here?" Spittle flew from his mouth.

"But how would I know that?" *Time, keep talking, distract him.* "After he died, his brother Thomas closed the house and never returned." Anger rose through my body, and as much as I knew this was the wrong path, I could not stop. "This house has passed down through my family—not yours!" As I spoke, my anger continued to rise to the top. "Besides, if he was so interested in having this house remain in the family hands, why did he allow Thomas to take his son away? Why didn't he keep that baby here? That baby that was a product of his adulterous affair with Ellen? And why did your ancestors sell the house back to mine?" *What is the matter with you, Charlotte! Stop before this gets any worse!*

Silence. I had just committed the biggest mistake I had ever made in my entire life. The muscles in Tom's arm grew tight and his fingers tightened around the wood. Words may have failed him, but I read fury in his eyes and his body. He raised the board high above his head and I did the only thing I could do. I rushed him, my head down, and I aimed for his torso. If I could throw him off balance, I might be able to gain a few moments to get away from him. If I couldn't, then I would suffer the consequences, but I had to do something.

I rammed into him, waiting for that 2 x 4 to come crashing down upon me. He did not fall, but my action startled him and sent him tripping backwards. He dropped the wood and staggered, off balance. I grabbed the weapon from the ground and swung around, not sure of the consequences of my action, when I felt a sudden thud and realized I had made contact. Tom fell backward and crumpled on the ground, where he remained still. My heartbeat increased as my heart pumped adrenaline through my body even when I stopped mid-step.

A sound drew my attention and I looked up to see Emmaline's vague figure suspended midway up the steps to the lighthouse. Emmaline slowly moved toward him until she hovered over him, within inches of his face. The air across the grounds became deadly quiet; nothing stirred, no night noises; it was as if the world stopped. Tom remained still, tucked close to the lighthouse steps. His eyes fluttered for a moment, then opened wide.

Emmaline looked at Tom, a calm anger in her face. *This is my house. It was never John's, never Ellen's, and never yours! It's Charlotte's now and forever!*

He heard her thoughts as I had, and terror settled across his face. Unable to move, he threw his arms across his face and screamed.

I skittered backward across the lawn, staring at the scene before me. At that same moment I heard the door to the manor open. I looked up just as Charlie raced out, slamming the door hard against the wall. He loped across the lawn toward me, then stopped as the picture before him clarified.

"What the…"

As he spoke, Emmaline turned and saw him. She said nothing, but I sensed a discourse between them that I was not privy to.

She lowered herself to the lawn and came toward me. *Yes, it is my body you found, and I am ready to leave.* She turned to Charlie, and said, *Thank you both. I will be forever grateful.*

I had no words, but a weary sadness wrapped around me as I realized this was the end of my relationship with Emmaline. She began to fade, but as she did, she seemed to lean in toward Charlie and brush him with her lips. And then she was gone.

The world slowed like the trickle of a stream, when a movement across the lawn drew us back into the present. Tom Greene was gone. In the distance I heard the sound of a siren shriek through the night, growing as it screamed up the driveway.

Lorelei raced around the house to the back lawn, gun in hand. "What's going on here?" she demanded.

Charlie drew her toward the house and explained about Tom's attack, but he pointedly did not refer to Emmaline's role in the event. Their voices floated to me from the distance, with words that were vague and at times indistinguishable, the tone clear and angry.

I sat on the top deck step and leaned my head against the stair rail. I stared at the bottom of the stairs, lost in my own thoughts when the sound of the kitchen door closing caught my attention and brought me back to the present.

"You okay?" Charlie asked as he sat one step below me.

"Yes, I'm fine. Stunned, but okay." I turned and stared at him, but the words stopped for a moment.

Charlie absorbed the quiet night before he continued, "I know. I don't believe it either, but it was real, and it happened as we saw it. Lorelei is putting out a BOLO for Tom. I doubt he'll get far."

"She's really gone now, isn't she?" I lost all thoughts of Tom and I felt my connection with Emmaline fading as we spoke.

Charlie lowered his head and nodded. "Yes, I believe she is." He then changed the subject. "Do you want me to stay?"

"No, not tonight. Let's talk tomorrow."

Charlie nodded, rose, and walked back through the house, leaving me with my thoughts. My gaze traveled back to the cliff and the lighthouse, and I listened to the roar of the river below.

I rose and turned toward the kitchen door, and in that moment, a sound—deep and dark—rumbled from the north. It started more as a distant storm, until it crept into a loud, thunderous growl. I turned and within a moment the earth began to tremble. A glow from the lighthouse quickly sparked into a bright vibrant blaze.

A figure appeared at the only unbroken window of the light room, shadowed by the fire behind it. I slowly lifted my hand to my mouth as if to stifle a scream when the entire lighthouse erupted into flames. I heard a gurgling shriek—a voice I recognized. Tom Greene stood far above me, his arms outstretched, as if giving himself up to death. All sound disappeared, as if sucked into the universe. Within moments the building collapsed into itself, a rubble of fire and ash. The heat from the fire and the noise of the explosion slammed across the yard; the house shook, I fell backwards onto the deck and the world went black.

* * *

The next day raced through me as if it were a dream. Lorelei returned late that morning and informed me that the fire department would further investigate the explosion once the ground and the remains of the lighthouse settled, and they would retrieve anything that remained of Tom Greene.

"I was surprised when I told Belinda," Lorelei said. "She was apparently quite relieved. Evidently, the relationship was not as close as it appeared. Seems Tom was only using her and her connection to the Historical Society to attempt to gain access to the Manor."

Before she left, Lorelei told me that Emmaline's remains were at the morgue for examination and she would let me know if any news emerged. I thought about Lorelei's comments as Charlie sat next to me on the deck.

"It seems that Belinda did not know why he was so interested in the manor," he said. "Perhaps she thought he wanted to buy it; she did know he didn't have the funds to do what your father did in restoring the manor. I guess he thought he would wait until all the work was done then put in his claim. If Belinda thought there was something more to the relationship, she would have been sorely disappointed."

He continued, "That also explains why he was so quick to want to help with work around here. At the open house, when he learned about that second picture, he must have convinced her that it would be good to have at the Historical Society. Really, he needed to find proof of his relationship to John, and hearing about the picture seemed to be what he was looking for."

"His connection to John would have no bearing on the ownership of the house," I said. "I've been assured that there is no question that it is mine."

I brought my attention to the remains of the lighthouse at the top of the cliff. It was nothing more than a smoldering pile of debris. "Good riddance to that building. It brought nothing but pain. So many accidents and deaths…" I let my thoughts wander to the events that seemed to haunt this house.

"Charlotte, no one knows anything about how these accidents happened. They were accidents, and I think you should leave them as that—just accidents."

I looked back at him. "You don't think that Emmaline…"

Charlie threw his hands up. "No, Charlotte. I do not think that Emmaline had anything to do with those events. You have to let go of them and you have to let go of Emmaline."

My attention diverted to the river beyond—it seemed especially beautiful today as the waves rolled forward against the rocks then withdrew. I leaned against Charlie's chest and he wrapped his arm around me. I took a deep breath and turned toward him. *I will have to put the struggle forward behind me.* He kissed me, and I thought, *perhaps the way forward won't be such a terrible struggle.*

Chapter Thirty-Nine

A week had passed since finding Emmaline's body and Tom's gruesome death, and I was not sure I could even remember what other events had occurred. I floated through the week and gradually began to surface back into the sun. My face and arms were scarred from the flying debris, but each day that passed, they hurt a little less.

Charlie sat in my kitchen and worked hard to take my thoughts away from the events of the prior week. "Here's where we are. The drive is cleaning up nicely. Eddie has removed most of the ground cover and his team has removed the bricks. We're getting ready to fill everything in and then lay the bricks to make a really fine driveway. We're still several weeks away from completion but well on the way."

I smiled. "Thanks for being here and helping life to go on."

He nodded but said nothing, just turned and looked out the window to the north and the graveyard. "Eddie is getting the ground ready for the sod and that should be finished in about a week."

I sighed. "I wish I could get excited about this. When I first moved here, I would have but today? Not so much."

Charlie coughed, an indication that he had something else on his mind. "We need to get rid of the remains of the lighthouse. The fire department removed Tom's remains; the ground has calmed enough for us to get to it. I think it should be removed and the ground totally cleaned up. That cliff is high enough that we might be able to build some kind of retreat there. Just a thought—get rid of all of the memories of the lighthouse."

"The fire marshal approached me yesterday as they were going through the debris." I rose and left the table and returned with a large bag. "They found this."

I reached into the bag and withdrew a piece of curved wood. Charlie took the wood out of my hands and looked at it, turning it over several times. He looked back at me, his eyes wide.

"This looks like a piece of the picture frame that John's picture was in."

"I suspect that's exactly what it is. Another mystery solved."

Charlie and I stared at the piece of wood when we were both caught by the sound of the front door opening. I thought of how comfortable people were in this community just walking into one another's houses. I realized I did not mind. As we both turned toward the sound, Lorelei walked into the kitchen. We smiled, but she didn't smile back.

"Is there something wrong, Lorelei?" I asked.

"Well, I don't know if 'wrong' is the word, but I *do* have some information."

Charlie and I both sat up straight.

"This is interesting news—the Bangor office has completed its testing on both bodies. They compared Tom's DNA with what is on file for John and Ellen and discovered the relationship existed."

Charlie thought for a moment then said, "He probably thought that once the DNA tests were clear, he could have his own DNA tested and if proved a match he could use that to strengthen his case for ownership to the manor."

Lorelei added, "However, something disturbing has come to light. If this was Emmaline, she did not commit suicide. The skull was badly damaged, and the right shoulder was almost totally disconnected from the skeleton. I don't think you could see the full extent of the damage when you picked her out of the ground because there was so much mud holding everything together. Once they got her cleaned up, they encountered massive trauma to the skull. We are fortunate to have very curious people in our office, and that curiosity paid off. They obtained DNA from a tooth and the hair from the locket and ran a DNA test against the blood on the carving board. The results were conclusive. I'm ready to definitely designate this as Emmaline and her death as a murder. Not bad for 145-year-old DNA and blood. Anyway, we're ready to return her to you. Just let me know when."

I was stunned. As with John and Ellen, I had given no thought to retrieving their bodies, now I had another one to consider. "Can you hold onto her for a bit? Let me figure this out?"

Lorelei put her hands on her hips and pursed her lips. "I can hold her for a *bit*, but don't take too long."

I nodded. Charlie saw Lorelei to the door and then returned. He poured a glass of wine for each of us and sat across from me.

"So?" he asked. "What's next?"

A chilly breeze rose from the river as I turned and looked out across the water. Autumn was approaching. I remained silent for several moments before I turned back to Charlie and said, "I need some time to think. But my thoughts are leaning toward selling the manor. I already feel as if there is something missing." My glance drifted out across the river before I resettled my attention on Charlie.

"Could I convince you to think at my place? Get you away from here? I have a nice widow's walk that's a great place for thinking. No obligations."

The speed of my answer surprised me. "I think that's a good idea. I'll pack some things and come this evening."

* * *

Over the next few weeks, my thoughts about Emmaline came and went with no organization to them and now my mind wandered back to her visits. I realized that I actually missed our conversations. As I moved through time I wondered if they ever really occurred at all. Much had changed; all for the better, and yet change brings with it a certain melancholy of things past, things lost, things never to be the same.

Charlie was correct about the widow's walk. As summer migrated into fall it became a morning sanctuary where I clutched warm mugs of coffee as the temperature dropped and for two weeks the trees became paintings of yellows, browns, reds, and greens. The air quickly moved from chilly to cold but could not drive me from my morning ritual of climbing the steps, retrieving the binoculars, and doing a 360° sweep around the town. My sweep always slowed as I moved my sight to the north, straining to visualize the manor.

The sale of Varcoe Manor to the State Historical Society moved quickly through the process. I stored most of the furniture and other belongings, and one condition of the sale was that Emmaline's photo should remain above the fireplace, unencumbered with any others around her, where she could continue to keep an eye on her house.

My decision to sell the manor was not without a deep sadness, but I felt the need to find some other retreat.

Reverend Smithers of the Methodist Church had approached me; it seemed his nose had been placed a wee bit out of joint when St. Aubin's church festival garnered a substantial profit with the addition of John and Ellen Varcoe to their grounds. When he learned of Emmaline's body being found, he asked what my plans were for her, and when I said I was not sure, he suggested that since she was, after all, a Methodist, it would be appropriate for her to be laid to rest in their cemetery. He showed a giddy side when he learned that she did not, indeed, commit suicide, but rather had been murdered. Although there was no definitive evidence regarding who murdered her, the rumor spread quickly and the town divided into two camps—the John and Ellen camp, and the Emmaline camp. I removed myself from either side but thought it fitting that Emmaline be given a proper burial in a proper place.

* * *

A week after the final sale of the property, and Emmaline's official burial, I was sitting in the widow's walk with a hot cup of coffee. The cold temperature assured me that this would be one of my last trips up to my favorite retreat. Charlie had offered me space and although the edginess of incomplete relationships seemed to keep us two steps apart, I was grateful for the growing friendship. I could not continue to impose on Charlie's good nature and as I contemplated my next move, my glance wandered to the two little porcelain piglets nestled in the middle of the table—*Supposed to be good luck, if I remember correctly*—one of the three items that had come with me when I left the manor. The other items were Emmaline's watch and the mysterious clothes tree. I lifted the watch and began setting the time. I wasn't looking at the time; I was looking at the watch and thinking about Emmaline when Charlie arrived. He was laughing.

"And just what is so funny?" I asked.

He sat next to me and we faced the river, watching the whitecaps rise and fall with a stiff late autumn wind. "You know, Charlotte, sometimes things just fall into place and everything is right with the world." He took a deep drink of his coffee. "I just learned that the state Historical Society is making some changes at the manor."

I sat forward, suddenly interested. "Really? What kind of changes?"

"As you know, the manor is being prepped as a museum and advertising is going out across New England to draw tourists here."

I squinted sideways at him. A frown of questions crossed my face. "Yes, and...?" I waited for the follow up.

He roared back with his deep throaty laugh. "And they are training Belinda to run it. They're moving all the local Historical Society files and furniture and whatnot into the manor."

I felt a twinge, but not anger, more curiosity.

"But that's not all. This is all being done on the condition that the Genealogical Society be given space, presumably the library, to assist Maine residents with family research." He bowled back and barked another huge laugh. "How ironic is that? Belinda and Peter will be working together. Who would ever have seen that coming!"

I smiled and nodded my approval. "I think that's good. Belinda may have used poor judgment, but she's dedicated to the history of the area and she'll certainly have a lot to work with. And Peter will keep her on her toes."

My mind turned to thoughts of moving forward. Charlie and I had come a long way over the past weeks but had not reached finality and I knew I could not remain here forever. He coughed and broke into my thoughts.

"I think it's time," he said, not finishing his thought; not looking directly at me, but at the two piglets on the table.

I wrinkled my brow. "Time for what?" I asked.

His glance moved from the table to the river. "Time for me to put Laura to rest." He moved close, put his arm around me, and kissed me. "And it's time we went to bed!"

"You know, Mr. Beasley, I think you may be right."

And now, I felt the heat rise.

49013302R00144